BLÀS

ACROSS THE MACHAIR

BLÀS
BOOK THREE

C C HUTTON

Leis deagh gach dhùrachdan
Ceitich x

BLÀTHS

COPYRIGHT

ISBN 978-1-7399745-2-7

Published by Blithe

ISBN 978-1-7399745-2-7

Blàths is an imprint of Dealan-de

BOOKS IN THE BLÀS SERIES

Book 1 Blàs of the Highlands

Book 2 Blàs Roots in the Soil

Some reviews of the Blàs series

"It reminds me of MC Beaton without the murders"

"A charming Highland tale full of warmth and some wicked comedy"

"This is the Highlands on toast, but it gives an insight into a way of life needing careful conservation"

"Excellent read"

"Enjoyable and uplifting"

"Heartwarming"

"Humour is never far away"

"A gentle ride though the Highland year sure to charm anyone with a taste for quirky, idiosyncratic human stories"

"The charming village of Blàs and its colourful residents are presented to us in a series of escapades involving all-knowing village women, gossip, cake and ceilidhs"

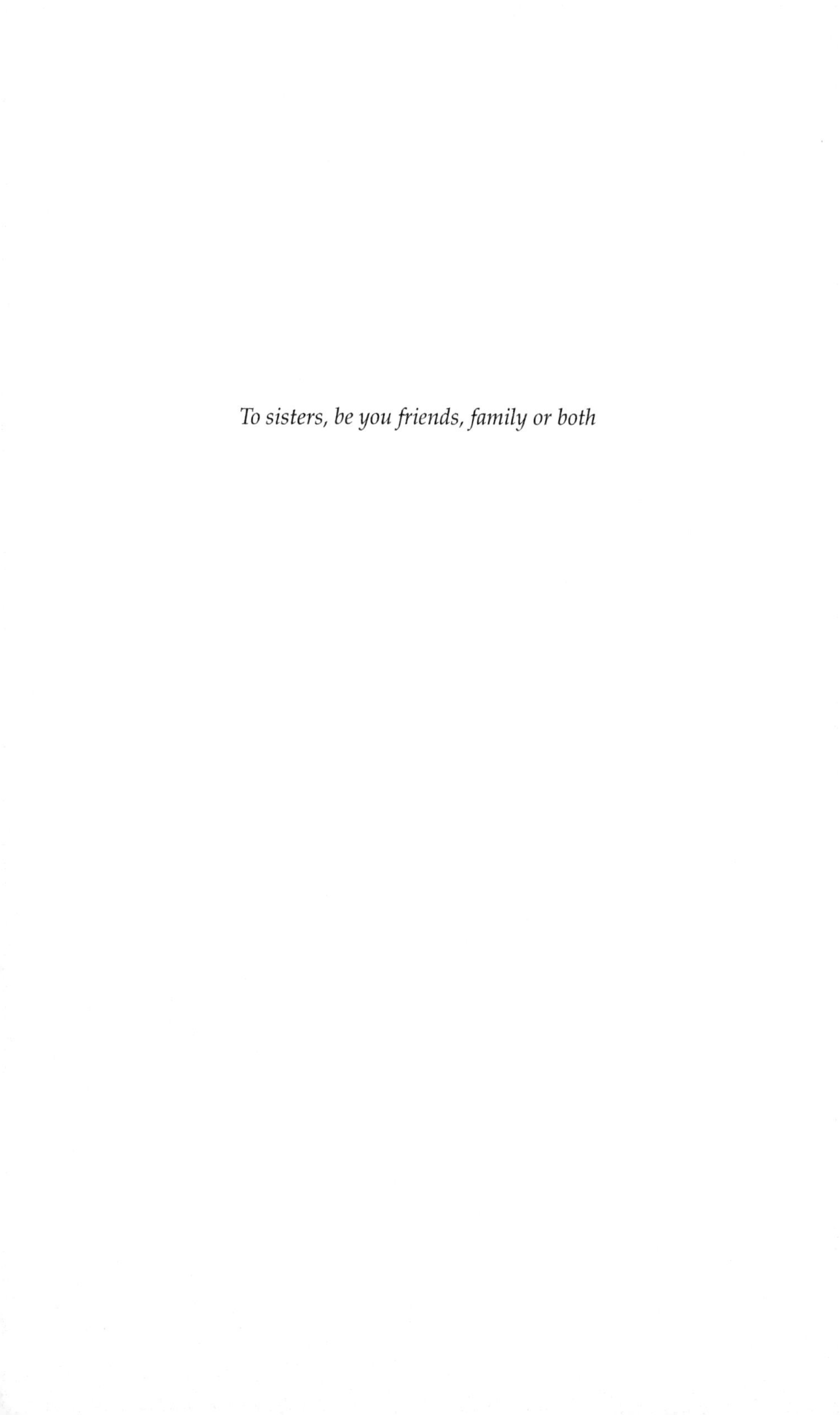

To sisters, be you friends, family or both

FOREWORD

Fàilte/welcome back to my fictional community of Blàs. Although this is the third Blàs book it can be enjoyed without having read *Blàs of the Highlands* or *Blàs Roots in the Soil*. Once more I have included notes at the end of the book that may interest you. Information on Brìde, the machair, the Ùraisg and our three native languages can all be found there. Thank you for allowing me to share the community of Blàs with you again.

A wee note to all you readers that tell me you are convinced Blàs is really your village in disguise. Honestly, it isn't…

Ceitidh xx

1

What on earth was she doing?

After a morning of online meetings, a walk had seemed a good idea to clear my head. Now I wasn't so sure as a cold blast hit me. I shivered inside my jacket, pulled my hat further onto my head and watched Mary.

She stood in the shallows resplendent in black wellies, her long coat just clear of the water. Small waves crowned in white foam broke up the grey that surrounded the rocks just beyond her. It was then I noticed the bucket anchored in the wet sand and immediately knew what she was up to.

"How's the gathering going, Mary? Did you get a good find?" I yelled over.

Hopefully, she would come out for a chat. I didn't know many other octogenarians who would be happy searching around the tide-line on such a bleak February day. The wind was bracing, mixing the salt and sand, and then throwing them towards anything close by. It left my lips tingling and salty grit in my mouth.

"Stroma, give me your hand there and a wee haul up." Mary picked up her wares and, nimble for one of her age, scrambled up the rocks towards me. I gave her one quick heave as she clasped my hand.

The scent of the sea drifted in the air all around her. Mary always seemed to reflect some part of nature.

Fresh air and pleasing rich smells of the earth were as much a part of her character as her ability to bring out the best in everyone she met. Her rewarding smile was craved by the many who knew her. People tended to be at their most charming in her company. Even dour Old Tam was often known to smile when he was with her.

She grabbed her bucket and headed for the bench that oversaw the shore. On a hot summer's day this seat was much sought after. Maureen, the local 'news crier', keeper of our folklore and friend to both myself and Mary was the only occupant that day, or rather her dog, Blether was. Maureen herself sat snuggled up in her wheelchair beside the bench. The cold weather was not deterring the most determined beach lovers.

"Ach it's yourself, Mary." Maureen smiled. "We were wondering who was guddling around in the water on such a fierce day, weren't we, Blether? You were so well wrapped up I couldn't make you out."

"Aye, Maureen, it's not the sort of day to be hanging around. I wasn't trying to catch fish right enough, but it's just the right time to be collecting this seaweed."

Mary placed the sandy bucket on Maureen's knee. She peered inside.

"What a collection you have there and so many colours." Maureen grimaced as she gently removed the bucket from her blanket and swept away the grains of sand. "It wouldn't be us, I'm telling you, wandering about in cold weather like this. Can't understand why anyone would want to be outside on a day like this." She sighed as she absently patted Blether and gazed out to sea apparently oblivious to the fact that she herself was doing just that.

"Have you heard about—" Maureen began, just as the drizzle was threatening to fall as rain.

"Home time I think, don't you, Stroma?" Mary interrupted her friend. "Well, Maureen, no doubt I'll see you this afternoon at the hall. I've a cake for the sale tomorrow so I'm hoping Ellen will be there and I can hand it over."

"We'll be there, won't we, *m'eudail*? *Tiugainn*, Blether, down you come." Maureen gently lifted her pup off the bench, onto her knee then let her slide to the ground. We watched as the two of them disappeared back into the village.

"That woman is getting ridiculous the way she treats that dog. *M'eudail* for goodness sake. It is no a bairn, it's a dog. What would my Angus have said to that?"

I shrugged, knowing she wasn't expecting an answer.

"Aye, it is getting a little wet. Do you fancy coming back with me for a nice wee cup of tea, Stroma. I just pulled a bran loaf from the oven before I came down, or are you wanting to get on?"

I should have, of course, gone back home to my office, but bakes and tea were a weakness of mine, especially anything that Mary baked.

I'd had to miss out on the afternoon hall gathering after my visit to Mary's. Work that I had skipped out on that morning had demanded my attention by lunchtime.

It turned out to be a very productive afternoon. GLADS (Gaelic Language and Development Schemes) courses were filling up fast. Auntie Lottie, my almost relative and close friend of both Mary and Maureen's, would be pleased that not only had we seen an increase in the number of students applying but that all her classes were proving so popular.

I'd delayed my afternoon cuppa and carried on until the rumbling of my stomach had started to distract me. After gobbling down a quick tea, the thought of spending the rest of my evening slumped in front of the telly and chilling out appealed greatly. Then came that familiar tapping on the door.

Maureen, there was no doubt, and she wasn't coming in which only meant one thing. I was expected to go out somewhere. I sighed, grabbed my coat, Malt's lead and we all met at the front door.

"Away, you daft wee dog, hold on, hold on, I'm just putting her down. Now you be careful of that nice wee scarf I have on her. I don't want it getting all dirty now, do I?" Maureen fussed over Malt while she helped Blether down from her lap.

Honestly, her dog was totally spoilt, and if my eyes didn't deceive me, that was yet another pink shiny thing wrapped around that poor dog's neck.

"Come on, Storm, they are all waiting. Ellen will have poured my tea by now and it will be getting cold, and Blether here will be looking forward to her wee bit of cake, won't you now, my wee pet?"

It wasn't worth pointing out to Maureen that I had no idea who was waiting or that no invitation has been issued before her appearance. Not that it would have been an invitation as such – when originating from Ellen, it was more of a directive.

Maureen being sent would mean that others would have received the same summons. I expected that Auntie Lottie would be there as well as Old Tam. Although his inclusion would depend on whether Ellen was prepared to put up with Shep's old doggie odours for the evening.

Thankfully, it wasn't dog but the sweet smell of warm baking that snuggled around me as I entered Ellen's house. If I was lucky, perhaps there would be an offering of hot chocolate.

"Ah, here you are at last, Stroma. We were wondering where you had got to." Ellen placed a hot mug of chocolate in front of me. I was too busy savouring it to mention the small detail that nobody had told me about this meeting.

"So that's agreed then. Stroma can get on to that first thing. In the meantime, Paul can forward us his dimensions while Maureen and Lottie set up a fundraising event. Everybody say aye and I can get this cake cut."

Above the shouts of aye, I raised my voice. "Excuse me, just what am I arranging, or if it comes to that, agreeing with?"

"Really, Stroma, please keep up." Ellen sighed. "Isn't it you that has been moaning about the lack of job opportunities around here and the lack of young people coming back or indeed staying?"

I had to agree, but I was always saying that. I didn't think I had mentioned it any more than usual.

"Well, we are simply agreeing to what we discussed at coffee time in the hall this afternoon—"

"I wasn't there," I interrupted.

"You weren't? Really? Well, we decided that you have been right all along. We need to offer more full-time job opportunities in our community. The seaweed factory and distillery are all well and good but they themselves just don't employ enough people. We need some new businesses.

"Mary, bless her, informed us of a new venture hoping to set up soon. They have requested our help and support to overcome some of their initial hurdles. They need suitable accommodation for a start. Paul of the Sheds has already offered to solve that challenge. Obviously, we need to have a community meeting about how to move things forward, but right now, we are putting our proposition in writing so we have a clearer understanding of how we can assist them."

I looked across at Mary who twinkled in the corner. She smiled sweetly at me. What had she been up to and what had she landed me with this time? I looked back at Ellen expectantly.

"Initially, it would employ two part-time people but eventually they hope to offer permanent full-time jobs for at least six people."

That sounded promising. Six full-time jobs in our village was a major development. Apart from the distillery and seaweed factory, much of the local work was seasonal and did nothing to encourage younger families to stay. More permanent full-time jobs would be a welcome boost to the area.

"Stroma, we need you to write a letter of support for the new venture and perhaps provide some help towards their funding application."

Oh no, here we go again, I groaned inwardly.

2

"So what do you think then?" I leaned into Auntie Lottie to try and hear what she had yelled above the roar of the sea. She gave up shouting and raised her finger pointing out a building further along the shore.

I rubbed my face. Blowing sand doing a better job of cleansing my pores than any beauty product could. Auntie Lottie grabbed my arm, and we plodded forward bent into the wind. She yelled something else, but its meaning disappeared mixed up in the swirl of salt, sea and sand.

She had insisted we walk along the beach instead of the road so we could exercise Madra, Paul of the Shed's otterhound. Paul, her husband, was attending yet another rescue. Not, thankfully, at sea this time. His dog was happily lolloping along the beach seemingly oblivious to the weather, ears flapping in the wind, while his nose enjoyed all the scents screaming towards him.

We struggled up the dunes and suddenly peace shattered the air.

"See, it's prefect." Auntie Lottie yelled into my face. "Oh, and apparently in a sheltered position," she continued in a more normal tone.

The building before us hadn't looked very large set within the beachscape. Once up close, though, its large dark-grey walls dwarfed us both. We headed around the corner and were immediately blasted again by the weather as Auntie Lottie struggled with her pockets which housed a large set of keys. I could barely see as my hair cascaded into my eyes. Key after key was thrust into the lock to no avail. I clasped my hood firmly to my head.

"Ah-ha." We rushed inside as the door sprang open. "Just hold on a moment while I fiddle with this. Stroma, shine the torch here." There were a few '*blast*'s, '*oops*'es and clangs, then like a reluctant dawn, a dim light grew feebly, stopping just before it managed to illuminate the inside properly.

"See, perfect." Auntie Lottie swung her arms around, a happy smile on her face. "It couldn't be more perfect."

I was finding it difficult to match the enthusiasm in her voice. Dust particulates vied with what little light there was, but at least the howling wind was barred from entering the building. It was indeed a massive space inside. Very little cluttered the area. A few bits of clothing hung forgotten on hooks, empty shelves lay forlorn awaiting long-discarded wellies or work boots.

"Paul says he doesn't use this building much at all now, so all we have to do is negotiate an acceptable rent."

Auntie Lottie had been right about the shed. From the little I had been able to find out, what was needed most was a large space. This shed was more like a big agricultural building than a mere hut. Looking out a dusty window, another larger building could be seen in the distance sitting beside a small inlet. Even in the worst of weather it was sheltered by the headland. A pier ran down to a smaller unit that still housed a couple of wee boats that the seaweed factory used.

The factory had been one of our successes but had taken years to set up. I found myself grinning as I remembered how Old Tam was convinced his granny from Dundee used to brew her own alcoholic drink from seaweed.

The success of the factory meant we were at the next stage of the project which left me with the challenge of how to celebrate the whole seaweed venture. I needed to talk with someone who thought a bit differently. Someone who could get others to part with their money. Someone who was always up for an adventure. Someone who had a little bit of knowledge regarding the environment and habitat. Someone who loved Blàs and could come up with a reason for partying even more. More than anything, I needed a mad scientist. Well, of course they didn't need to be mad, but the one I knew and loved was a little offbeat to say the least.

But how could I persuade her to come home for a wee while at least, to help? I had my own little biochemist in the family, now all I had to do was entice her to return. I would have to get in touch with Iona, my wandering sister.

Today, though, I had to put the seaweed factory to the back of my mind and focus on our latest project, which in reality, I knew little about. According to Ellen we needed a big shed, hopefully close to the seaweed factory. Right now, where Auntie Lottie and I were standing seemed to fit the bill in every way. Ellen had been a bit reluctant to give me too many details about the investors, but I had enough information at this stage to work with. However, I had to point out to Ellen that I would need more information soon.

"The interested party wants to keep their idea under wraps for now so I can't say too much, only what sort of accommodation they are looking for."

"Ellen, if you want me to help and find any sort of funding for this project, I need to know what it is. No one is going to invest in something they know nothing about."

"Well, we are investing, and I know what it's about so please just go and check out the shed and see if it matches what they have asked for." Ellen's background was in accounting and she was a shrewd investor, so I knew I could trust her judgement.

I couldn't understand what all the secrecy was about, and quite frankly, I found it very frustrating not knowing. I was right though – grant-funding bodies would not give a penny to anyone who wasn't prepared to say what the business was going to be. I knew, however, it would only be a matter of time before I found out.

Meanwhile, I needed to contact Jim our development officer with HIE, Highlands and Islands Enterprise. They had invested in a number of our Development Trust projects around Blàs. If we wanted this new venture to be successful, his support would be vital.

Since the shed seemed to fit our requirements, it was time to start laying down the foundations with someone who could champion our cause within HIE. I knew Jim had a soft spot for Blàs, and if he could help, he would. Although after him spending so much time in Blàs on our various projects before, he had been conspicuous in his absence lately. Due, no doubt, to his recent break-up with Grace.

Despite the weather, Jim appeared enthusiastic about our projects as I showed him the key areas around Blàs. Given the personal circumstances, him being the ex-lover of one of my best friends, he had been friendly and his usual efficient self. That was until it came to parting company.

"I thought I might take a look at the hall to see how it's all progressing. The exhibition space will take time, but I wanted to reacquaint myself with the dimensions. Do you fancy catching a cup of coffee before I head back? Maybe if we're lucky they'll be serving some of their delicious cakes."

I had been surprised, thinking that once our business was done he would disappear straight back to Inverness.

Most of the elderly had thankfully disappeared for the day, having partaken of their morning catch-up complete with tea and cake. This then tended to roll into a lunch of soup, more chatter and sandwiches before they headed away.

Goodness knows what they would have made of Jim and myself arriving together. They were always on the lookout for some good speculation and blatant tongue-wagging. Old Tam was just leaving with Shep when we arrived.

"Ach, ye are that late th day, Stroma, wer awh heidin hame. Juist a couple o ous stragglers left. Best *greas ort* if ye are wantin te." Old Tam often mixed his Dundonian and Gaelic together. It made for a colourful way of speaking. He was right that most people had left. Although Maureen was just heading our way.

"Ach, I was just leaving but I can stay if you want some company."

"Nah, that's okay, Maureen, I see Ellen's still there – she can get us anything we need."

Maureen wheeled past. No doubt she wouldn't be happy not having the latest news to deliver, but I couldn't be doing with her probing poor Jim for information. We had to keep him on our side if we were to progress our plans further.

"Thanks for that. I don't think I'm ready for an inquisition by Maureen right now." Jim placed two cakes, a coffee and tea on the table. "Not much choice left I'm afraid, but the good thing is, even with little to choose from, I know they will taste great. I'd forgotten how much I missed this place." He sounded really nostalgic.

He and one of my school friends Grace had surprisingly quickly become a couple the year before. Even Cavan, Grace's young son had seemed to love him. Jim, it had to be said, had immersed himself in Blàs when living here. Then, equally abruptly, the romance between him and Grace had ended. Thankfully, his love for Blàs had survived. It wasn't only Grace he would be missing but also being part of this community.

As if reading my thoughts, he asked, "Look, Stroma, I know you are one of Grace's oldest friends and this is completely off the record but I need to talk to someone about this. I just don't understand where I went wrong. We seemed to be getting along really well. Even Cavan seemed to like me. And then suddenly she's telling me we're over and I have to leave. I've tried calling her, sent her flowers, emailed her even, and she had just blocked me at every turn. I need to know what I've done wrong. I just don't understand."

Gone was the smart, professional image of our development officer, and in its place was a miserable male looking forlorn and upset.

"You have to help me, Stroma. If only I knew what I'd done I could maybe set it right. She will have talked to you – please, you have to help me."

What could I do? My loyalties would always lie with Grace, even if I wanted to help him. In truth, I knew about as much as he did.

"I'm sorry, Jim, but she hasn't said a word to me or Karen." Karen was the third member of our school trio. Certainly, Karen hadn't said anything to me. The pair had drawn closer in some respects, mainly due to the fact they were both mothers now, but this was something different. I was fairly sure, if Grace hadn't confided in me, she wouldn't have done so with Karen, either.

"She must talk to someone surely."

An image of Auntie Lottie flashed through my head. She was technically Grace's stepmother, being married to Paul of the Sheds, Grace's father. She was the last person who would give Grace sensible advice on the relationship side of things. It had practically taken the strength of the entire community to finally get Auntie Lottie to walk down the aisle… or rather, a lovely blossom-encased path in the woods.

There were four people in the whole area who would run before committing to a long-term relationship, and three of them were in Grace's family. The fourth was Iona.

Mary was the only person we all went to when seeking non-judgemental advice. She was older, could keep a secret and could be relied upon for hugs and wise counsel.

Unfortunately, she couldn't be trusted not to meddle if she thought it was what was needed, but even then, she mostly got that right too. Even if Grace hadn't confided in her, if Mary saw the unhappiness flowing from Grace and Jim, she wouldn't be able to stop herself from trying to help. I expected that, in the not too distant future, I would be getting a summons to attend supper or a late cuppa at Mary's croft.

3

A few days later my prediction came true. Grace, Karen and myself were sitting once more in Mary's kitchen. She had requested our company for the evening with the excuse that she missed having us all visiting together. We had all dutifully made our way to her back door.

"Ach, the evenings are that long on my own now. My Angus took up such a big space in the house. His stories rattled off the roof and clattered around my kitchen. All this silence is deafening. I get right fed up listening to my own breathing."

Auntie Lottie and Paul of the Sheds were babysitting Cavan. Jack, Karen's husband was thankfully home from the rigs. He was looking after his own children allowing Karen a well-deserved evening out. I had briefly wondered, given that both Karen and Grace had a night off from motherhood, whether they begrudged spending it in Mary's kitchen and would rather be in the pub.

"Thanks, Mary, I don't often get the chance to be out on a school night, even when Jack is home."

"Well, lass, I just thought you would appreciate a nice wee quiet night without the bairns, and no hangover the next morning." Mary twinkled across at Karen and placed some passion cake in front of her. "It's quite a while since I had all three of you here at once."

She was right. Between work commitments with GLADS and the Development Trust, it was difficult to find time to fit everything in. Lately, I had met up with my friends but not in this particular grouping. The three of us together in Mary's kitchen always took me back to our younger days when we would fall though her back door for plasters, understanding hugs and comforting silence – in fact, whatever was needed. If we fell out with each other, we knew at some point we would be summoned to Mary and Angus' kitchen to talk it over.

Karen, Grace and myself had never left this house without a better awareness of our friendship with each other and our love for that amazing couple. How they got to be so understanding of our needs when they were childless themselves surprised me. *Then again,* I mused, *maybe they had the patience that parents couldn't always offer, given the pressures on them.*

"Stroma, come back to us." Grace laughed at me. "Honestly, I always thought, with all that daydreaming you did, you were bound to be a writer of some kind. But you are not prepared to share your thoughts with anyone."

"Ha, you're one to talk. How long did it take you to tell us you were pregnant with Cavan?"

"Now, now, girls, no need for that. You are here to keep me company. I have no desire to be a referee. Speaking of desires, Stroma, why don't you tell us what young Jim was talking to you so earnestly about at the hall cafe? You seemed very... friendly. I'm led to believe it wasn't all about the Development Trust now, was it?"

This woman was a witch. How on earth did she know? It couldn't be Maureen. She had left before Jim and I had had our little tête-à-tête. Ellen wouldn't have told her. I racked my brain some more. There was no one else in the hall. We had left together. Jim to get his car which was parked right outside. He had pleaded once more for me to try and find out what he had done to annoy Grace so much.

I had replied I would try, and he dropped a light kiss on my cheek as a way of thanks and off he went. Malt had then dragged me towards Blether whose paws were eating up the distance between us, her Dandie ears flapping wildly. Pure joy erupted as the litter mates bound around together. There was no sign of Maureen. Eventually she wheeled into sight.

"Ach, Tam and I were just catching up, then this here little lady jumped down and ran off. I should've known you were around somewhere. Blether, will you leave Malt alone? You know I have just the right pretty collar that would suit your little Malt to a tee. You're welcome to it; my wee Blether has plenty of her own – she wouldn't miss one."

"That's very kind of you, Maureen, but me and Malt are quite happy with what's she got." Maureen looked a bit put out. She would have been more upset if I had said what I really thought. There is no way Malt was wearing one of Blether's ornate contraptions. In a bid to appease her, I finished, "Anyway, Iona would be upset if I was to use anything else on Malt – she did buy this collar, after all."

"Yes, well, my Blether is a bit more refined than your wee hooligan, aren't you, my precious?" Blether by now was back in her favourite spot, cosied into Maureen on top of her knees.

"I haven't seen anything of Ellen's nephew around lately. Have you, Stroma?" Maureen glanced up from adjusting Blether's bow. "Only, there are not that many young, unattached men around here. So if one drops by, you should grab your chance. Well, we're off, see you soon. Bye, Malt."

I had watched as she wheeled away. Why did everyone think I needed a man in my life? The ironic thing was it appeared it was those who didn't have a partner of their own who were so intent on me having one.

I had assumed Maureen had been referring to Scott, Ellen's nephew, with her last remarks. I forced myself away from that thought. It would only result in lowering my mood. He had left Blàs, he was away, and any thoughts of him had to be put aside for now.

Only, looking back, maybe Maureen had not actually been referring to Scott with her last remarks; maybe she had been aiming them at Jim. Perhaps she had seen Jim and me talking before he got into his car. It was possible, even if I hadn't seen her. And if she saw that little kiss he gave me on my cheek, that would definitely have been reported back to Mary and many others…

I could feel Grace's eyes boring into me.

"Well, if you got that information from Maureen, you know how much truth there is wrapped around that."

Karen slowly munched her way through her cake. Her eyes flitting between myself and Grace. I swore I felt the anger flowing in waves from Grace as she sat there immobile.

"Ach, well, you could be right there, Stroma, but it wasn't only Maureen that was saying how cosy and friendly you and young Jim looked together. A handsome couple, I believe was one remark I heard. Of course, you are right about Maureen, bless her – she may not always be totally accurate; she does have a tendency to get her signals a little muddled at times."

Mary sat there looking all sweet and innocent, but she wasn't helping one little bit. In fact, quite the reverse. Grace's gaze was fixed on a spot on the table. What was Mary up to? Instead of putting out any potential fire, she was fuelling it. This was immediately confirmed with her addition of, "I'd have to agree with the sentiment that you'd make a handsome couple, I must say. Don't you agree, girls? I'm sorry, Grace, do you want to say something I didn't quite catch that?" Mary took a small sip of tea and smiled sweetly across at Grace who mumbled something incoherently under her breath.

"Now, Stroma, just look at all you have in common. You both like the environment, you're into community involvement. More importantly, you love Blàs. And we could all see he loved children. Grace here can vouch for that, can't you, lass? He was that good with your Cavan, I expect the wee soul will be missing Jim's presence a little. Here, Karen, have some more tea to wash that cake down."

Karen was furiously nibbling tiny pieces of cake and regarding the three of us as if we were a tennis match, her eyes flicking from one to the other but not saying a word. At the point when the silence felt more dangerous than the conversation, Mary continued with, "Well, he won't be around for long, I'll wager. Some nice lass will come along, I've no doubt, so why not have it be one of our own? I quite miss him myself. Always had time for a cup of tea and a chat with me. You're finished with him anyway, Grace, so what would it matter to you if our Stroma got a look in." Mary finished triumphantly.

The silence deepened. "Well, Grace, aren't you quite finished with the poor man? He is free to do what he wants with whom he wants." Mary paused and stared at an increasingly uneasy Grace. Mary continued, "I was going to say he's free and happy, but I think we all know he's not happy, don't we, Stroma?"

Mary looked meaningfully at me. She had manoeuvred this whole situation around and back towards me. "Stroma," she said more gently, "why don't you tell us all what Jim was so anxious to say?"

Grace refused to meet my eyes, but I ploughed forth, if only so she knew I had no interest in Jim other than as a friend.

"Well, Grace, to be honest, he has no idea what he did wrong. He's heartbroken. He wanted me to find out from you what happened." She glanced in my direction. "Honestly, Grace, he has no interest in me other than the projects. In fact, I would say he has no interest in any women apart from you." She finally looked me in the eyes, her own sparkling with unshed tears.

"I wouldn't have told him anything about you, Grace, I wouldn't. Firstly, much as I like Jim, you are my friend so I would never betray your trust, but honestly, I couldn't have told him anything as I have no idea what he did. I don't know what went wrong with your relationship. And much as I would like to help, it's up to you, if you want my help."

I looked significantly towards Mary at this point who, rather than look abashed, simply winked at me and smiled. She was a menace – you just couldn't stop her when she decided she wanted to interfere. Karen shrugged her shoulders and continued eating her cake. How had she made it last that long?

"Grace," Mary probed, "are you going to tell us, lass? What did Jim do? I have a feeling, right enough, that I know, but I'm asking you, lass, to trust us."

"It's not about trust, as you know well enough, Mary. You should just leave me alone. I'm not a teenager anymore. You can't make me tell you things. I'm an adult, a mother, a grown woman, I'm... well... I... well, I... well, he's just an idiot."

Karen put down her teacup and looked her friend firmly in the eye. "Oh my, Grace, he did, didn't he? My God, he did! What a prize idiot – how could he stoop so low. He asked you, didn't he? He asked you to marry him and you shut down, turned around and threw him out. So tell me, Grace, does that make us all idiots for loving you too?"

I could have hugged Karen.

Grace looked shocked. "No, of course not. That's not the same at all. Of course not."

"Okay then, Grace, you tell us what the difference is? What makes us loving you so different from Jim loving and wanting to be with you?"

"You of all people should know, Karen. You're married to Jack. You're tied down; you can't make a decision without consulting him. What if I want to travel again or move away or just do something else?"

I felt my anger rising on behalf of Karen. I knew Grace was hurting, but really, she shouldn't be distaining Karen's choices. To my surprise, Karen started to laugh. A free joyful laugh. She wiped her eyes and looked at Grace.

"You absolute nutter. Jack doesn't tie me down, or at least not in that way…" She smirked, looked across at Mary and immediately reddened. "Yes, I consult him, in the same way I would ask you lot about things. He doesn't cage me, Grace – far from it. He knew who he'd married. He encourages me to be me. Yes, I can moan about him not doing the dishes and things, but that's just normal. If you and I lived together, you can bet your bottom dollar I would find plenty to moan about you. How can you have got things so wrong? Well, look at your dad, I suppose we don't have so far to look. Look, I'm not saying marry the man. If you don't love him then definitely don't, but for the love of God, don't follow in your dad's footsteps. You are not him."

"Well, that isn't true. She is exactly like her dad," said Mary. "I can't think of any better examples of how not to behave when you are in love than Paul of the Sheds and Lottie. Those two only ever had eyes for each other and did nothing about it, absolutely nothing for years. Him sewing his oats, her taking on all her travels and lovers. Running away, the pair of them scared to commit, and where did that leave them? Only putting off the inevitable, one broken marriage, numerous lovers, and eventually, they are finally both happy. Silly pair could have been together for years if they had had an ounce of sense between them."

I wasn't sure Auntie Lottie or Paul of the Sheds, if it came to that, would agree with Mary. I would have said both had thoroughly enjoyed their lives apart *and* together. But I wasn't going to dispute Mary's take on things.

We would just have to wait and see how Grace would react. Whichever path she chose, we would all be there for her, and she knew that too.

4

"What do you mean he is coming for a visit?"

I thought that was fairly self-explanatory myself.

"Just how many visits does he have to make, Stroma? I really don't want to see him. How could you do this to me? I thought I had made it plain I didn't want to see him."

Well, actually, she hadn't. Grace had quickly changed the subject that night in Mary's kitchen. She had then excused herself from our company as soon as she could.

"Ah well, that's it sorted." Mary had sighed contentedly as the front door closed. "All we have to do is wait a wee while."

I hadn't been so sure we had resolved anything that night.

Now here we were again in another Blàs kitchen, this time Ellen's. Normally this signalled that the subjects to be discussed would involve the Development Trust. Not Grace's relationship with Jim, but Grace had hijacked it around to her situation once more. I was finding my patience with her fast waning, and I wasn't the only one.

Grace was making a drama out of the simplest of things. She had known Jim was our HIE Project Officer when she linked up with him. In fact, if he hadn't been, they probably would never have met in the first place. He had spent a good deal of time in

Blàs for our previous projects which is when their relationship had blossomed. It wasn't my fault they had since fallen out. His job meant he was still very much connected to Blàs and its inhabitants. Grace may not like it, but Jim would still be spending time here while our current projects developed.

"I mean, look at me, how can you do this to me?" She waved her hands up and down her body. It wasn't as if she had suddenly sprouted two heads. In fact, I couldn't see anything wrong with how she was looking. Okay, she may have had dark circles under her eyes, but she had a young child – looking tired when you had a child under three was quite normal in my book.

"What am I going to tell him? How am I going to avoid him? This is going to make it so much worse, now. He is going to be even more persistent."

It would appear Karen had been right about why their relationship had sunk. Grace's fear of being tied down was almost as bad as Auntie Lottie's had been. At least, having a best friend and 'auntie' with these issues, I was used to this sort of thinking, even if I didn't completely understand it myself.

"Grace, will you please sit down," Ellen intoned. "I've made you a cup of that stuff you call tea. Take a sip and try to relax. We need to be getting on with the meeting." Grace thumped back down into her seat, scowling at anyone who looked in her direction.

Ellen moved us along. "A chef is coming from one of the hotels to give us a class on seaweed cookery," she stated. "We can open that up to the public and charge a small entry fee. We thought we could probably theme one of our markets around seaweed. Now that we are harvesting our own, I feel we need to push this a little further. Karen says the school are keen to develop their 'harvest from the sea' project. The factory folks are keen to move on to the next step. Now, Stroma, how is your task coming along?"

I had been dreading that very question. Truth be told I'd been avoiding my designated task quite well as far as I was concerned. Catching up with Iona was always fun... so long as certain unwritten protocols were not breeched. This meant no mention of her returning to Blàs for the long term. Asking her to come and stay here in Blàs for an unspecified length of time was not a question I wanted to broach with her. She would feel I was trying to trap her. I only had to mention the possibility of how well the community was doing for her to break in with comments like:

"Stroma, I don't care how many great nights you are all having – I'm not coming home to Blàs to stay. I like my freedom. Nobody knows what I am doing, and I continually meet new people."

Before I could stop myself, I would be defending our community to her:

"We're not all bad you know. I just thought you might like to hear how people were doing. I'm not giving you this news to entice you home. Why do you always think that?"

And from there the conversation would descend to avoidance of any mention of Blàs.

I found it difficult to understand why she thought I would want her to return here permanently. I was busy living my own life. I had a job that was both time-consuming and that I loved. Any spare minute I had from that was spent working for the Blàs Development Trust. I needed to keep busy – I didn't want my mind wandering into what had been before Scott had left. If I could keep my thoughts away from Scott, my life in general was full and interesting. I loved it, mostly.

I positively revelled in the fact I was no longer responsible for Iona's choices or her life. Malt was enough company for me, I told myself often. I didn't want or have time to interfere in Iona's life. All I wanted was for her to maybe come home a bit more often for a visit. Realistically, I couldn't see myself living with her again. We would both go mad.

Unfortunately, Iona didn't see it that way. She seemed to live under the illusion that my biggest desire was to have her back home and me looking after her – nothing could have been further from the truth.

Perhaps it was because I'd had to be part sister, part guardian and part parent once we had lost our own parents. I had moved happily beyond that particular role. She, however, still regarded me as a sort of captor, and someone who could call time on any of the exploits she would frequently get herself involved in.

❧

"I can see from that look you haven't mentioned it to her yet, have you?" Ellen fixed me under her gaze. I turned bright red and shuffled in my seat. Mary looked across and winked.

"Well, Ellen, she has no need to do that. I've been speaking with the lass myself. She even got me on to messaging her face to face. Myself, I'd rather use the email. It's more like letter writing, but Iona insisted she wanted to see me. Misses seeing me, I think."

Everyone was transfixed, staring across at Mary as she calmly gave us the information. It was uncanny how easily she had taken to technology. Many half her age weren't as good.

"Anyway, as Stroma will tell you herself, she will be picking our Iona up on Saturday afternoon. Or knowing Iona, at some point in the next few days."

What? I didn't know that, and by the silence and looks being passed around, neither did anyone else.

"She was more than happy to come when I explained. Luckily for us, she has just finished a contract and was looking around for something else. I told her the Trust had accommodation for a biochemist so she would have her own place but may have to stay with Stroma, just until it is ready."

❧

"You didn't know, did you?" Karen asked as we walked home together.

"Nope. She never said a word to me. Well, actually, neither of them said anything. I still can't believe Mary spoke to Iona about the position – never mind Iona agreeing to come home for it." I sighed.

How had Mary managed that? I was pretty certain that Iona wouldn't have heeded my call to arms. Karen, as always, appeared to have read my mind.

"You know Mary is a shrewd *cailleach*. She knew that your Iona would have twisted like a fish on a hook if you had asked her to come home. Mary has the most sway with her, you know that. That woman back there – she is not so different from your sister you know. Don't forget how many exploits she is behind in the village. She understands your sister better than Iona does herself. Why do you think she was able to handle her so well as a teen when nobody else could?"

I hadn't thought of it like that. How had I never spotted that shared wildness and freedom of spirit before? Maybe the many years between them had stopped me. But Karen was right. Mary had recognised the same streak that ran through Iona. No wonder they had got on so well.

Now it would appear, all I had to do was try and live with Iona again at least for a little while. First, though, I had to hope she would show up at the appointed time in Inverness. Well, there was always a first time, but I wasn't going to hold my breath.

❧

Iona texted me briefly on the Saturday, thankfully before I had left for Inverness. Something had come up – nothing unusual, in that something always did. She wouldn't be arriving today as expected. Once more, nothing out of the ordinary for Iona. She would get in touch and let me know when her travel plans were finalised.

What was unique about all this was the fact that she had messaged me at all. Normally, I would be left waiting, wandering around until she would suddenly appear unannounced and without apologies. What had happened to my sister for this seismic change to occur?

5

Malt was whining and pacing beside the bedroom door. It was pitch-black outside, rain crashed like pebbles battering against my window. Wiping the sleep from my eyes, I fumbled and tripped my way downstairs, rammed my feet into my boots and grabbed my jacket on my way to the door. Why it was always on a horrible night like this that Malt decided she couldn't wait till morning was beyond me. She needed out and now.

"Okay, okay, Malt, give me a minute. I'll let you out." I shouldn't have complained, even as a young pup Malt hadn't got me out of bed often during the night.

Her whole body by now was wriggling, her wagging tail throwing her off balance at the mere thought of getting out. Poor wee thing was obviously desperate given the noise she was making. Rain lashed in as I opened the door and slung my jacket on too late to stop myself from getting soaked. Fighting with my hair, I reached for the outdoor light and switched it on. Malt wouldn't be out long in this. No one with any sense would be out on such a night.

A voice rang out, proving me wrong. "At last, I thought I was going to be stuck out here till morning. What's a person got to do to wake you up?"

"Holy shit, Iona, you near give me a heart attack." I was engulfed in a dripping wet hug. The March rain had now turned to sleet, Iona was freezing and now so was I. Malt was jumping up and down at knee-height, then rolling onto her back, unsure what to do in her excitement at greeting Iona again.

"Well, are you going to let us in?" She motioned to a car behind her. A figure appeared at her side.

"This is Stuart. He's on his way home to visit someone in Durness. He offered to bring me and my stuff home. Not that I've got that much, like. But still easier than carting it all the way on public transport. Anyway, I told him we could give him a bed for the night, and he can head away sometime tomorrow. Any chance of something hot to drink and toast or something?"

Iona still didn't appear to have any concept of time. I was up now anyway, so might as well put the kettle on. I ushered them both inside, dwelling on the fact that some things never changed. Iona, late home and with someone in tow needing fed and a bed. My quiet, orderly life was definitely going to suffer with her return to Blàs.

"Look, Iona, you know where the extra bedding and things are, but I'm heading back to bed. I'm off out sharp in the morning," I informed them as I put the kettle on. "There's bread over there and some lasagne in the fridge you can heat up if you want."

I left Malt with them, knowing she wouldn't settle now there was the chance of more company, and perhaps even food, and headed back to bed.

❧

After a quick early-morning walk with Malt, I grabbed a coffee and climbed into my car. There was no sign of my housemates. I had heard Stuart gently snoring in the sitting room. Of Iona there was no sight or sound. I left a brief note explaining I had a meeting up north and I wouldn't be back until after tea.

I had considered leaving Malt in Iona's care but wasn't sure of her plans or when she would surface. For now, apart from the note, I would act as if I was still living on my own. Malt would be accompanying me on my journey north.

The roads since the marketing of the tourist route, the North Coast 500, had never reverted to the quiet stream of cars that used to frequent these parts. Blàs had also suffered from over-tourism at one stage. A combination of a pilot television series and the finding of a significant treasure trove had resulted in blocked roads, numerous tourist buses and an altogether unpleasant experience. The village had been invaded way beyond its capacity for such numbers.

We had reverted to our more normal rhythm after some deception on our part which had resulted in the television series moving filming to the nearest town of Inbhirasgaidh. For once we had been happy to lose out to our closest rivals. Luckily, the deluge of people interested in the treasure had fallen to a more manageable number as well. We still had our usual small trickle of tourists coming for a short spell. Most people visiting the area, however, now stayed in and around Inbhirasgaidh.

Once I had joined the main road north, it was easy to gauge from the volume of traffic that today wasn't one of the busy ones. No lines of traffic or traffic jams. Perhaps leaving so sharp in the morning had helped.

We followed the road as the volumes of traffic slowly increased. Malt insisted on stopping a few times. Thankfully, I had built that possibility into the journey, and we lingered in Scourie – Malt to chase along the shoreline and me to watch the birds and stretch my legs.

As I turned onto the main track again, a car tooted and a hand waved. It was Stuart. Sutherland was still small enough in population to pass familiar faces during the day. The fact that it was still possible brought a smile to my face.

Iona might grudge staying a little longer in the more remote parts of the Highlands, but I knew where my home was and it was right here. I couldn't envisage living anywhere else.

I knew I would have to tackle her reluctance when I got home. Mary may have managed to persuade her to come back for a while, but I knew that Iona wouldn't be happy for long in a place that thought it knew your every move.

I didn't know how long the seaweed factory needed her, for this next stage yet. That still had to be worked out. I just hoped that we would be able keep her interest long enough. Though I had to admit, if the increase in house prices was due to high demand, we shouldn't have much of a problem finding a more permanent scientist interested in the job when Iona decided to move on.

❧

After a successful trip up north, Malt and I finally arrived home. No lights were shining from my little house to welcome us back. A surge of sadness overwhelmed me. Sensing the change, Malt called out from the back.

"Just coming, girl." I picked her up and we entered the house, switching on every light we passed. A note was stuck to the fridge.

Gone out to meet friends, don't wait up. I've eaten xx.

The disappointment was real. I hadn't realised how much I had been looking forward to seeing Iona waiting for me at home, but I should have anticipated this.

I had been looking forward to a nice meal together or even maybe going out to the pub for supper, a few drinks and a catch-up. But Iona was never going to wait around for anybody, not even me.

"Well, Malt, just you and me for tea." Malt wagged her tail and placed her front paws just below my knee. I rubbed her head. "Come on, pup, supper and a cuddle is just what we need."

After tea, Malt and I sat together on the couch, a blazing fire warming the room and music playing softly in the background. I turned the page on my book and Malt snuggled further onto my lap. Idly, I stroked her back and we breathed a contented sigh together as the wind howled outside. Lights twinkled from the houses around the village and merrymakers laughed and shared stories in the pub, but we didn't notice. We had just what we needed right here.

6

The next few days passed in a flurry of activity. Between my waged job and the Development Trust, I was kept busy. I barely saw Iona. She breezed in and out of the house at all times and disappeared most evenings to meet up with friends. Unsurprisingly, it was a summoning from Mary that forced us to spend some time together. Maureen delivered the invitation.

"Ah, it's yourself, Stroma. I was just heading your way. Blether, now that is enough." Maureen lifted her wriggling puppy down so she could run around with Malt.

Sand flew under their paws as they raced back and forth along the beach, jumping on top of each other in excitement. The bright yellow bandana around Blether's neck didn't seem to hamper her movements. It would be ruined by the time they were finished dashing around, not that Maureen seemed concerned – but then she would have lots more doggie paraphernalia at home.

A movement beyond the dogs caught my eye. Mary was out among the rocks again with her bucket collecting more seaweed. Her classes were due to start soon so she was probably getting some more samples ready for any students that had signed up. There was someone on her other side.

"See your sister has agreed to help Mary. Not that she had much choice, mark you. Mary doesn't give you much option when she has made up her mind, does she? Which reminds me, Mary said six o'clock sharp, tea will be on the table. Just make sure that Malt has had hers before you come along."

"I don't remember Mary asking me along for tea. I have other arrangements for this evening." Nothing, to be honest, that I couldn't change, but still, it was a big presumption expecting me to drop everything and go. I had thought I might try and get Iona on her own for a while to catch up and ask how things were going, or at least find out how she felt about staying in Blàs for the foreseeable future.

"Now, Stroma, regard this more like a summons than an invitation. Your sister has already been persuaded, by herself, to stay on for tea." She nodded towards Mary.

The figure beside her looked up and give a quick wave before looking down again at something Mary had in her hands.

"See, she's working her magic with Iona right there. Before you know it, she will have her settled here for the next wee while."

"I can't see that happening, Maureen. You know how much Iona values her life away from here. We may only need her for a few months anyway. She'll be desperate to get away before long, you know that."

I looked across at my sister. I often wished she lived a bit closer. I understood why she chose to have a life outside of Blàs, but even if her visits were a little bit longer, it would be better, for me at least. Despite all my friends here, I did miss her company, and since Scott had left, I missed my sister even more.

"Well, Stroma, she wouldn't be the first to set up a life elsewhere and then come back. The village is full of people like her. Off to travel and see the bright lights, only to find out, when it comes to putting down roots, they had never really pulled them out to begin with. Prime example, I am. Was younger than your Iona when I came back. Still miss the warm sunshine in winter, mind, but I missed the people here more. Oh, did I tell you about Rumba Tracy's latest shenanigans?"

No, she hadn't, and I didn't want to know, so I informed her I had to get some more work done if I was expected at Mary's by six. No doubt, whatever Rumba Tracy had been up to, I would hear about it soon enough.

❧

I heard Iona in the shower while I was on a video call. She rushed in and out so fast that I actually only caught up with her when I entered Mary's kitchen.

Homely, warm and inviting were the feelings I always got on entering Mary's. She had never modernised her home like so many others had. A big range still took up a large area in the room. On either side sat two big comfy chairs.

It had taken a long time for anyone to sit in Angus' chair. Eventually, Mary had asked Jill, one of our local craftswomen, to make a throw for it from shirts and jumpers Angus had often worn. Jill had then made a tapestry with threaded pictures and sayings that many of Angus' friends supplied.

The 'wrap' had developed into a patchwork effect that Mary loved. Mary had then switched the chairs around and now she sat in her husband's old one surrounded by the beautiful wrap that Jill had created. Iona sat in Mary's original chair.

Mary stood up. "Ah, Stroma, at last. I'll just pop the kettle on. But first, here, have a wee drink of this and tell me what you think?"

I gave Iona a quick hug and sat down on one of the kitchen chairs. Mary handed me a wee nip, light brown in colour. I give it a brief sniff but all I smelt was alcohol with a slight sweet hint. It burnt softly as it went down. Not the usual mind-blowing feeling you got from Mary and Angus' 'wee nips'. It was actually quite nice, rather than burning and lethal.

"Is it some kind of sherry, Mary? I never figured on you being one of the sherry set." I laughed.

Mary smiled "Aye, you'd be right there, Storm, but it's no sherry you have there, lass."

"Really, so what is it then?"

"You'll never guess, Stroma – even I was taken aback. It's quite exciting really," Iona said, taking a small sip from her glass.

I was intrigued by now. I hadn't seen Iona this excited about a drink before. Going out for one, yes, but she had never shown an interest in any of our many 'cottage' breweries before. Per population head, we probably had many more inhabitants who made one sort of alcoholic concoction or other than anywhere else I knew.

"Well, lass, you saw me collecting some of the ingredients this afternoon. It is seaweed wine.' Mary's eyes twinkled as she watched my astonished expression.

"Can you imagine, Stroma?" said Iona. "Wine that tastes like sherry, made from our own seaweed right here. Just think how that opens up possibilities. If we can't gather enough seaweed ourselves from the sea, we could buy it directly from our seaweed factory. They have enough going on, what with the animal feed and beauty products I'm developing for them. They have no intention of developing any alcohol, but we could. We could have a line of beers and wine. Just think, an endless supply of ingredients. This is definitely an idea to run with."

"When you say we, Iona, I take it you mean the Development Trust."

"Well, no, not at all. Well, maybe a wee bit. They have offered to take a few shares to help us get started."

"Have we? I don't remember that. The only thing we have agreed to lately is the new business venture that Ellen..." I looked over at my sister, who was grinning like an over-happy puppy, as I realised what had been happening right under my nose.

Iona was the person behind the new business venture looking for premises in Blàs. She was the one who had had Auntie Lottie and myself checking out the big shed near the beach.

"I can't believe you didn't tell me, any of you." I looked at Mary and Iona. Why hadn't they told me before? I was failing to stamp down on the feeling of hurt at being left out of this big secret.

"Now, lass," Mary said, recognising my look of dismay. "Iona wanted to be sure she could pull all the bits and pieces together before she told you. She knew you would be disappointed if it didn't come off and she left again. I told her to tell you, but she wanted it to be a surprise. A nice surprise – which it is, isn't it?"

I swallowed the words fighting to get out. Didn't she trust I would be happy for her? Would I really have been that upset if it hadn't worked out and she left again? I breathed deeply and recognised the truth in Mary's words. I would have been devastated if I had thought Iona had come home for good and then she had to leave again. Even so, I still felt that drag of loneliness pulling me down at the thought that at least Mary and Ellen had known who was behind the new business but had said nothing to me.

I looked over at my little sister, enthusiasm flowed in waves of happiness from her. I knew she wouldn't understand my sense of being left out.

"I can't wait to get started on this project. This is going to be amazing for us."

I thought back to what Maureen had said about the possibility of Iona staying for a while, and felt that dull space inside starting to fill with tiny bubbles of excitement. Mary stood up.

"Right, girls, the tatties should be ready. Iona, refresh the glasses please. Stroma, things are looking up for us, wouldn't you say?"

Her eyes sparkled as she winked at me. It was difficult not to be swept up in their enthusiasm. I worried for my sister though. She had barely started her new job, and she was already looking at something new and exciting. The one thing I did know for sure, with Iona being involved, it would be unpredictable.

7

The rain was lashing down, although it was difficult to tell with the waves breaking over the bow of the ferry. At this time of year it would normally be quiet, but the increase in tourists had not just happened on the mainland. Floods of them had descended on the islands as well.

At one time I could have sprawled out across a few seats and relaxed for a couple of hours. Not anymore. Families and dogs were everywhere, dotted among the locals and lorry drivers. I sipped my tea and glanced out into the grey again, thankful for a rest from the talking that I had been assaulted with during the drive west.

I had finally got used to Auntie Lottie hitching a lift on my work visits. She had friends dotted all over the Highlands, it would seem, and the chance of a free lift to see them was too good an opportunity to miss. Now I had Iona coming along too. Her role in the seaweed factory allowed her to check out the Hebridean Seaweed Company on Lewis.

I used to enjoy my solitary drives all over the Highlands and Islands. Much as I loved living in Blàs, it was always nice to get away from the people who knew you and thought they knew everything you got up to. When I was out and about, people took me for who I was at that moment which was their development officer or language course coordinator. No one in these communities knew or cared why I had bought extra milk and food over a weekend or if I had visited the local doctor or been spotted 'sneaking', as some would see it, back to my house at some ridiculous time in the morning.

My private life was hardly, if ever, thought of outside of Blàs. Once Auntie Lottie had started coming along, bits and pieces of my life in Blàs invariably began slipping out courtesy of my passenger. It happened often enough to pip the interest of some I visited in these communities. After all, they normally had their equivalent of Maureen living there.

Now I had the addition of Iona entering the communities I worked with. I was hoping this would be a one-off journey. To be honest, although I had looked forward to her returning on a more permanent basis to Blàs, I hadn't really grasped the impact it would have on my life.

My privacy in my own home had gone, to a large extent. It wasn't that Iona trespassed on my personal life. It was merely, she was there or around. I never knew if she was in or not so couldn't plan anything private.

It felt very much like back to the early days of Auntie Lottie when she had returned home. She had settled in with me when the renovations on her cottage had been seriously delayed. In many ways, Auntie Lottie and Iona were alike, in that they would disappear for hours or even not be seen at home for days. Then suddenly, they would appear for breakfast or tea.

"It's freezing out there." Iona dropped into the seat beside me, disturbing my daydreaming again. "Does that woman know everyone in the Highlands, do you think? She bumped into one of the crew and is having a great chinwag with him. Honestly, she is some woman."

"I take it, by 'that woman' you mean Auntie Lottie?" I passed Iona a serviette to wipe up some of the tea she had spilt. "I don't think I've been anywhere with Auntie Lottie where she hasn't seen someone she knows. She is almost as bad as Maureen who seems to be related to everyone except, funnily enough, Auntie Lottie and us."

Iona laughed. "And now you can understand why I had to get away. I don't know how you stayed all these years. I used to find it so claustrophobic at times."

"I get that, Iona, I really do, but I have always worked outside the village too. I'm often away in some other community that only knows me through work. I have the best job. I love it and love coming back to Blàs."

"I hadn't really thought of that. I just used to think there you were, all cosy in Blàs. It never occurred to me that you spent so much time away. Although, I have noticed this time, but maybe that's because I've already been here longer than normal."

"How are you getting on being 'stuck' with us for so long?" I asked.

Mary would be happy we had finally got the chance to both stay in one place and ask those questions that had hung in the air since her return.

"Ach well, to be honest, I had already decided to come home at least for a while before the factory job came up."

What? This was news to me. I'd had no idea Iona had considered coming home before the seaweed job had been offered to her. I thought her interest in the microbrewery had developed after she had been offered the work at the factory. It seemed I had got it wrong. This was a major shift in how she normally regarded Blàs. Short visits home were the norm with strictly no discussions of her staying longer. What had caused this complete turnaround?

"Don't look so shocked Stroma. Mary told you I'd been speaking with her on and off for a while. She knew I was unhappy in my last job. You know what she's like. Before I realised it, I was telling her I was glad the contract was coming to an end and I couldn't see anything else that filled me with excitement. I shouldn't have said anything of course as that was all it took. She started asking if I had considered this or that then reminded me of an old idea I'd discussed with Angus. And that was it, I found myself agreeing to come home to check out the possibility of setting up a microbrewery. Later she phoned and mentioned the factory job as an added incentive, to be sure I didn't change my mind. Then she pulled in the real boss, Ellen video-called me. Didn't once pull out the 'I was friends with you mum card' but talked to me like a job interviewer would. Stated where I would fit in as far as she could tell and asked some really in-depth questions about where my particular skills lay. Actually, at one point she wasn't at all sure I was suitable, so she left me to think about it. She wanted to check herself that I was the right person for the job. By that time, my interest was really growing. I had already made up my mind I was coming home anyway and here was a job just made for my skill set. It was meant to be."

"I take it she phoned you back to offer it to you then?"

"Oh no, Ellen is way more crafty than that, as you know. I had another call from Mary telling me how proud Angus would have been and how he would have loved seeing me back looking into setting up a brewery, the very thing we had discussed together. Honestly, I knew what she was doing, and she knew I knew too. I was giggling by the time we logged off. Then Auntie Lottie phoned just for a wee catch-up." Iona pulled a face. "She understands me too well. She also thought her cottage might be vacant soon, and if so, she's offered it to me for a peppercorn rent. Then I believe Grace phoned to say she had heard I may be coming home and was looking forward to a catch-up.

"My boyfriend asked if I felt I was being stalked. I ditched him right after that. He wasn't up to much. We were more a convenience than a real relationship. Then I believe Ellen finally got back to me. She still wasn't sure if I was right for the job but I persuaded her. I needed somewhere else to live and hadn't looked at another contract. I think you were maybe the only one who didn't phone. Why was that? Don't you want me cramping your style?"

I blushed, not so much at what she was asking, but more to do with the thought that Auntie Lottie's cottage may be coming up for rent. Scott had been living in it before he left, and I knew he still had some of his belongings there. Just how much did Iona know about what had been going on in my private life? I thought I had been discreet, but in Blàs, it was not easy keeping my personal life out of public speculation.

"Stroma." Iona burst into my thoughts. "Come back! I've just asked if I cramp your style and you haven't said no. Well, do I? Would you rather, after all this time of wanting me back, I hadn't come?"

"Away and don't be so daft." I nudged her with my elbow. "It's strange you finally coming home for longer than a few days. But so far, we have kicked along pretty well. I've hardly seen you."

There was still no sign of Auntie Lottie, who no doubt was catching up on news of her own. Iona and I settled down with another cup of tea and got caught up in the tide of news. By the time we left the ferry, we had reconnected with each other and our lives.

8

Not only was I now sharing my house in Blàs with Iona, but on this trip we were sharing a bedroom. It was strange, after so long, to be sleeping in the same room as her. I had forgotten what a disturbed sleeper she was. Her arms were flung around and her legs were constantly kicking the covers. Little murmurs escaped her mouth as she took part in one-sided conversations with herself. I finally fell asleep to be woken at three o'clock to find her stripping her bed then lying on the floor under the bedclothes.

"Sorry did I disturb you?"

"Only a little. I thought by now you might have learnt to stay asleep or at least not thrash around so much," I whispered.

"It's so annoying. I'm hoping I find the floor so uncomfy that when I go back into the bed I will finally fall sound asleep." Iona lay down on the hard floor and pulled up the covers. "Wish me luck," she said as I felt myself fall back to sleep.

It must have worked because when I woke up she was out for the count and snuggled down in bed again.

Auntie Lottie was meeting us for breakfast before going off to call in on yet another friend. Iona was off to speak to the

Hebridean Seaweed Company. She was keen to make sure we were harvesting in the most environmentally friendly way.

That both the Hebridean Seaweed Company's factory and our own had received grants from HIE had made the visit easier to organise. Both organisations were keen to have good sustainable and green credentials. In the longer term, it would feed into how our factory wanted to be perceived and fitted in perfectly with Iona's personal views.

"I know they use a harvester which only takes off the top of the seaweed. It allows the plants to grow back quicker but I'm not sure how that affects the habitat for the sea life. Although, harvesting by hand has its drawbacks too and can do more damage sometimes. I know it takes longer for the plants to recover that way. I can't wait to see them at work. They have been at this so much longer than we have. I'm hoping we might fit in a swim later."

"You can count me out, wetsuit or not. It's way too cold for swimming in the sea right now. Anyway, think what it would do to my hair." Auntie Lottie patted down her well-groomed locks.

"Well, I can't do this afternoon. I'll be in a meeting till lunchtime then I'm going to visit a parent group after that," I added.

We arranged to meet up for tea, before having a quiet night, as we were leaving on the early ferry the following morning. The worst thing about visiting Lewis for work was that often I had to be up sharp to catch the 7 a.m. ferry. At least now, though, there was a lovely covered walkway that took you from the terminal to the ferry. When we were younger, there had been nothing. The wind at the pier had buffeted while the lashing rain had soaked us as we hurried along, heads bent. The shelter provided as we entered the ferry had been wonderfully warm and dry. Perhaps that was one of the reasons I always had a soft spot for travelling by boat. The reminder of the timely shelter it had given from the horrendous weather.

I arrived back at the hotel after a successful day. The parents who had decided to learn Gaelic were keen and full of motivation. The meeting in the morning had been between the many professionals who worked in various areas of childcare development and education. We had come to a consensus that would help both Na h-Eileanan Siar and the rural areas of the Scottish mainland with their Gaelic challenges. With so many knowledgeable people in the room it had led to some interesting outcomes all of which would be fed into the Scottish Government think-tank.

I was enjoying a nice quiet coffee when Iona arrived back, her eyes sparkling.

"What a day. I can't wait to get started on the next phase. They were so helpful. The labs are brilliant; I can't see us getting to that level anytime soon, but if we can build up, step by step, it will be amazing. I'm clearer on what our next products will be. And I get to develop these new ones. It was so interesting you should have come and visited, Stroma – you would have loved seeing all their labs and what they intend to do."

It was strange to see Iona so enthused about something like this, but then again, I didn't normally see her when she was involved in her work. This project certainly seemed to have inspired her. It was another piece of her life I was getting to see and be involved in. She went off to shower as I ordered her a coffee.

There was still no sign of Auntie Lottie. Iona and I blethered companionably together for a while longer. Auntie Lottie was still nowhere to be seen. I tried to phone her but it kept going straight to 'please leave a message'.

"Well, her phone has either run out of battery or she is somewhere where she hasn't got a signal."

"Do you know where she went or even who she was meeting up with?"

Just then a draft blew in from the opening front door. In came a policeman, and following him: Auntie Lottie.

"Come on, let's see what's she has been up to." Iona sprung out of her chair and hurried towards a rather bedraggled and wet Auntie Lottie. Gone were the impeccable hairstyle and neat clothes. Mud and grass dripped down onto the hotel carpet.

"Are you okay, Auntie Lottie, what happened, are you hurt?"

"Aye, well, I see you are in fine hands now, so I'll be saying goodbye. Remember now, be careful where you're going and no more little adventures while you're here."

"Thank you, Robert, yes, of course, I'll be more careful. Please give my regards to your dad. I haven't seen him in a long time."

"Aye, I'll do that right enough. I'll be telling him exactly how you are. Ladies." Robert nodded to both myself and Iona before he left us in silence.

Iona burst out laughing.

"I hardly think this is a laughing matter, Iona. I could have died," Auntie Lottie stated.

"I'm sorry. It's not you. Are you okay?"

"Well, if you are not laughing at me, what are you finding so funny then?"

"The policeman, Robert, or rather, Bobbie the Bobby." And off she went again.

"Oh, for goodness sake, Iona, I hardly think that's so funny." By now, even Auntie Lottie was smiling slightly.

"Just what did happen, Auntie Lottie?" I asked as Iona tried to get herself under control.

"I need a shower first. Come with me while I get cleaned up, and I will tell you what happened. It is all Janet's fault, needless to say. That woman has never grown up."

And off she squelched to her room. Mud, grass, Iona and me trailing in her wake.

Auntie Lottie hadn't visited Janet on the island for years. Before her eventual return to Blàs, Auntie Lottie had lived, worked and played in and around various places in Scotland, only returning to Blàs for short visits. Janet, on the other hand, had often stayed with Auntie Lottie when she lived in one of our cities.

Like many islanders, Janet loved her rural home but also enjoyed the hustle and bustle of a large town with the choice of shops, theatres and eating places on hand. Today, it had been Auntie Lottie's turn to visit her friend in her own house. Instead of them having a wild and wonderful time in a city setting, they had decided to have a calm and cosy chat while they wandered around the Lochs area.

Janet however had been afraid that Auntie Lottie might get a bit bored. After all, each time she had visited her friend in the busy city they had spent the time careering around going to shows, concerts and exhibitions. They would hardly stop for breath before it was time for Janet to head home again.

Janet thought she should arrange at least one activity for them to do. She had organised a bit of fishing at one of the smaller lochs up on the moor. Unfortunately, to get there they had to make their way across an old peatbog.

"Now, Janet said to me, just follow in my footsteps and you will be okay. Don't go jumping on any turfs that don't look firm, or you will find yourself at the bottom of the bog."

Auntie Lottie had rejoined us in her room – clean, warm and full of her normal sparkle. "Only, we were so busy blethering, and you know one bit of turf looks so like another piece. Anyway, I was watching a heron taking off with a fish in its mouth and overbalanced. I didn't want to fall face-flat in the bog – my hair, you know." Auntie Lottie involuntary reached up to her hair. "Anyway, I wouldn't have heard the end of it if I had fallen face-first. So I put my foot down and it sort of kept on going – down, down and down. I felt like I was going to hell, I tell you. I just wasn't stopping. The next thing I knew I was waist-deep in wet slime and Janet was doubled over laughing. I think it was shock as much as anything. She was just so relieved I had finally stopped sinking down. She always was a bit giggly when she was nervous. In fact, she laughed so much that she slipped and did a face plant herself. I can't tell you how satisfying that was. That stopped her laughing."

"Oh my goodness, was she alright, did she sink too?"

"No, thankfully, Stroma," Auntie Lottie continued, "or we would both have been in a right pickle. She was wet and dripping but managed to get out. The problem was I couldn't. She tried getting me to grab on to her. Had her arms wrapped around my body but I was stuck fast. It was pretty scary, I can tell you. She phoned Keven the Splice, and he immediately phoned the Fire and Rescue – he's part of their team anyway and wasn't prepared to come out on his own in case he couldn't get me out either."

"Oh, I heard the sirens leaving Stornoway earlier! Were they for you then? Wow, you certainly know how to leave your mark on places, don't you?"

"Anyway, Iona, if you would let me finish," sniffed Auntie Lottie. "They arrived and seemed to just mill around a lot, until eventually they wrapped a rope around me and heaved me out. I was that cold and miserable then but happy to be out. Missed my whole day with Janet. Although we did a lot of catching up while we waited for me to be rescued. If only my Paul had been about; I know he would have got to me quickly. I just wanted to go home after that. We dropped Janet home on the way. She was still soaking too from her fall." Auntie Lottie sounded a little lost.

"So that's how you got the lift from that policeman," I said "And you're okay now, no damage? I'm sure Paul of the Sheds will give you a big hug when he sees you."

"How is it you know Bobbie the Bobby's father then?" Iona asked, still struggling to keep a straight face.

"Oh well," Auntie Lottie said, sounding more like herself, "that is another story entirely. I don't know if I am ready to tell you all about that right now. Come on, girls, I'm starving, let's go down for tea. I'll give Janet a ring after I've eaten, to check she is feeling a bit warmer. I need to thank her again for ringing the services and getting me out. She must have been frozen herself."

9

Thankfully, the weather in Blàs was much improved on our return from Na h-Eileanan Siar. No rain lashed down and the wind was minimal. Iona had arranged a meeting with Jim, to update him on her trip and how her findings fitted in with her new position at our seaweed factory.

No doubt, Grace would be keeping herself scarce if she knew Jim was about. She would have to face him eventually; I just wished she would get it over with as it was making me feel a bit tense when I was in his company. I had to work with him, and Grace's attitude towards him had added an edge to our relationship that I didn't like.

Iona was also going to ask Jim's advice about help from HIE or other organisations that might invest in her seaweed brewery. She knew she needed to raise some money which would allow her to access further help from grants. Jim would be able to advise her further. I wasn't sure if her seaweed brewery would get much traction with Jim. Although, I wouldn't put it past Iona to spin a brewery into something grant-worthy. As if Blàs needed more to drink!

I was off to Ellen's. Maureen would be there already, and I was impatient to see how Malt had behaved. Auntie Lottie, on the other hand, was anxious about going home. She knew she would need to explain to Paul of the Sheds what had happened.

"He won't be happy, you know. I will get scant sympathy. Knowing him, he'll get all moody and upset about me going up onto the peatbog in the first place. Well, he better not get too short with me as I don't need any more lectures." And off she stomped.

The fact that she was so touchy about the subject was evidence enough that she still felt a little frightened about the 'bog mishap' – as she was now referring to the events of the previous day.

Ellen's kitchen oozed its normal smell of homebaking. The added scent of melting chocolate laced the atmosphere. Giulietta's presence in the household was changing the flavour of Ellen's home for the better. Delicious though it was before, we all knew that the addition of Giulietta had enlivened Ellen's home and brought back the laughter after her previous partner Helen had so tragically died. Yet another sad statistic to add to the many motorbike accidents in the Highlands.

The noise of dogs erupted as I stepped into the kitchen. Malt just beat Blether as they threw themselves joyfully at my legs. Both whined and bounced around on their stumpy legs, accompanied by constant ecstatic barking. They had lost any semblance of control. It took a good five minutes before we managed to restore any kind of order. Blether, with her enormous yellow-and-gold bow adorning her head, had been firmly placed on Maureen's lap, where Maureen adjusted the fashion accessory back to its original place.

"For goodness sake, Stroma, sit down and tell us how it went. I can't hear myself think with all this commotion."

"Is Giulietta joining us?"

"No, she's developing another chocolate inspired by what we're doing in Blàs again," Ellen informed us.

"Really?" I said, "Don't tell me she's making a chocolate out of seaweed."

"Well, if someone can do it, Giulietta can," Ellen informed me with a smile on her face. "But I think it more likely seaweed will merely feature in the flavour. Right, Stroma, fill us in with all your news from Na h-Eileanan Siar."

I relayed Iona's information regarding their laboratories and their product development.

"Obviously, we can't copy their products. HIE, being one of their funders, were happy to encourage them to let us see their operations, but neither HIE nor the Hebridean Seaweed Company would be happy if we ended up competing with each other. Our factory is not on the same scale, and we definitely don't want to be aiming for exactly the same markets. It has taken a long time for them to get where they are now. In that respect, we're coming into the market just as things appear to be on the up..."

"Well, that all sounds very positive, doesn't it, poppet." I looked around at Maureen more than a little shocked at the way she had addressed me and was relieved to see she was actually speaking to Blether. "They've had a productive trip, it would appear, haven't they, precious." No one could remember when Maureen had started making conversation through Blether, but it was gradually getting worse. After readjusting Blether's bow yet again, she addressed her next remark to me. "Are you not leaving out the important bit, Stroma?"

Her eyes zoomed in on me. Having had everything up until now relayed through Blether, it was a shock to have her pinpoint me with her question.

"No, no I don't think so," I stammered, doing a quick recall of all I had said.

"Oh, we think you have, don't we, Blether? What of Lottie and her need to be rescued then, hmm? We've heard about that, you know, but I'd rather get the true facts from someone who was there." Maureen was stroking Blether gently, resembling a Bond villain. I gulped. How had Maureen found out so quickly? We were just back from the ferry ourselves, even Paul of the Sheds hadn't been told. Well, he would know by now, but that still didn't explain how Maureen had heard the news so fast.

"What's that?" Ellen intervened. "What on earth has she been up to now?"

Before I could open my mouth, Maureen input, "Ach, well she only got herself stuck in a peatbog and they had to call out the rescue services to free her."

"Oh my goodness, Stroma, is that true? She didn't, did she, get stuck in a bog? Oh my, that could have turned out badly."

Ellen looked shocked. I suppose after losing Helen to an accident, events that others may find entertaining had become serious and foreboding to her.

I explained what had happened, playing down any sort of danger there had been to Auntie Lottie. Ellen was right, in a way – some of these bogs are very dangerous and deep.

"Anyway, of course Auntie Lottie knew Bobbie the Bobby's dad, but she wouldn't say how she knew him," I finished.

"Who on earth is Bobbie the Bobby?" asked Maureen.

"Sorry, his name was Robert MacTaggart. Auntie Lottie seemed to know his dad Robert MacRobert, MacCèol Mòr. Played the bagpipes, apparently, but that was all Auntie Lottie was prepared to say."

"Oh him." Ellen and Maureen exchanged looks and both burst out laughing but neither would come out and explain why. Annoyingly, Maureen stated, "That is a story for another time."

10

Blue sky with a brisk wind hailed our first big community beach clean. Along with the March storms and spring tides, rubbish had been swept in. Now tins, bottles and other unpleasant things discarded by thoughtless beachgoers were scattered along the sand. In an effort to keep our beach pristine our local community was stepping in to help.

Waves crashed well out from shore as we all gathered on the seafront. Maureen and Blether positioned themselves beside the bench once more. Maureen was determined to help out so would be cleaning up the long grasses that edged the road and the shore. Paul of the Sheds, always mindful of safety, had reminded everyone taking part about the dangers of the tide, slippery rocks and potential sharp objects among the debris. After all, if things went wrong, he would be the person who would be sent to rescue anyone in difficulty.

It was Iona, however, who was in charge of the event. Her own thoughts on the environment made it a good fit with her. She had arranged it as part of a publicity drive to highlight the seaweed factory. Iona had persuaded them to provide the equipment needed for the day as well as a contribution towards refreshments. Our local paper was covering the story and BBC

Alba had sent a reporter along to interview some of our Gaelic speakers.

"Okay, everyone has their grippers, bags and gloves. Please put whatever you find into the correct recycling bins. We have a few hours, then we'll take a break before we do the last clean-up. Thank you again for coming. Enjoy your day." Iona turned to me and grinned before heading off in search of someone else's rubbish.

I'd only ever seen the non-working Iona. The Iona who wasn't bothered if she was late and never planned anything in advance. Only, it would seem that was just when she wasn't working. She was two different people: the working Iona and a carefree soul with the ability to switch off any sort of responsibility. I envied her that ability. I wondered if it was possible to maybe try and be a bit more like her in my downtime.

"Penny for your thoughts, Stroma." Mary broke into my musing.

"Ach, I was just thinking maybe I should relax a bit more." She followed my gaze.

"She is a right mixed bag your sister and I wouldn't have her any other way. The stories we have about her will be remembered for a long time. But thankfully, you are not her, Stroma; I don't think our nerves could cope with another Iona in our midst. It is nice to be able to relax and know things will get done when we expect them. Many love having Iona about but it is you we would all turn too if we needed help, and we wouldn't have it any other way. Your mum would be proud of you both for who you are. Right, I'm off to help get some food ready. It looks like they have managed to get the tent up. Drop by for a snack when you are ready – I have something I want to ask you."

And off Mary went. It would be a while before she reached the tent, I could see. People stopped her as she went past to ask how she was and no doubt pass the time of day.

Mary was the closest we had to royalty or indeed celebrity status. I was mulling over what she wanted to ask me while I helped to tidy up the beach. She was renowned for getting people to do things for her, and on many occasion, they found themselves in all sorts of bother, myself among them. Karen hailed me at that point, and I soon forgot my musings as I became engrossed in helping with the clean-up.

By lunchtime, we were all more than ready for some sustenance. The smell of homemade lentil soup mingled with the salty air. Rough home-baked oatcakes accompanied the soup.

I walked over to Maureen who was talking to Old Tam. Shep lay at his feet. Having given up on moving forward, the old sheepdog had fallen asleep.

"Eh telt ye," Old Tam stated, "and Maureen here wull bear meh oot, thars an *ùraisg* somewhar here aboot. Eh mind meh mum tellin meh."

"Aye, he's right in some of what he says," Maureen agreed. "Well before our time, right enough. They say there used to be a right old church around here somewhere, predates Christianity, or so they say."

"Aye that's right enough, ye ken," Old Tam interrupted. "Meh mum telt meh it waz afore then. She reckoned in Celtic or Pictish times, thay were awh aboot. Ye dinnae want tae be messing wi' them. Got awh sort o strange goin ons awh them auld religions dae, so thay dae." Old Tam shook his head slowly. "Eh've been warnin folk th day takin peirt tae be careful at wat thay pul up. Onything cauld be cursed. We dinnae want a repeat o that bad luck thon auld skull brought ous, ye ken."

Some local children had found a rare Scottish sapphire and an old skull after a landslide last year – the result, as it turned out, of climate change. Old Tam with his dour predictions and character had convinced as many people as he could that the skull was cursed. Anything that had gone wrong or happened unexpectedly he blamed on the skull.

When all was said and done, you only had to scratch lightly beneath the surface of any modern techno-savvy-highlander to find the layers of superstition running deep.

"Don't you start your nonsense again, Tam. Nobody is going looking for treasure. No one is digging around the dunes, no ùraisg has been seen for years. And furthermore, there are no curses associated with that ancient church wherever it is. Anyway, nobody knows for certain where that old church was."

Mary came over. "My Angus reckoned it's here about on the beach, that old church… or rather, place of worship. It was too ancient to be a church my Angus said. There were some right old tales about it and the *ùraisg*. But they were lost with him. Perhaps, Maureen, you could find some of these old tales somewhere."

We all looked over at Maureen and then down towards the beach. *It must be awful not being able to access nature in the way we all take for granted,* I thought. Everyone knows the benefits for our wellbeing of being close to nature, beaches and woods. The others must have been having similar thoughts by the looks on their faces.

Before I could say anything, one of our local children appeared, quickly followed by his twin sister Fawn and their dog. Our pups had all come from the same litter, so they bounced around with glee, barked and ran off down the beach, jumping and circling around each other. We all watched them go, none of them had a care in the world.

"Me brofers good at finding treasure, sure you are, Stag?" Fawn said.

"I am, yes, I am. I am the bestest treasure-hunter you will efer find. Mind, I finded the skull and the brooch"

"No, you nefer. I found the brooch." Fawn stamped her foot and thumped her arms dramatically on her hips.

"Okay, we bofe found them then. Okay?" Stag relented. "And we can bofe find more treasure. Come on, Fawn, let's go." Stag ran off down the beach after the dogs, sand blowing a dust cloud around him.

But Fawn lingered. "Maureen, when we find the next treasure, we will buy you a special wheelchair. They have great big enormous wheels, like big and massive, way bigger than your ones. They are like great big balloons. I sawed them on Dornoch beach. We'll sell our treasure and buy you one all of your own, and you can come down and build sandcastles wif us." Fawn turned her head when she heard her brother calling. "Bye." She waved and run off after Stag.

"That wee lass is the sweetest thing," Mary said.

"Aye, she is that, Mary," Maureen added, wiping a tear from her eye. "This damned wind is making my eyes water."

We all knew it wasn't that, although the wind was getting up again.

"Well, if onybody is goin tae find ony treasure, it wull be that twa right enough. We all ken thay did no bad the last time." Old Tam ruffled Shep's head. "Come on, *balach,* time Eh got ye hame, afore the weather gets worse."

Shep struggled to his feet. I didn't know how old the dog was, but he seemed to have been ancient for as long as I could remember.

"Eh'll see ye awh at the ceilidh th night," Old Tam said as he headed off.

It was my cue to go off down the beach again to retrieve my wayward puppy. But the twins and the dogs were nowhere in sight.

11

The beach ceilidh at the pub proved as wild as the storm that raged outside. Many of the adults who had attended the clean-up with their families had left the children at home to come along and enjoy the evening's entertainment.

Drink flowed as the rain streamed down the windowpanes. Inside, wild dancers knocked over chairs, while outside, the wind toppled the benches. Crisps and nuts were crushed underfoot indoors while pebbles and seaweed swirled together and were dumped onto the roads. Singing and laughter were so loud inside the pub that no one realised until it was time to leave just how bad the storm outside was.

If we had stopped to notice, we would have seen how people had struggled to open the door to leave, and that a slight vacuum seemed to suck the air out of the room before the door closed again.

At the lock-in (reserved for the chosen favourites of Pete the Froth the owner), when no one technically paid for a drink (but in reality, the money and booze continued to flow), the numbers remaining inside consisted of the usual few. Mary was seldom seen in the pub at night since Angus' death and Auntie Lottie was on babysitting duties. That left: myself and Iona, Old Tam, the Twa Pinters (Archie and Sandy, so called as two pints of beer was all they ever asked for), Grace, Karen and a couple of younger males who had nipped into the toilet to avoid being thrown out with the rest at closing time.

The music and singing had ceased. Old Tam had found his stride again. "Eh'm tellin ye, the auld kirk waz somewhar atween here"—he placed his pint on the bar—"an here, thon big shed that Paul hiv given tae that new brewery."

"Oi, I'm no caring where the old kirk was – that's my pint." Archie grabbed back his drink.

"Wull, if ye wauld come wi' meh, Eh'll show ye juist whar Eh ken that auld kirk waz. Come on noo, or are ye feart?"

Before Archie could reply, the side door banged open and Paul of the Sheds hurried inside.

"What's wrong? Is Cavan okay, Dad?" Grace's face had drained of colour.

"Ach, there's nothing wrong with the wee lad. He's nice and cosy, tucked up in his bed. Out for the count, so he is," Paul reassured his daughter. "Lottie is keeping a close eye on him."

Pete the Froth passed over a drink to Paul of the Sheds. "On the house, like," he said.

I doubted whether Paul of the Sheds ever paid for a drink. He was so involved in the community. He helped most people who asked and those who didn't but should have. His involvement in our local rescue service meant that he had probably either helped a person or someone from their family at one time or other. When he entered a pub or party, everyone bought him a drink like a continuing thank you for all he did. It would appear tonight he was on duty again.

"I've just been down at the harbour checking on the boats. The fishermen are all either tethered up here or Inbhirasgaidh. I've already checked, but it's a wicked night. There's going to be damage somewhere." As if to confirm his statement, the lights flickered twice and went out.

"Damn, that's my pint sloshed all over the place."

"Will you watch what you're doing? You've just stood on my toe."

There was a scraping as a chair was moved, and I heard someone walking towards us. It was a little spooky. A beam of light suddenly blinded me, then two large beams flickered on beside the bar. Pete the Froth placed two more further along.

"Right, I think it's time everyone went home. So I'll bid you *oidhche mhath*. Be careful how you go – that's not hailstones we're hearing; that's the sand from the beach."

As we left the pub, Paul of the Sheds had already switched on his head torch. He stretched out his hands to Grace, Karen, Iona and myself as we left, hunkered down inside our coats.

"Right, girls, keep a good grip of each other. I'll walk you all home, starting with you, Karen, and before you say there's no need, I'm doing it. I'll not sleep safe in my bed if I don't know you all got home safely," Paul of the Sheds said.

"Your dad's so sweet," Karen said as we stepped out. "He's never going to accept we've grown up. Ouch."

Debris hit us as we left the shelter of the building. There was no point in talking as the howling of the wind was so loud we wouldn't have heard each other. Our heads bowed as if we were praying. We bent into the storm and headed to Karen's, before we arrived – soaked and shivering – at our house. We waved Grace and Paul of the Sheds off and fell into the house.

Something was wrong. I could feel it, but I couldn't put my finger on what. The howling had stopped, but we could still hear the storm trying to rip its way inside. I started to take off my coat, the feeling of disquiet still there. It was Iona who came up with the right question.

"Where's Malt? She's normally jumping up and down whining like a lunatic when we get back."

She was right. There was no sound inside the cottage at all. I should have been tripping up over her.

"Malt," I yelled as I fumbled with the cupboard to pull out a torch. "Malt. Where are you, Malt?"

I could hear the worry in my voice. I handed another torch to Iona and thanked myself for always making sure they were ready for use. Power cuts were not unusual in bad weather. In Blàs we had to be prepared.

"Well, she can't have got out. The doors were all shut, and besides, she was exhausted after her run about with Gillie Dubh all afternoon. She's probably just huffing somewhere because you didn't take her to the pub," Iona said, but I could hear she was concerned too.

I wished I had taken her to the pub. We checked out all the rooms and couldn't find her anywhere. She wasn't in any of her usual places. Her bed lay empty, as did mine which was her preferred choice given the chance. We were still in my bedroom when the lights reluctantly came back on.

"I didn't think we would see them back on tonight, but maybe now we might find that daft dog. Malt, Malt, where are you?"

We heard a rather pathetic yelp and both fell to our knees to check under the bed. And there she was, tucked right up at the back looking very nervous and half wagging her tail.

"Here, you silly dog. Come on, come on, Malt, come on out." Relief flooded through me.

Malt slowly crept forward and crawled out from her hidey hole. I cuddled her as Iona came around to see her.

"Here you daft thing, did you get a fright when the lights went out?" Malt rolled over onto her back and wagged her tail as Iona rubbed her belly.

As we stood up, Malt suddenly came to life and started jumping up and down and greeting us in her normal excited way. The horrors of being in the dark in a cosy house as a howling gale raged outside forgotten.

"Jeez, Stroma, I hope you're not depending on her as a guard dog. I don't think she would be much use. Imagine being afraid of the dark. What a pathetic excuse of a dog you are."

Iona bundled Malt up and hugged her close, a satisfied smile on her face. "Just as well we love you, little one. You can sleep with me tonight on my bed and I'll protect you. *Oidhche mhath,* Stroma, *chi mi sa mhadainn thu.*" She pecked my cheek and disappeared with my not so brave guard dog.

12

"Coffee," I groaned, my brain registering the sound of bashing and thumping as four paws scrambled for traction on the stairs. Malt's head appeared intermittently as she jumped up and down at the side of my bed. Ears flat out each time she leapt. She was doing a good impression of Dumbo in flight.

"Okay, okay, I'm getting up. Just wait a minute." I threw back the covers and grabbed my clothes. The shower could wait. We had another day planned for the beach clean-up – I would want to wash away the sand and salt once we were finished.

I sneaked a look outside expecting to see rubbish still blowing in the wind. Stillness and devastation met my gaze. Seaweed blown up from the beach hung on fences and telegraph wires. Sand and broken shells were scattered all around. Burst balls, tin cans and rags littered the ground. A trampoline lay on its side, buckled. Goodness knows where that had come from; no one I knew owned one.

"Morning, you ready for another day tidying up the beach?" Iona handed me a coffee. "Thankfully that storm has passed. *Greas ort,* folk will be making their way there now." Iona popped on a rather colourful hat. Her round dark glasses made her look even younger than she was.

"I like the tammy, sis."

She laughed. "It was the only one I could get at the time. It's warm so I'm not going to complain about the colour, or colours, I suppose."

We finished breakfast and headed out.

As we walked towards the beach, we spotted the obligatory single sock and shoe. Why was there always one shoe? I never saw a pair of shoes lost together – it was always one, never mind where I went. To my knowledge, I wasn't aware of lots of people hopping around with one shoe off and one shoe on.

We arrived at the beach and joined a small group of people. Many were looking out towards the waves crashing and tearing themselves apart as they rushed up the shore. Seagulls swooped and rode the currents. My hair blew from my face now that we had left the shelter of the houses.

"Meh, wull ye nae look at that?" Old Tam shook his head and stared along the length of the sand. The whole aspect had changed. The bench so loved by everyone was broken and imbedded in what was left of a dune. Huge tufts of grass had been ripped from the natural wall of sand that had protected the shore. The beach landscape was barely recognisable as that of the day before. Great heaps of sand had shifted. It was as if baby dunes had been made to replace the large ones that had been destroyed.

Malt disappeared down to investigate the new smells created in the wake of the chaos.

"Well, it looks like we have even more of a litter crisis than we expected," Iona said as she pointed out the vast amounts of plastic bottles and general rubbish that had been thrown into a sheltered area.

"Oh, *mo chreach*!" Old Tam said. "Eh cauld o waited until th day. Eh shauldnae hiv picked up onything yesterday. Wat a waste o time."

"Ah, come on, Tam, it's not as bad as that," Iona said. "It looks like most of it has ended up in just a few places rather than all over the beach. Any newcomers for today, please go and sign in with Paul over there and the rest of you come with me. We've got some tasty soup you can have at lunchtime then we should be finished. Thank you all again for coming."

"Stroma, can we take Malt with us? Gillie Dubh likes playing with her and we want to go further along the beach."

It was Swallow, the twin's big sister. She had a soft spot for Malt and was always looking for ways to add her to their household.

"Well, you have to look after her and yourselves. There are a lot of broken things about so be careful."

"It's okay. Dad is coming down later to join us. Come on Malt, come and see Gillie Dubh." And off my so-called loyal companion went. That was twice in less than twenty-four hours she had chosen to go off with someone else. Well, she wasn't the only one, my treacherous thoughts reminded me.

My stomach was rumbling but I could still hear the excited voices of the children along the beach. It must be near lunchtime by now. I looked up and there were the twins, Swallow and their big brother Lark bounding towards us, the pups running alongside them. You felt their excitement even from a distance. As they drew closer the smiles on their faces were evident.

"Wull, at least they hivnae fallen intae a hole this time," Old Tam droned beside me.

"What's all the excitement about?" Iona said joining us. Other members of the clean-up party were also moving towards us as the children drew nearer.

"Dad… Dad… Dad…" Lark gasped out.

"Juist tak yer time, wee mun. Breathe noo and wait a bitty." Old Tam placed his hand on Lark's shoulders. Although there were no tears this time, we had seen this all before – after the landslide the previous year which had unearthed the Scottish sapphire and the 'skull of doom' – as Old Tam liked to call it. It was so reminiscent it felt a bit eerie.

"Dad said to let you know what we found."

"Jeez." Ellen had joined us. "I hope it is not another skull or something else dead."

"And what would that something be?" Paul of the Sheds had come out of the refreshment tent when he heard the commotion. He was probably as relieved as we were that it appeared everyone was okay and no accidents had occurred.

"No, no, it's the beach. The beach has collapsed. It's massive, the hole, like really big. Somebody could fall right in, Stroma." Lark, unusually for him, was looking serious. No doubt remembering when his little brother and sister had tumbled down together with the landslip.

Stag burst out, "Dad is waiting for youse to come along. He doesn't want to leave. He said it needed fenced off or somefink. Me, I wanted to look and see if there was treasure inside but he said it was too dangerous. But, just fink, there could be another skull—"

So Stag was not so bothered about falling in then. He just wanted to be allowed to check out this new hole.

"Alright, Stag," Ellen interrupted. "Perhaps we should come along and take a look."

"Come on, come on, hurry. I don't want Stag going and looking for treasure without me." Fawn took off after her siblings along the beach. Malt and Gillie Dubh running behind them.

"If he turns up with another bloody skull I'm resigning from the school. I don't think I could stand another year of Stag and a skull," Karen said.

"Eh wauldnae worry, lass. Nae skull wull be there. Eh wauld ken. Eh wauld feel it in meh bones." Old Tam turned and made his way up towards the tea tents. "Youse can let meh know whut awh the fuss is aboot when youse come back. Eh'm off tae get some of thon broth – it smells right good. *Tiugainn,* Shep, *àm biadh.*"

"Well, there you go then – there isn't going to be a skull. Let's just hope someone hasn't buried one of their dead pets or a sheep there; the twins would be so unhappy," Iona said. "It's probably why Ralph sent them here, so he could check it out before the twins got back."

"And juist mind, it waz meh that telt ye if ony treasure waz tae be fooound it wid be thon bairns that fooound it," Old Tam shouted at us as we filed along the beach after the children.

"Aye, well he did say that," Ellen said. "But don't tell him I said that, will you? Hopefully, this collapse is not too bad. We don't want to have to close off part of the beach. It would be a devil of a job to police, anyway."

"Hopefully Iona is right and it's just a manmade hole for someone's poor pet remains," I pointed out. "What are the chances of finding something else of value in the one area. If I remember right, even the rainbow has only one pot of gold."

"Oh, come on, Stroma, it's exciting – just think, another skull maybe." Iona's infectious laughter trickled around as we went to see what 'fortune' was about to be revealed this time.

13

Conversation was buzzing around the rafters of the hall. Our elderly had left behind their normal competitive topics. Most other days their various afflictions were their preferred subjects. The winner was the one who had the most ailments but carried on as normal despite all that besieged them. The ultimate champion, however, was the one left alive after all their friends had departed. Unfortunately for them, that meant none of their friends were around to witness their victory.

Today, though, the subjects of ingrowing toenails, bowel movements and what doctor said what had been left unexplored. Ironically, given their normal topics of conversation, the subject up for debate was a six-foot-deep hole. However, not one in the graveyard this time but on the beach.

"Ach, *uil ma tha,* it's just as well we can't get down that beach. We wouldn't be wanting any of us falling in there before our time. Mark you, a nice sandy wee resting place with a sea view wouldn't be a bad spot to spend eternity." Catherine Cailleach laughed. "Aye, Crabbit, Meg loved that part of the beach, sure she did. Swore that was where she saw that *ùraisg*."

"You leave my Meg out of this," Crabbit answered. "I'll no have anyone speak ill of her."

"She's no dead, Crabbit, and she's hardly your Meg now. Maybe if you'd found your way to doing some housework, Meg may well no have left you for that foreign gentleman."

"I hardly think someone from Inverness can be called foreign, Cailleach. If he had been from Nairn, well maybe, but not Inverness, surely." Ben the Stump slurped his tea, his little finger raised delicately in the air.

Old Tam shuffled past their table. Tam had never joined the 'elderlies' of the village, although he would fit into the group in so many ways. He wasn't that old in comparison to some. His title had come about more to do with his attitude than the number of years he had been on the planet. Old Shep, as ever, was following up behind.

"Wull, Eh telt ye, if someane was gaein tae find something it wauld be them twins. Eh ken Eh wauld be right." He sat down slowly, lifted the cake off his plate and broke it in two before picking up his mug of tea. After pouring a little tea onto the plate, he added a wee drop of milk to cool it down before placing the plate on the ground. Shep continued to look up at him with pleading eyes. "Aye wull, ye be wantin yer wee bit o cake then, *mo ghraidh*."

He patted Shep's head and fed him the smallest piece of lemon cake from the table. Mary watched patiently, well used to Old Tam's routine. Maureen, however, tutted and held Blether tight.

"You better watch what you are feeding him, Tam, or the vet will be getting on to you for his weight," Maureen said as she sorted the pink shiny ribbon around Blether's neck.

"Dinnae be so daft," Old Tam said "Shep here is an athlete when eeh's nae hivin eeh's tea. Runs it all af, so eeh does. Nae like that spoilt wee lass of yers."

"I'll have you know Blether is not spoilt. It's her genes. We just have to watch what she eats from now on."

Our local vet was renowned for keeping a check on his doggie clients' weight. In the same way human doctors appeared to blame every ailment on smoking, our vet blamed many of the illnesses in the local dogs on weight gain. In Blether's case, he was probably right.

"It has nothing to do with her genes, thank you very much," Auntie Lottie shrieked. "As her breeder, I can vouch for that. If you would only let that poor thing walk some of the time, she wouldn't look so pudgy."

"She's not pudgy; she is delicate. Aren't you, my wee treasure? You love sitting up here on your mummy's knees, don't you?" Maureen clapped Blether under her chin as Auntie Lottie sighed heavily and shook her head.

"Speaking of the beach..." Mary drew everyone back to the main subject of conversation. "What are we going to do about that collapse? We can't keep it cordoned off for ever. It's near the area my Angus said was where that ancient worship used to take place. Said he used to have conversations with Parnell an Spuit there. If only we still had those archaeology students here, we could have asked them to take a look. You never know what could be there.

"Well, Mary, given that nothing has turned up yet, I think we will have to accept that nothing probably will. What we need to decide now is how to move forward."

There was no question that something had to be done. The storm had ripped away a large section of dune and left a hole and a drop onto the beach. We would have to get repairs carried out before someone fell into it.

It was decided that, in the short term, Paul of the Sheds would put up a warning sign. In the meantime, I would look into finding funding to repair that part of the beach. I'd have to talk to Digger Dodd; she would know how to go about it and probably give me a quote for the work at the same time.

Karen would be approached so the school could warn the children about entering areas that were fenced off. For children who were free to roam and play among the moorland, woods and beach, we knew the warnings could go unheeded.

14

"Come on Stroma, you've got to help. It's all in the... It's science." Iona poured out a greenish brown liquid. "I followed Mary's suggestions... almost to the letter."

That was the bit that was worrying me: the 'almost to the letter'. Iona had added a few wee improvements, or so she thought, to Mary's original ingredients. My glass sparkled.

"I'm not so keen on the colour." I hesitated.

"Ach, I can fix that. I just need you to taste it and tell me what you think."

It had been a hard day of driving finished with a rather tension-filled committee meeting. I'd rather have been going for a long walk with Malt followed by an early night.

"Come on, I'm not going to poison my own sister now, am I?" she persisted.

Malt's walk would have to wait. She had already been down to the beach anyway. Iona had taken her when she was checking out more areas for different varieties of seaweed.

Malt was fast becoming a community dog. Whoever could offer her the comfiest bed, the best treat or an interesting walk, got her loyalty. In that respect, she wasn't a typical Dandie. Although sociable, they tended to stick to their pack or family.

Malt had decided that most of the community were her 'family'. She went between myself and Iona which was fair enough, but she was also willing to go with many others within the community. Of course they all had some sort of added attraction.

Auntie Lottie and Paul of the Sheds had Malt's mum Whisky and Paul's daft young otterhound Madra; Old Tam with Shep could be relied upon for treats and a ruffle of the head, and Maureen completely spoilt both Malt and her sister Blether. Ellen and Mary had been known to open the door to her scratching, take her in and offer her enough tummy tickles to please any Dandie Dinmont Terrier. The Smiths had the added attraction of Gillie Dubh and could be relied upon for some adventure or other with the bairns. Being a dog owner was not turning out to be what I had expected. She came less and less with me on my journeys and spent more time in Blàs. On the days I was away, she was happy to stay with anyone who was available to see to her needs, as she saw it.

I could feel that familiar wave of loneliness creeping up and quickly quashed it. I gave myself an internal shake, closed my eyes and took a sip of my beer. A slight smell of the sea assaulted my nostrils. It wasn't unpleasant just a gentle reminder, a nudge to my memory. The cold liquid passed down my throat. I was still alive which was a bonus. There was a tickle of freshness left on my tongue.

"Well?" asked Iona expediently.

"Actually, it's not bad, not bad at all… if you can get past the colour." I drank some more. "This would be nice with some oysters sitting on the beach with a campfire on a summer's night."

"Don't aim so low, Stroma. I know that's something we can enjoy but I'm thinking more of selling it to some high-end hotel or restaurant as an accompaniment to our superb fresh Scottish shellfish. I reckon if we went upmarket, we could aim for a bigger profit on a lower turnover."

"We? I'm not sure I actually agreed to this, did I? I thought this was all your little business adventure."

"Well, you didn't say no so I took that as a yes. Like I said on the ferry, opening a microbrewery is something I have been considering for a while. It fits my skill set. I just needed the push. Ellen offering me the factory job was a bonus. I could develop my beer and still be pulling in a wage. And what's more with the seaweed factory specialising in health and beauty, I knew they wouldn't be considering alcoholic drinks. Producing alcohol would just not fit in with the healthy image they are trying to foster. Also, Mary gave me strict instructions that her wine recipe was ours alone, that is: yours and mine. We need to make something like beer in the short term but hopefully we can also offer wine or sherry later. I never considered you wouldn't be part of it all."

This was news to me. Mary had obviously been discussing my involvement with Iona. I hadn't ever considered starting my own business, let alone one with Iona, not until she had mentioned it that night at Mary's. When would I have the time? If Iona left again, I would be left here doing it all on my own.

"Look, I've being going over figures. I've talked it over with Ellen and you know how good she is with numbers. Auntie Lottie said Paul of the Sheds would help increase my knowledge regarding brewing. Mary has given me her blessing. I've even got a chef interested up at Ruadh Lodge. He wants me to take some beer along when I've perfected the recipe. Come on, Stroma, have another one and we can talk about it."

Ruadh Lodge was about as upmarket as you could get. They didn't cater for the regular tourist but for well-moneyed individuals who spent their whole lives experiencing the joys of what the world could offer those with enough in the bank to buy a small country.

Iona was excited, I saw that, but would that wear off after a while? I didn't need anything else in my busy life. She refilled my glass and we sat back to talk about it. After all, what harm could come out of a few beers and a sisterly chat?

❧

"Oh my God, it's bloody freezing." My breath froze in my chest as the water lapped around me.

"Relax, Stroma, just breathe – it's not that bad. Lean back, look at the stars. It's so beautiful."

Lifting my feet from the seabed, I tipped onto my back. Cold numbed my head. She was right – the sky was amazing. The sea lapped around my ears as I gently floated in the inky water. I lifted my arm and watched the droplets fall like crystals back into the water. A satellite moved across the heavens surrounded by millions of tiny lights. I sat up, looked into Iona's shiny face, and we smiled and laughed together in sheer joy at the universe.

"It seems Malt has finally stopped barking. Hopefully, she's sitting quietly beside our towels."

"Doesn't the village look so different from here? Look at the lights reflecting on the waves."

We took a few minutes to consider our home. This late in the evening on such a dark spring night few lights could be seen. Curtains had been drawn and many inhabitants would already be asleep in their beds. Rose cottage where the Smiths stayed had, as always, a light streaming from their upper window marking out where the twins slept.

"Oh, look, Stroma, look. I have so missed that." Iona pointed and I turned out to sea, away for my beloved village and towards the north. Green light shone across the sky, the Northern Lights as we called them, officially the Aurora Borealis, glittered and illuminated the sky above us. We fell back into the water and floated there for a while enjoying the magical scene. We clashed hands and simply stayed there, once more connected to each other, this place we called home and the spectacle that nature gifted us.

Waves started to increase gently at first, then frantic splashing nearby intensified their size. Something was breaking the water around us, I heard the water sloshing and plodding beside us, then a thump and a scratch of a paw. I stood up.

"Malt, you maniac, what are you doing?" Iona also broke the water and laughed. She grabbed the dog and sent her back the way she had come.

"Hey, you two, what the hell are you doing swimming at this time of night?" Paul of the Sheds shouted as Madra his otter-hound splashed his way towards us. The magic dispersing as the cold air engulfed our bodies.

"Hi, Paul, you're out late walking," I said, as I grabbed the towel he held out to me and wrapped it around myself.

"Well, it wasn't planned, I can tell you. I was in my bed when Madra started to howl and pace around. I thought he had a sore tummy or something. Anyway, he was desperate to get out, so I got dressed – only he ran to the bottom of the garden highly excited. I went over and there was Malt wriggling around. She kept going out of reach every time I tried to grab her. I was up anyway so decided, on such a nice night, why not follow her. Your door was open, did you know? I closed it on the way past. Malt came down here and I saw your towels. Is it no a bit late to be swimming? Did you take note of the tide? You're both shivering – you know you lose body temperature very fast in the sea."

"Paul." Iona hugged his arm. "You taught us well. We didn't take any risks. We stayed well in our depth. We're going back for hot chocolate. Are you coming?"

"No, no, lass. I'm going to take this lump back with me. I'm thinking your wee Malt may have the better instinct for rescuing than this one here." He ruffled Madra's head. "I'll say *oidhche mhath* to you both." He stopped to rub Malt's head and strolled back up the beach.

"Do you think he smelt the beer on us?" I asked as we made our way up the beach.

"Ach, if he did, he won't say anything. We're alright and that's what matters to him. I'm thinking, though, I'd better check the strength of that beer before I make any more. I barely remember coming here."

"Good idea," I said as we made our way home.

"Only, I do remember you saying, 'Wouldn't it be great to go for a swim right now,'" she added with a smirk, which was more than I remembered.

15

Along with the howling gale, another little treasure made its way into the light of the day. Rowan Smith arrived, when expected, in a fairly orderly manner in a maternity unit. Given the births I had witnessed with my friends, this was an unusual occurrence. Road closures, early arrivals and extreme personality changes in the mothers were more the norm in my experience. Excitement levels within the Smith household had filtered out into Blàs itself. The community were looking forward to welcoming wee Rowan and Jill home.

"We're not the youngest anymore; we're big. We are big ones," Stag proudly told Maureen who was probably trying to get as much information about the birth as she could. "I'm a big brofer." And he stuck out his chest, proud of this achievement.

Blether and Gillie Dubh were tangled together with their leads.

"Can you just pick up Blether there for me? Mind her back now... That's right, support her there. My, you are going to make a fine big brother right enough. And are you getting any new visitors coming to stay?"

"Wow, would you look at that." Stag watched as a large four-by-four drove past. Its windows darkened. "Fancy car, and look, it's stopping at Auntie Lottie's door."

The car pulled up and the driver walked around to open one of the back doors. Auntie Lottie emerged, turned back to say something to the people inside, waved, and closed the door. The car slowly made its way back out of the village.

Maureen was frowning, torn between the need to know who was in the car and having to acknowledge that Auntie Lottie obviously already knew.

"Do you fink that's her new car?" Fawn asked.

"No." Maureen was ruffling Blether's hair backwards and forwards. She stopped suddenly, a decision having been made. "Right, you two, I'm off to catch up with Lottie. I'll find out about the car for you, Stag, don't you worry." And she wheeled off like she was taking part in a car rally.

The summons came on the one night I was finally alone in the house with only Malt for company. Since our discussion on the microbrewery and our late-night swim, my feelings of loneliness had been dispersing. I could feel myself regarding things in a more positive light. Even Scott's decision to leave Blàs for a time was sitting better with me. I had understood his reasons – his parents needed him – but that didn't mean it still hadn't hurt.

I had just emptied a bucket of logs beside the fire when Malt ran past me and started jumping up and down at the kitchen door. I recognised the knocking of Maureen's walking stick immediately. Bucket in hand, I opened the door.

"Ah, Malt, wee soul. Meeting at Ellen's." She turned to go.

"What, right now?" I asked.

"Yes, why not? Oh, and bring that bucket with you – that's perfect."

"So much for our quiet night in then, Malt." I had no idea why I had been summoned again. This wasn't a scheduled meeting, so something had happened. And why did I have to take a bucket, for goodness sake? Maybe someone had a leak.

I grabbed Malt's lead and we marched over to Ellen's. Opening the door, I was wondering what cake I would be offered; I smelt something had been baking but couldn't work out what.

The usual suspects were there. Mary sat in the comfiest seat, next to her sat Auntie Lottie with Whisky at her feet. Ellen was busy cutting up a delicious-looking cake, and Giulietta was pouring out tea.

"Paul is at Grace's speaking with Iona about the huts, rents and beer," Auntie Lottie said, "so I thought I would join you all here."

"Why has a meeting been called? What's happened?" I asked.

"Stroma, will you put that bucket down and come grab a piece of cake and your tea." Ellen passed around plates to the others. "Well, according to Lottie, we seem to have a celebrity in our midst. A film star, no less. He is the new owner of Gleann Liath Lodge and is looking to invest in something that could help the community – something that would be inclusive and help locals, maybe to do with the environment or at least take in some aspect of the beauty of the area."

I looked across at Auntie Lottie. How on earth had she found someone like that? Was it their car she was seen getting out of earlier? Maureen had done the rounds, so everyone now knew there was someone new with expensive taste in cars. But that was about all the information I had heard.

Ellen continued. "I thought perhaps we could look at something we had put to one side while we focused on our big projects. I mean, almost instant money – you can't say no to that. What do you think, Stroma?"

"Well, of course, if we had the offer of money with no ties, we could well re-look at something that could be completed quicker without too much fuss. We have that list of improvements people rated from one of our earlier surveys. But I warn you, there are always ties, Ellen, even from philanthropists."

I was still more curious about how Auntie Lottie knew the film star and why she hadn't mentioned them before. "Do we know how much and whether it is for revenue or capital costs?"

"Well, I expected you would have some questions regarding the money and any conditions, Stroma." Auntie Lottie looked at me as she patted her hair. "However, I know Maureen is even more desperate to find out about our new resident and new benefactor."

"I am not. I expect he is just one of your ex-lovers," Maureen stated, before adding with a smirk on her face, "or more likely, the grandson of a distant lover from somewhere."

Auntie Lottie seemed to freeze for a second before giving an indignant huff.

Mary intervened. "Well, I've no doubt there could be some truth in that, but whatever the connection, that is Lottie's *affair*. I'm sure we would all agree." Mary stared straight at Maureen daring her to disagree. "We need to thank you Lottie for using whatever influence you had to our advantage. If this person is willing to help, who are we to say no? After all, with the purchase of Gleann Liath Lodge, he is now a part of this community too. Are you happy to continue to speak with them on our behalf, Lottie?"

Auntie Lottie smiled at Mary and nodded her head. I saw Maureen was struggling. Tension flowed from her in waves. Not knowing all the facts about our new neighbour and, worse still, Auntie Lottie seeming to know everything about him, did not sit well with her.

Ellen added, "I think Stroma should go along to any meeting. After all, she looks after the money. Or even Iona, if she has a mind. Right, I'll leave you to sort out the best date for that. I will want a report and we need to know what, if any, hoops we have to go through."

"Ellen, I have two things I would like to know," Mary said.

"Firstly, what kind of cake is this? I can taste the apple, right enough, but I just can't place the other flavour."

"Oh, yes, I was just trying it out. It goes perfectly with our theme. It is apple and seaweed. I thought we could sell some of it at our next market. What do you think, ladies? Do you like it?"

We all agreed it was delicious. Apple and seaweed – we certainly were going all out on our beach and shore theme.

"The second thing"—Mary broke into my thoughts—"is why have you brought a bucket, Stroma?" Her gaze twinkled across to Maureen who smiled back.

"I can't believe you fell for that again," laughed Maureen. "Last time I got her to bring a wooden spoon."

Damn, I thought as I joined in the laughter. *I won't be caught again. Next time I am summoned it will just be me and nothing else.*

Only, next time, something else was needed.

16

Nobody had seen Old Tam for two days. Like many older people he was a person of habit. You could tell what time of the day it was when you saw Old Tam and Shep around.

Bright and early in the morning before many of us were even out of bed, they would make their way to the local shop for rolls. Mid-morning and they could be seen again off to check out the newspapers, have a wee blether with the owner of the shop, buy some granny sookers (better known as pan drops by most), a wee treat for Old Shep, then they made their way back home with some fresh purchase for his mid-morning snack.

"Perhaps he has changed his routine for some reason."

Maureen scowled across at me for entertaining the thought.

"Do you think he went off with Morag?" Maureen said meekly. Morag, Old Tam's granddaughter, and Struan her young son were away for the weekend.

"I've no idea. Have you tried the house?" I asked.

"Of course, but there is no reply. Only I'm sure I would have remembered if he said he was going with them." Maureen patted Blether as much to comfort herself as anything else.

"He's not been in the shop and nobody has seen either himself or Shep around. I'm worried, Stroma, and so is Mary.

She asked me to find you. You know where Morag hides her spare key."

Old Tam's cottage and some of his outbuildings had been converted so both he and Morag had a place of their own. "I think we should take a look inside."

I was reluctant to do that. After all, Old Tam could well be down the road seeing his family with Morag. It felt like an intrusion to be going into their house without good cause.

"Stroma, what if he has fallen and Morag comes back and we haven't checked on him? Can you imagine the fright she would get and the disappointment that we hadn't noticed he was missing or hadn't checked up on them?"

"You know I could always phone and ask her."

"Don't be daft. What if he didn't go with her? She would be that worried and we would have spoilt her weekend for nothing. Come on now, it will only take a second or two." As if on cue a blast of heavy metal music filled the air. "Hold on, that's my phone."

I left Maureen to her one-sided conversation. Honestly, sometimes there was no privacy in this place. What if Old Tam had a wee thing going this weekend that he hadn't told us about and we spoilt it by sneaking into his house? He probably had gone with Morag – after all, it was his family too she was visiting. Anyway, I didn't need Maureen's permission to call Morag. As soon as Maureen was off her phone, I vowed I would do just that.

"Right, right, okay, right see you in a wee minute. *Tìoraidh an-drasta*. Okay, we've got to collect Mary first."

What had changed? It was her who had sent Maureen to find me. If Mary was worried enough that she wanted to come along too then the choice had been taken out of my hands. "Morag has been in touch with Mary. He's not answering his phone."

I felt a flutter in my stomach. The signs were not good. Old Tam normally didn't hesitate to answer his phone when he knew it was Morag on the other end. We dropped by Mary's, finding her standing waiting in her coat and wellies.

"Okay, let's go. I hope Tam is alright. I don't like to think we have lost another character from the village."

"Ach, I'm sure he's fine. If something had happened to Old Tam, we would hear Shep howling," I said.

We arrived at the cottage and all seemed quiet. I searched around for the key.

"Wait." Maureen grabbed my arm. "Wait, Stroma, oh no, no, poor Tam, poor, poor Tam. He's here Stroma."

I turned slowly expecting to see Old Tam sprawled out in the garden but instead I watched him coming towards us. There appeared to be a silent crowd following him. Others joined in behind as he passed them. The old man was carrying something in his arms. A quiet bundle of black-and-white fur. Old Shep no longer limping at his side. His days of shadowing his master were over. Old Tam, tears streaming down his face, gently held his loyal companion in his arms.

"Eh took eem up tae the auld sheep pen," he sobbed. "It wer eez favourite place."

"How long have you been there, Tam?" Mary gently held his arm.

"Yesterday, Eh think. Eh knew it wer comin. Eh wrapped eem up warm, ye ken, and carried eem up. But Eh cauldnae leave eem thar, eftir, ye ken. Eh juist cauldnae."

I had found the key and opened the door. Mary ushered Old Tam inside. He was sheet white. The cold oozed from him as he walked past, clutching his old friend close.

Mary searched around for cups as we waited for the kettle to boil. Old Tam gently placed Shep in his warm bed and covered him with a blanket. He ruffled his head once and sat down exhausted, as much by the emotional strain as the effort it would have taken him to carry his companion home. I hurried over and placed a warm rug over Old Tam's shoulders.

"Thank ye, lass," he said, wiping a stray tear away from his face. "Ee waz a guid companion, Eh'll say that fur eem. A right loyal dug, ye ken. Cauldnae hiv asked fae a better ane, Eh juist cauldnae."

"Here you go, Tam, take a hold of this. You will be needing it." Mary placed a mug in his hands. There was a distinct smell of alcohol coming from the hot drink.

Paul of the Sheds walked in and offered Old Tam his hand. "I heard. How you doing, Tam?" The atmosphere changed as it so often did when Paul of the Sheds was around. An air of order and calm seemed to follow him wherever he went. That was unless he was dealing with Auntie Lottie when even he seemed bemused by her goings-on. Still, he took most of that in his stride as well.

"When you're ready, Tam, we will have to place him in his final resting place. He can't stay here for long."

"Paul, leave the man in peace. He has just spent a night outside. He needs to warm up," Mary rebuked.

"It's okay, Mary. Ees right. Eh wauldnae want auld Shep left here or'er lang. Ee needs to be awa playing wi' th sheeps and runnin or'er th moors like ee waz when ee waz a pup. Eh need tae let eem go." Old Tam stood up slowly as if crippled and ageing in grief. Every step seemed to hurt him.

"Where are we going, Tam? Have you thought of a place?"

"Aye Eh hiv. Eh'm puttin eem under thon apple tree in the garden. Ee loved to laze thar and watch ous. It wull gie eem shade in the sun an Eh can still come oot an speak tae eem when Eh want tae."

"Right, you stay here and get warm. I'll go and sort it out, then you can all come out when you are ready."

By the time Paul of the Sheds had dug Old Shep's final resting place, Tam's colour had improved.

Villagers stood on the hill that overlooked the garden. Iona was there with Malt. In fact, almost all the village dogs were there. They must have felt the sadness as they all lay down quietly or stood silent at their family's side.

Peter the Pipes stood alone. As we entered the garden, he played a mournful tune. Old Tam followed us out, Shep in his arms for the last time, wrapped in his favourite blanket.

Maureen in that short time had managed to compose a short tribute to our village's oldest pet. It was both melancholic and humorous, capturing the spirit of Old Shep one last time.

Blàs said goodbye to one of its favourite, most loyal and loveable, albeit smelly, friends in its own fitting way. We would all miss him limping along and shadowing Old Tam. We could only hope that Old Tam's heart could be mended somehow after this.

17

"Well, we have to do something, I can't even get Grandad to take the bairn for a walk in his pushchair. He's ageing before my eyes." Morag looked distraught. She was used to Old Tam being a pessimist, but this was something else.

Mary picked up Struan and placed him on her knee singing softly the traditional *Gàidhlig* lullaby 'An Coineachan'.

Hò-bhan, hò-bhan, Goiridh òg O,
Goiridh òg O, Goiridh òg O
Hò-bhan, hò-bhan, Goiridh òg O,
Gu'n dh'fhalbh mo ghaoil 's gu'n dh'fhag e mi.

"*Ach m' eudail,* you have nothing to worry about, we won't leave you anywhere. Such a *balach math.*"

Morag smiled, besotted. "Aye, he is that right enough, Mary. *Mo bhalach math.* Grandad loves him dearly as well. How could he not? Only now it seems he would do anything for him but leave the house. He hasn't gone out since he buried Shep. I should have been here. I knew Old Shep was getting done."

"Not at all Morag. You needed to see your family and so did you *a ghràidh*." Mary looked into Struan's large eyes. "Shep had been on his last legs for years now. Nobody could have known he was going to go when he did."

"Grandad did," Morag answered stubbornly.

I chimed in, "Aye, well it was his dog, so he would."

"It's not healthy, Mary," Maureen added "Tam keeping indoors. I've tried to get him to take Blether out or at least accompany me for a walk, but he is having none of it, stubborn old fool."

"Aye well, you'll be missing his gossip, Maureen. I can't remember the last time I saw your heads together discussing the community's little secrets."

I helped myself to another scone waiting for Maureen to say something, only she didn't. *She must be worried if she's stuck for words*, I thought.

"Is he not going out at all, Morag, not even for his weekly paper?"

"No, well, that's not entirely true. He goes out into the garden and talks to Shep under the tree but nowhere else. I've had the twins at my door asking to see him to come out and walk the beach with them, but he won't go out the front door at all."

"It may be that another dog is the answer," Mary mused.

"Well, you can forget that, Mary. I already suggested it. Even found out where we could get a new collie. He wouldn't even go and visit them. So I took photos and he just looked and said, 'Aye very nice. Em noo wantin aneithir dug,' and went off into the garden and stood under Shep's tree."

"Could we not just get him one? He would have to feed it and look after it. Old Tam wouldn't let it starve."

He was stubborn I knew, but he was also a dog lover, and even if he was mourning his beloved Shep, he wouldn't harm a dog. Still, I wasn't at all sure this was the right thing to do.

"Maybe we should get a rescue dog with something wrong

with it. You know – a missing eye or leg or ear or really ugly. Tam's an old softy, he would take special care of something that was needing looking after." Maureen's suggestion wasn't a bad idea exactly. However, I was feeling more and more uneasy about the whole proposition. Thankfully, I mused, what dog rescue centre would be willing to hand over an animal without meeting up with the prospective new owner? No reputable centre would. I breathed a sigh of relief knowing her proposal wouldn't work.

"You know, Morag," Mary said, handing back Struan and picking up her tea. "This wee bairn of yours is missing out. He was just telling me how much he would love a new dog."

"Away with you, Mary. Between this little man and my work, I have quite enough to do. The last thing I need is a puppy or dog to cope with too. And this wee mite hasn't said his first word yet never mind stringing a whole sentence together."

"Ach well, that's because he told me in Gaelic, did you not *laochan*? *A 'Mhairi, tha mi ag iarraidh cu,* you all heard him." Mary looked around at us, her blue eyes twinkling.

Morag burst out laughing. "You are incorrigible, Mary. He did not say *cu*."

Only, as children often do, Struan almost proved her wrong and out came a cry that sounded very much like the word *cu*.

"There we go then," said Mary. "That's it sorted. Morag, you need to get a dog for this poor bairn. The thing is, do you get a collie or is that too close to Old Shep or something else mad and family friendly."

"Jeez, Mary, you don't give up – I'm not getting a dog."

"Not you, Morag, I didn't say you, did I? I said—"

"Ach, he is way too young for a dog, and you know it. It would be down to me to look after it."

"Blether and I could help you there," Maureen said.

"NO, no and no. I am not getting a dog." Morag was adamant.

"Of course you are not." Mary said. "Struan is getting a dog. Is his birthday not coming up?"

"His birthday is months away yet, as you well know, Mary," Morag informed her.

However, Mary was well into her stride. "I mean, everyone knows that having a dog helps children understand empathy, teaches them responsibilities, and more importantly, we can all see how much he is missing Old Shep. Yes, a dog will help him come to terms. It's just a great shame you wouldn't be able to cope. You'll be overtired, going back to work to deliver all these new babies. You'll have to give the dog back, of course, unless someone can help out, wouldn't you say, Stroma?"

Before I could answer, Maureen said rather indignantly, "I've already offered to help. You can't be sending that poor puppy back, not after you just got it. That would be cruel. In fact, I'll take it. Just give the dog to me and I will look after it. Blether would soon get used to another dog."

We all stared at Maureen, until Morag said, "Maureen, are you forgetting I don't actually have a dog?"

"What, oh yes, sorry, of course you don't. Mary, what are you talking about making me think these things?"

"Tam needs to be reminded of all these things, Morag, after you get your dog. Then you tell him you have to put the dog back unless you get some help. That should wake him out of his grief, and before you know it, the new dog will be sleeping and eating in Tam's part of the cottage. Yes, this should work well."

Mary closed her mouth and dared anyone of us to question her logic. I didn't like it at all. If Old Tam didn't want another dog, we should respect that. However, trying to cross Mary when she was meddling would make no difference, no matter what I said.

"And what if he doesn't offer to help, Mary, what then?" Morag asked.

"Well, Maureen here has already offered to take it off your hands," Mary said, with a gleam in her eyes. "Only you have to remember, Morag, Tam is stubborn and prone to wallow in self-pity even when things are going well for him. The only time I have ever known him to sound happy was when he transformed in that ridiculous bright yellow tartan suit the year he was the Chieftain at the Highland Games."

We all thought back to that day, when dour Old Tam wowed the crowds with his joy and loud suit. His favourite hat for the first and only time had been taken off and in place of it sat an oversized tammy in a matching yellow tartan. The most enormous feather reached for the sky from the side. No one had seen Old Tam smile and joke as much as he had on that day. However, as soon at that suit came off, there stood our loveable old pessimistic Tam. We were all smiling together as we remembered.

"Okay, okay, Mary, you win but I am telling you if this doesn't work it will be to your door that I will be coming. So you had better get a dog basket here just in case."

"Ach, I've no worries there, lass. Tam will be all over the new dog pretty quickly, you mark my words. He's just needing a little push or should I say a little wet furry nose."

As we walked back together, Morag said, "I've no idea when I will get a dog or what kind. The one thing I do know is that I am desperate enough to try anything to get Grandad out and about again so don't be surprised if you see me with a four-legged beast the next time we meet up."

I assured her I wouldn't, and we both went our separate ways.

"Well, what do you think, Malt? Will she get a dog?" Malt wagged her tail and placed her two front paws below my knee "You haven't a clue either. Well, we will just have to wait and see."

18

The air seemed to sparkle around Iona, matching the light in her eyes. A soft flush infused her cheeks. I couldn't put this down to the time she was spending outdoors. Given our weather, her face would have been glowing a robust red scoured by the wind. The reason for her barely concealed excitement soon became obvious.

"Honestly, Stroma, he's a magician. No wonder they ask these ridiculous prices for his food." Iona had finally met up with the chef from the exclusive and highly expensive Ruadh Lodge near Blàs.

It was one of those places where if you needed to ask the price of a meal you simply didn't go. People came from all over the world to stay at this exclusive retreat. We had a few well-known folk who owned houses in the area, and when around, they would frequent the restaurant at Ruadh Lodge. It was a world away from Blàs, unless you worked there. It was highly improbable that any of us would ever eat there.

"I mean, we can harvest some of the same seafood ourselves and just cook it for nothing. But I have to admit he does have a way with food. I'm off to visit him in his kitchen tomorrow after-noon. The lodge is closed right now so he is going to give me a tasting session. He loves the thought of our seaweed beer and is interested in supplying it to his clientele. He uses seaweed in many of his dishes anyway so is open to what we could supply him with, once we are up and running."

Iona had met up and spent the afternoon on the beach with Mateo the chef. It hadn't been the warmest of spring days but that hadn't stopped them from diving for scallops. Iona then took him to see the seaweed factory, after which they spent a few hours showing each other their favourite spots for harvesting the different types of seaweed around the area. Their afternoon had been topped off with a small firepit on the beach, cooking the various foods they had collected.

"Like me, he loves foraging," Iona continued. "I can't tell you how fantastic his cooking was. You could taste the sea. It gave me such a thrill to be able to eat what we had gathered."

It wasn't as if we hadn't ever eaten seafood before or, if it came to that, couldn't get fresh seafood ourselves but I knew what Iona meant. I could cook up a tasty enough meal but there were certain people who could take the same ingredients and make it special. Mateo, according to Iona, was one of them.

Mateo hadn't been that long in the area, therefore word of his cooking skills was only just beginning to get around. I had never been to Ruadh Lodge's restaurant and had certainly never tasted Mateo's food. It was way above my price range, and I had to admit, there had been no occasions recently to warrant a special meal anyway.

I had become a bit lazy regarding going out, apart from to the pub or walks with Malt. After a day's work away, I looked forward to simply getting home. My idea of a perfect evening was taking Malt for a nice walk, followed by a home-cooked meal and a cuddle with my dog on the sofa. Well, that was when I wasn't being summoned to either Mary or Ellen's house. Perhaps it was about time I made more of an effort and headed out to somewhere special occasionally.

As if reading my thoughts Iona said, "I'd offer to take you

with me but figured you'd be too busy. I'll report back to you once I find out from him what he needs from either us or the factory in terms of ingredients."

"Are you sure you'll report back everything, Iona," I replied with a smirk. "You seem quite smitten with Mateo."

Iona looked indignant for a moment "Well, I could argue the toss with you, Stroma, but you wouldn't believe me. To be honest, I do think he is very talented and we had an interesting afternoon. I'll say this: I wouldn't say no if he offered me something a bit more personal." She grinned. "So don't wait up, and do me a favour: don't turn into Auntie Lottie or the others. If I thought for one moment you were trying to match me up with anyone, you wouldn't see me for dust or, in this case, sand." She kissed my cheek and ran upstairs to shower leaving the scent of sea and fresh air in her wake.

"I haven't seen Iona around for a couple of days." Maureen had cornered me at the shop a few days later.

"Ach well, you know what she's like, busy, busy, busy." I tried not to blush.

"Only I had heard she was seen having a cosy little time with that new chef, near the seaweed factory. Nice wee fire they had going and I'm not talking about the ones that burn logs either."

"Now, Maureen, that's how rumours start. I'm hoping you're not about to do that. We need Iona here; she hasn't finished with her role in the seaweed factory yet. If you carry on like this, you'll scare her away and we don't want that, do we?"

I hadn't noticed Mary joining us. I had been too busy trying to form an appropriate retort.

"I expect Iona was just doing her job. Researching and developing – after all, the factory is expanding their health food range. Is that not what she is employed to do, Stroma?"

I nodded.

"Well, if that is the case where is she now then?" Maureen persisted.

"Looking into more products and testing out machinery as far as I am aware. Iona is her own person as you know, Maureen, and she has lots of research to do. Please don't read any more into it."

Maureen huffed "Well, Blether, I see we are not going to get any more information for these two. But I'm seldom wrong, Stroma. I just don't want our wee lass to get hurt by some Jack the lad. I'll see you at the meeting tonight. Oh, and remember to bring along that bucket of yours. Or at least a plate with a cover." She laughed and wheeled off. I wasn't about to fall for that again, my bucket would be staying where it was.

I just hoped Iona was going to make it back in time for the meeting. She sent a text the night before to say she wouldn't be home that night so I knew she was fine.

"I don't think Maureen quite understands our wee Iona. If anyone is going to get burnt from a relationship, it won't be our girl. I sometimes wonder if she will ever be able to accept Iona has grown up." Mary smiled across at me. "She'll be back in time, don't you worry. Let's just hope that will put a stop to any wagging tongues. Hopefully, that poor Chef Mateo knows what he is getting into. See you tonight, Stroma, and you too, I expect, Malt."

Mary slowly walked away. Blàs was small and its residents always seemed to know what was happening in the area. But how they knew so quickly was always a puzzle. How on earth had these two known about Iona staying over at Mateo's? The way news travelled in these parts always made me feel bewildered.

Neither Mary nor Maureen left the village often and they certainly didn't go far, so how did they know what was going on outside its boundaries?

A vision of a network of local spies reporting to them made me glance around at the people walking by in a different way.

Could they really have something like that going on? Probably, I reasoned, but not in any formalised way, more an informal good-intention spreading of news type of thing. It was, however, just as effective as any spy network.

Mary, thankfully, was right though. I wasn't overly concerned about Iona ending up with a broken heart. She enjoyed herself and, rather like Auntie Lottie before her marriage, she rarely had what most would call a relationship, more a succession of lovers.

As I mused this over, it struck me she was like her in another way as well. Any use of the word long-term or relationship and she'd be off as soon as the words were out of your mouth. Perhaps I should have taken a leaf out of her book, then maybe Auntie Lottie would stop trying to pair me off with every single male in the area.

19

Iona barely had time to shower and change before we left for the Development Trust meeting. Our Trust owned and managed the factory so a regular report was expected. Tonight was Iona's turn.

"I take it your research was a success then?" I ventured as we walked towards Ellen's, Malt marching along between us.

"Oh, I think I can comfortably say it was a great success," she smirked.

"Jeez, Iona, you better wipe that grin off your face and try not to look so smug or Maureen and Auntie Lottie will be all over you."

"Ach, let them. Auntie Lottie will be fine about it, and Maureen, well she is putty in my hands when I want her to be."

"Don't underestimate their desire to match you off. Remember, Auntie Lottie is happily married now and that has changed her view a little."

Iona stopped walking "Really?" She wasn't looking so confident now.

"Look, I'll try and head off any remarks. You keep filling them full of facts and formulas – that should keep their minds occupied."

"I've missed that so much." Iona inhaled the smell of home-baking as we entered Ellen's kitchen. I recognised the apple and seaweed cake but saw what looked like carrot muffins on the table as well. Ellen had obviously stopped experimenting with seaweed and was returning to recipes she had already tried. She had baked, and we had tasted, dozens of different recipes so far.

"Ah, here you both are." Ellen came over and embraced us both. "I hear you have been busy, Iona. The trustees are really pleased with how things are going. I can feed whatever you tell us tonight into their next meeting tomorrow morning. Now, help yourself to cakes everyone. The muffins are carrot and seaweed."

So not quite *finished with our favourite theme of the moment then.*

We all listened patiently while Iona brought us up to speed on how far along we were with the seaweed beauty products and the general workings of the factory.

"So, the seeding has gone well this year and we are continuing to develop our products. That's why I'm here, after all. One of our main enterprises will be to supply high-end beauty products. From exclusive spas to high-star hotels, we intend to supply each with their own range of exclusive creams and beauty products that they can gift and sell to their clients. There is a demand out there which we should be able tap into. Locally, as you know, we have a few hidden away lodges and high-class hotels that are frequented by the wealthy. We've already made contact and are actively pursuing contracts to supply them. We will need to increase our range as we develop but supplying high-end markets means we don't have to have such a big turnover. My report regarding progress has, as Ellen already pointed out, been presented to the trustees on the seaweed factory board. The reason for tonight's meeting to is advise you on where we want to diversify and add more social enterprise within the community."

Once again, I was taken aback by Iona in 'work mode'. No jokes or clever quips, no slapdash comments. I was seeing her in an entirely different light. She was scary in her efficiency. I thought I was the one who was organised, up to speed and good at my job, but seeing Iona deliver her report was making me re-evaluate both myself and her. There was no doubt she was great at what she did.

"I've spoken at length with the trustees and Ellen. It will take us a few years to get more established, and we need to focus on our chosen products and be sure we can produce enough seaweed in terms of variety and amount to develop our range. At the same time, we hope to continue to develop our health food range and supply the same organisations with seaweed and other seaweed-based products that they can use within their establishments. Both these lines will give us the best possible chance of surviving and thriving.

"Another product line that we considered and have since rejected is beer. Two reasons. One is it doesn't fit well with our 'health' theme and the other is, quite frankly, we won't have the time to develop anything along these lines at the moment. This leaves a gap in a potentially lucrative market, which is where Stroma and I come in."

I stopped eating my cake. I hadn't been expecting her to present our thoughts on a brewery so soon. We were still at such an early stage, and if truth be told, a part of me still regarded it as just one of Iona's crazy ideas that she would soon become bored with. Even the tastings we had shared hadn't convinced me that she was in it for the long term. I knew she had already sounded Ellen out about it. But now I was finding out that she had also talked with the trustees of the factory as well.

"So, given that we want to encourage new growth and cottage industries in the area. The board has agreed to own a small part of the brewery that Stroma and I will set up. This way, hopefully both organisations can benefit from each other. I've already spoken to Paul of the Sheds. He's willing to let us rent one of his redundant buildings at a reasonable rate. It is well big enough for our immediate start and will still allow for growth.

There's more land we can put other buildings on if we find we need the space. We've already got some organisations interested in our product."

We do? I thought. *Since when?* Perhaps I should have been paying more attention to what Iona had been telling me about this proposal.

Iona sat down beside me and immediately broke the professional persona by winking at me, grabbing a piece of my cake and giving me one of her blazing smiles.

I protected the rest of my cake from wandering hands.

"Stroma, have you anything to add?" Ellen asked.

I shook my head. I felt a bit shell-shocked, to be honest – due to a combination of my little sister being an amazing presenter and the dawning reality that I was to become a part-owner of a seaweed brewery. When had my mad scientist of a sister turned into an entrepreneur?

Auntie Lottie broke in. "Before we close the meeting, Maureen will have asked you all to bring along a container, so if you can pop them up here, I'll drop in some of the shellfish my Paul and the fishermen handed in. The market was slow in Inbhirasgaidh, so they were left with quite a bit of extra fish. You can leave a donation if you want, and it will go to the fishermen's mission. They are always looking for money."

"Stroma, where is your bucket?" I blushed and looked over at Maureen who was smiling mischievously at me.

"Well, I told her to bring it along. Did you forget, then?" Maureen's smile was wide and full of humour. She'd known fine well I wouldn't bring one, especially after last time.

"Never mind, lass," Mary twinkled. "Here you go, I brought a spare one, just in case."

I looked between the pair of them. They'd known this would happen. This would now be their standing joke. I had just added to their repertoire of enjoyable mischief. I mean, who brings an extra bucket to a meeting? Actually, who would bring a bucket along to a meeting anyway? I looked around. It would seem a number of people had. Bother! How would I know whether or not to bring something along the next time?

20

Something wasn't right with the picture in front of me. I was on my way to the shop – nothing new there. Locals were dotted around the place, a few speaking in small groups while others were getting on with their normal everyday business. Old Tam and Shep… except… it wasn't Old Shep. However, there *was* a sheepdog at Old Tam's side.

As they drew nearer, I saw this dog was a lot younger and livelier than Shep had been for many a year. The dog also didn't have that leaning tilt Shep had had. This collie's coat appeared healthy and thick. I hid a smile as Old Tam approached. It was good to see him out and about. He hadn't been seen around the village for ages. Morag had waited longer than I had expected before introducing a new dog into the household. Something must have changed for her to have thought the timing was now right.

"*Madainn mhath,* Tam, and who is this, then?" Malt had jumped up at the new dog in greeting. The collie immediately moved forward into a play bow, having recognised the arrival of another young spirit.

"Ee's Morag's. Eh'm juist lookin eftir eem."

"That's kind of you. Where did he come from?"

I bent down and rubbed the collie's ears, immediately making a new friend for life.

"Ach, it wer Radical Sandy. Seid th pair dug wer useless at the sheeps. Nae like meh pair auld Shep. Ee wer the best dug ever at the sheeps."

That explained it then. Radical Sandy was well known for breeding and training sheepdogs to look after flocks. He was famed throughout the farming and crofting community for his dogs. It was said if he entered any dog into the sheepdog trials there was no point in anyone else even trying. Second spot was the best other competitors could hope for. However, there was no saying, despite the sire and bitch, whether a dog would be good with sheep. Sometimes a dog just didn't hit the mark, no matter who its parents were. Obviously, this rather lovely sheepdog had not displayed the right signs. Radical Sandy would have been happy to give it away to someone he knew as long as it wasn't to be bred from.

There was no way Morag would want her dog involved in creating more puppies and certainly Old Tam wasn't about to go down the road of dog-breeding.

As if reading my mind, he continued. "Pair wee thing cannae hiv pups either. Had a bit o a problem an had tae be done, ye ken. That's why eez so wee, ye ken."

Compared to Malt he didn't look small at all, but I suppose, thinking back on Old Shep, he was quite wee for a border collie.

"Have you named him yet, Tam?"

"No, Eh've no. It's meh Morag what's come up wi' ees name. Eez nae mine. Eh'm nae gettin another yin. Eh telt ye that."

"Yes, sorry you did." I smiled into the dog's coat – Old Tam could be as stubborn as any of us.

"So, what name did Morag pick, then?"

"Nae meh choice mind," he reminded me. It must be an unusual name for him to be so coy about it, but then again, Old Tam was set in his ways. If this new dog wasn't called Jim, Shep (mark two), Fly or Glen, any name would sound racy to him.

"It can't be that bad, Tam. Come on, what is it?" Surely, she wouldn't have called it Sparkle or anything like that. Morag just wasn't that kind of woman.

Old Tam looked over his shoulder making sure nobody was around to hear him. Nobody was taking any notice of us.

"She's ca'd eem Dundee. Wauld ye credit it? She's only named th pair wee sowel eftir a city – Dundee." He'd raised his voice in disgust. The collie looked up at him and wagged his tail. Old Tam bent down and rubbed the dog's head, once more talking in a softer tone. "Eh ken, Eh ken, it's nae yer fault. There's naethin wrang wi' the city, ye ken, but it's nae right fur a dug. Ay no, pal. Dundee, Eh ask ye."

"Maybe she's honouring you and your mum, Tam. You know, paying homage to your heritage." Personally, I thought it was both a unique and thoughtful name.

"Eh dinnae care why she done it. It's juist nae right." He looked around as if expecting Morag to jump out at him any minute. "Eem and meh's got an understanding though. Eh'm cawin eem a different name and ees a lot happier wi' it."

"Oh, and what's that then, Tam?" I was dreading him saying Shep – it wasn't unheard of for people who owned working dogs to either keep using the same name or alternate it with just one other choice. So, once one Shep died, maybe they would call their new dog Glen, and once Glen died, you would be right back to Shep for the next dog.

"Dìleas." The dog jumped up and extracted a pat from Old Tam. Old Tam smiled down at Dundee or Dìleas. "See, ee likes meh name fur eem a lot better, ye ken."

I had to admit I liked his choice but saw no problem with Morag's either. I found myself wondering if Morag had forced this choice on Old Tam. Had she chosen the name Dundee knowing it would annoy her grandfather?

Having his own name for the dog would strengthen their bond, that was for sure. Mary popped into my head – this was exactly the sort of thing she would have done to encourage the relationship between Old Tam and the collie without him even being aware of it. I reminded myself how alike Mary and Morag were in nature, and how, although distant they were in fact related.

"I like that, Tam. Dìleas. I may stick with your choice if Morag doesn't mind."

"Ach, Eh dinnae think she'll object tae much. Eh've herd eer mistakenly caw eem that already. Eh'm hopin afore onybody gets tae grips wi' that ither name Eh'll hiv changed eer mind aroond to meh way o thinkin."

So, Morag was already using Old Tam's name for the dog, as if by accident. She knew what she was doing. The dog may be a bit muddled for a short while but that would soon pass.

Dìleas was Gaelic and probably one of the oldest and most common names for a dog. Dìleas, faithful, or the equivalent, as many others would say, to Fido.

I was looking forward to seeing Old Tam out and about more again.

I knew Maureen had been missing their chats too. She had been visiting him on a regular basis, but nothing had seemed capable of shifting him out of his chair other than the urge to speak to his beloved Old Shep who now lay at rest in his garden.

Dìleas had already managed to get Old Tam out and about. I had no doubt the collie would help to heal that sore bit in his soul as well. It was only a matter of time before we would be hearing Old Tam's dour predictions again. Strangely, that thought didn't bother me as much as I expected.

21

Stopping in at the hall for my mid-afternoon cuppa was always entertaining. The elderlies' combined sense of the inevitable laced their humour. No one was safe from it, be they young or old.

Now that Old Tam was back in the fold, he was their target for the day. Their continued badgering of him showed just how much they had all missed his presence, to say nothing of his dog.

Most of our older community had been dog owners at some point in their lives. Growing old had meant once their canine companions had died, they had to make difficult decisions on whether to get another dog or not.

Some found it difficult enough walking on their own without trying to negotiate a lead and the four paws walking beside them. Many weren't able to go for long walks anymore. The added hazard of being pulled off balance and getting hurt was a good enough reason for some to give up being dog owners. Others didn't like the thought of their four-legged friends being left on their own without them to give the care and attention that only the elderly could.

It never stopped them being dog lovers. They fussed and clapped other people's dog. Any dog friendly enough to pay them attention was almost adopted by them all. Old Shep had been no exception. After he had finished his own little feast from Old Tam, he would often make his way over to the elderlies' table and receive more pats and cuddles and, if he was lucky, extra pieces of cake.

Old Tam's return had sparked a conversation once more about their hard times and how much better equipped they were than the younger generations.

"*Ach uil ma tha,* you young ones just have no idea how difficult life can be. All that fuss for a dog, and here you have gone and got another one." Alex Nail (so named for his tendency to proclaim that anything could be fixed purely by the addition of a few more nails) knew fine and well who really owned Dìleas.

"Aye wull, ye ken fine wull th dug is nae mine," Old Tam said as he placed a small plate with milky tea and a piece of scone on the ground for his borrowed companion.

Dìleas gratefully received his gift and gobbled it down, splashing liquid all over the floor. Being a pup, his excitement was rather overpowering.

"Jeez, young Tam, that dog's got no manners; Old Shep wouldn't have done that," Crabbit O'Neil said.

"Aye wull, ye juist keep Shep oot o this."

"Mind, he had a coat you could smell at a hundred yards," Crabbit continued, with the rest nodding sagely beside him. "We thought you were going to be following him for a while there. Not by your smell right enough, but man you fair closed off yourself. I've had to buy Ronnie here a cake. I lost the bet, you see. You didn't die after all. Not that I wanted you dead, right enough, but still, you being here has cost me a tea and a slice of cake. At least I suppose you have made one person happy – is that no right, Ronnie?"

Ronnie raised his cup to Old Tam and gave him a toothless grin. I sincerely hoped the cake he had won was soft enough for him to gum away at it.

Old Tam humphed and tried to ignore their conversation.

Mary had heard enough ribbing of Old Tam. "Now, Crabbit, what was that I was hearing about your young Clara running after our postie? Heard she was asking all sorts of questions and has been lying in wait for the little red van."

The collective immediately pounced on this piece of information and began ruthlessly bombarding Crabbit with questions about his daughter.

"I haven't heard anything about that." Maureen leant over to Mary. "I would have thought Litir the Post would have been a bit too old for her. Mark you, he is quite fit with all that walking he does. Nice legs too in them shorts. My, but he does make me shiver." We all looked at Maureen. "No, no, not in that way. I meant in winter when he still wears those shorts even with six feet of snow on the ground. Nice head of hair, though, and all his own too. So Mary, why hadn't I heard about this?"

"Well of course you wouldn't have heard," Mary said, "but they needed a distraction."

"Mary!" Maureen was shocked. "You've started a rumour. That's not good. Poor Clara, word about her will be around like wildfire. And it's not even true!"

"It will soon blow over. It was nothing, Maureen. She *was* seen running after the postie – only it was because we have a new postie who had given Clara all *Claire* O'Neil's mail instead of her own for *Clara* O'Neil. Easy enough mistake, so you see, I wasn't wrong – she ran after the *new* postie, who by the way is a woman. I'm sure Crabbit O'Neil will stop the rumour quickly enough. They are probably onto someone else already." Mary lifted her tea, a gleam in her eye.

Maureen was still looking slightly shocked at her friend's behaviour. When no one said anything, she turned again to Old Tam.

"Now then, Tam, are you going to be taking this lovely young pup here to the beach ceilidh on Saturday? Blether has got a special outfit especially for the day. Haven't you, my wee precious?" Maureen gave her dog an extra hug. "I'm right looking forward to going myself, and I'm sure Blether here would be happy to play along with Dìleas wouldn't you now?"

Old Tam pondered for a few moments, "Wull, Eh don't rightly ken. Morag might want tae do somethin wi' eem."

"Ach, I wouldn't bother yourself with Morag. I expect she will have enough to do looking after her wee bairn, after all," Maureen said. "Only, I know Blether will want to play on the beach with the others. As you know, I can't get down there. At least not in my wheelchair. I'll have to stay in amongst the stalls and food. Not that I'm complaining mind. It just would be nice if I knew someone was prepared to look after her and take her for a wee trip down to the sea. She likes the sea when she gets the chance."

Maureen never did complain about the restrictions a wheelchair often meant. It hadn't stopped her doing most things, as far I as could remember, so it was strange to hear her say she wouldn't be able to take part in something.

I had never considered it before – how we took for granted the extra effort she had to make. After all, she had still managed to be there, whatever we were doing, even taking the occasional trip into the woods at night. Though, the last time, we did have to call on Paul of the Sheds to come and rescue her and her wheelchair.

I looked across the room to where the elderlies were laughing again, at some morbid joke, no doubt. Many of them had mobility challenges. How would they enjoy our beach day? Would they even be able to get access properly?

I felt someone staring at me. Looking up, Mary met my gaze and smiled softly. I remembered well the last time she was gathering seaweed from the shore and how she had needed me to help pull her up. Mary would be finding it more difficult to get down the beach herself the older she got. Now with that deep hole and part of the dunes missing, it had become even more difficult in places. What we needed was someone to design a route that was safe for people with mobility challenges.

If we could do that, maybe our elderly would be able to come down and share in their beach again. What a gift we could give the community, if only we could find a way to fund it and make it happen quickly – before summer even. What we needed was a beneficiary, someone who was willing to fund a project like this or at least enough to kickstart it.

"Auntie Lottie, just who was that celebrity you hitched a lift from? You know that funding they offered? I think I may have found the perfect project."

I couldn't believe I hadn't thought of this before. It would fit exactly with the funding being offered and benefit all the community. Dornoch, a small town near us, had developed a project that allowed access to their expansive beach for wheelchair users. Beach Wheelchairs was exactly what we needed for Blàs. We could get rid of the damage caused by the storm at the same time by developing that area as one of the access points for the beach. We could also provide beach wheelchairs and a suitable shed to house them in. I just had to find out from the people involved in the Dornoch project about costs and how to go about getting permission for creating such an area. In the end it would mean better accessibility for all.

I turned to Maureen who seemed to know most people and was related to even more in the area. "Maureen, you must know someone in Dornoch."

"Well, of course I do. There's Fred. He is my mother's stepbrother's nephew's wee boy. Oh, and there is Pauline – she was related to Calum. You remember him, Mary? Big strong lad, used to deliver coal, nice boy but dour, really dour, even more pessimistic than our Tam here."

"Ach, I can't see that being true, Maureen – our Tam takes a lot of beating in the dour stakes. Even with a new dog," Mary added with a smile on her face.

"Eh telt ye, ees nae meh dug," Old Tam said, as he absently ruffled Dìleas' head.

"Oh, and then there is—" Maureen started to say again.

"It's okay, Maureen, one contact will do fine. Someone involved in their beach wheelchair project. If you give me their details, I'll do the rest."

Mary rose from the table, came over to me and squeezed my shoulders. "You go and do this, Stroma. It is what we all need for the community. Well done, lass."

I watched her make her way out of the hall. She wasn't as spritely on her feet as she once was. This project would help her as much as anyone. Then it slowly filtered into my brain – did she know that? Had she once more brought me around to her way of thinking?

She knew as I had that the community of Dornoch had recently funded and purchased some wheelchairs specifically for use on their beaches. Mary was a woman who knew not only what she wanted but what she would need and, it would appear, who could make it work for her.

"Why are you shaking your head, Stroma?" Maureen burst into my thoughts.

"Ach, it's nothing, Maureen. Just Mary, you know."

She followed my gaze.

"Aye, she is quite some woman. Now, you will keep me up to date on what you find out, won't you, about them wheelchairs?"

"Ach, of course"

"Well, that's okay then, just mind that you do."

Satisfied she would be the first with any news, she renewed her attention towards finding out the latest gossip doing the rounds.

22

Blue sky and the ideal level of wind for surfing on the sand or on the water were all good signs for the start of our beach ceilidh day. Early risers were already enjoying what nature could offer. More families were expected later to take part in our beachcombing session. Our beach ranger had arrived and was enjoying some quiet time before taking charge for the rest of the day.

A massive game of rounders was due to take place just before lunch. Stalls were set up on either side of the road that ran along the grassy dunes. Harvest straight from the sea would be exhibited in these colourful tents. Local producers offered everything from fresh shellfish to seaweed crisps. There was enough variety to tempt even the fussiest eater and no end of free tasty samples. For those who couldn't be persuaded to try some of our sea harvest, burgers could still be found cooking on an enormous barbecue. Coffee and cake were amongst the many food and drink stalls.

For anyone not so beach orientated, they could work up their appetite by following our annual scarecrow trail around the village. Our theme this year followed our beach topic. Everyone's display had to be made from whatever could be found either in the sea or washed-up on the shore. This meant that many scarecrows had hair made out of the different seaweeds that grew nearby.

I had gone around to see what the Smiths had managed this year. Jill was so busy with Rowan, their new baby, I was surprised that they had undertaken to display anything at all. Their previous scarecrow had been so amazing that it was difficult to imagine them coming up with anything remotely as brilliant. But I had to admit to being impressed yet again. Where Jill had found the time to supervise the children with their creation, I couldn't comprehend. A mermaid adorned with shells and all kinds of flotsam and jetsam, including the remains of an old fishing net, was displayed on their fence. As I got closer, I saw tiny fish made out of tin cans the children had collected from the beach. Jellyfish dangled daintily from the old fishing net, made up of tiny pieces of coloured plastic cut out into small sizes. The mermaid's eyes were bottle tops placed inside large bright shells. Her tail was covered in different fabrics gathered from our beach clean earlier in the year.

All along the fence, different sea creatures were displayed, made from other people's rubbish. The Smiths had turned what had been destructive and ugly junk into a beautiful design adorning their property.

Their handiwork appeared to float in the sea breeze that gently blew up from the shore. It felt like the sand and the sea were swelling all around their mermaid. Once more, the family had outdone themselves. I couldn't see anyone beating their entry. It truly was a work of art.

It put Iona's and my effort to shame. Thankfully, our half-hearted attempt was displayed nowhere near the Smith's. We had found one wellie and one odd shoe then teamed this up with a large piece of plastic to create a whale. The wellie and shoe were placed as if someone was being swallowed. It was the best we could come up with, given the time we felt we could spend on it.

Thankfully, most others in the village had made a bit more of an effort. I wandered around inspecting the various structures. Another entry stopped me in my tracks. It would definitely give the Smiths' some real competition. Surprisingly, it was Morag and Old Tam's effort that impressed me so much. Old Tam may not be able to croft in the way he used to, but it was still in his blood. It showed in the subject he had chosen.

Not a sea monster or anything even connected with the sea – unless you counted when they went for a paddle. Outside their house stood a large Highland cow, its shaggy coat made up of tonnes of bladder-wrack seaweed. The seaweed's olive brown appearance looked surprisingly perfect for our iconic Highland beast. It was helped, no doubt, by the seaweed's splayed fronds that housed air-filled pockets which resembled bubble wrap. Old Tam and Morag had used scallop shells for the cow's eyes and pieces of thin sticks for its large eyelashes. An empty sea urchin shell represented its nose.

It was without doubt my favourite 'scare-sea-crow'. I had a soft spot for the real thing anyway. It had to be the bonniest cow on the planet. I was glad again that the judging was not one of my responsibilities.

A thump on my legs nearly knocked me over as Cavan threw himself around my lower body.

"Hi *balach beag*, have you come to say *madainn mhath* to Old Tam's new cow?" I asked, as his mother hurried towards me.

"He loves this Highland cow. I have to take a detour here on my way home every day." Grace laughed and scooped up her son.

"It's quite magnificent. Who'd have thought Old Tam was so creative."

"I think you are forgetting about his Highland Games suit." Grace laughed.

Old Tam's suit, we reckoned, could have been spotted from outer space. He hid his colourful taste most of the time, but when let loose, he had an artistic flair.

"When are you heading down to the beach, by the way?" I asked Grace.

"I'm just about to go home and grab our matching bag." She smiled and pointed to my backpack. "Only, mine is stuffed for the day. So, we won't be far behind you. I take it you're on your way now?"

I confirmed I was and watched her go as I adjusted the strap on my bag. I was looking forward to some downtime and fun. Iona was meeting up with some of her friends, and no doubt, I would catch up with her later. Maureen and Mary would be waiting for me right now in one of the snack tents. Ellen would be down the beach making sure everyone was where they should be and hopefully enjoying themselves. Now was the time for me to take a few minutes, catch up on the latest news and enjoy my friends' company.

The beach events were a huge success with families and individuals alike. Most people took part in the game of rounders which went on for longer than anyone had anticipated. I had found myself waiting in the queue next to Jim. He had come over from Inverness on the pretence that he was checking out how well our beach event would do. After all, his organisation, HIE, was funding some of the elements of our fun day. We were also working on a joint project aimed at highlighting what the coastline combined with our culture could offer tourists and locals alike. GLADS was involved, as well, by allowing me to donate some of my work time.

In reality, though, Jim was here to see Grace and Cavan. He loved Grace and had also formed a strong bond with her son. He missed being part of that ready-made family. Jim had blended into the community so seamlessly it was if he had lived here for years. I knew he still could not fathom what he had done wrong, why Grace had suddenly ended their relationship.

"One minute, she's being nice and friendly, and the next, I don't know where I stand with her. Have you spoken to her yet?" he asked, as we awaited our turn to bat.

What could I say? It wasn't my place to tell him she was just scared of commitment. I couldn't spill out that information. Grace was first and foremost my friend. On the other hand, she wasn't exactly happy about the split. Was there a way I could help them both? Probably not, but I wasn't going to put him off either.

"Look, Jim, you are going to have to talk to her yourself. I know, I know you have tried. What I can say is this: she can be prickly; she's been hurt before. But from what I know of Grace, I wouldn't give up on her. I can't say more than that, but if I were you, I'd bide my time. Take it slowly, but don't give up on her."

He leaned down and kissed my cheek, whispering, "Stroma, you have made my day. Coming from you as one of her best friends, it means that all is not lost. Thank you, I'll be patient. Right, I'm up next – I'm going for a home run."

Oh dear, I hoped I had done the right thing. I hadn't said how Grace felt. I didn't say exactly what Grace had said. I felt sure she'd be glad, if they did sort out their differences, that I had said something to Jim to keep him encouraged.

Watching Jim career around the pitch, sand flying in all directions, I noticed Grace. She couldn't take her eyes off him as his hair streamed out in the air.

Cheering was coming from the crowd; people stamped their feet and clapped their hands. Jim was going for the home run as he'd said. He skidded over the home line to a massive shout that echoed around the beach. The first home run of the day. He was a determined man, that was for sure. When he set his mind to it, he got results. Hopefully, that would bode well for his, Grace and Cavan's future. Only time and a lot of patience on his part would tell.

23

"Stroma, Ellen's, five minutes. Oh, and make sure you bring your phone." A familiar bang then silence. At least Maureen hadn't asked me to bring anything strange this time.

It was early evening and I had been considering taking Malt for a walk anyway so I would pop into Ellen's on my way. Malt wouldn't object to visiting Ellen's, especially if Blether was going to be there too.

A crowd of people were hanging around the middle of the village. Not an usual sight, only most seemed to have come from the cars that were either parked or abandoned nearby. Was there some sort of car meet-up?

At this time in the evening most people in the village tended to walk. You could indulge in the odd pint that way and just meander home, or spend a few pleasant hours clustered in gentle conversation.

These people did not give out the 'I've all the time in the world' vibes. People were marching around, looking at mobile phones or trying to get a signal. Others appeared tense and were continually looking out towards the entrance to the village. These folk were expecting something… or someone.

I waved as I heard my name being shouted but continued on

to Ellen's. I quickly put them out of my mind. This meeting at Ellen's was one of those unplanned ones so something had happened or was happening I should probably know about.

Paul of the Sheds was already in Ellen's kitchen – he was standing in for Auntie Lottie. Maureen was busying feeding cake to Blether while Giulietta passed around some of her chocolates. After the initial loud greeting between the dogs, Ellen placed her usual cup of tea on the table.

"Right, Stroma, have you heard from either Mary or Lottie today?"

"Nope, but then again, I wasn't expecting to. Aren't they both on the old folks' outing?"

Paul cleared his throat. "Not quite, Stroma, remember my Lottie is helping them. I just want to make it clear, as she would want it, that she is not part of the old folks' outing. She is only there as a helper, nothing to do with her age."

Ellen gave him one of her looks. He immediately reddened and added, "I'm just saying. My Lottie would have wanted me to make that point clear."

He was right – any suggestion that Auntie Lottie would qualify for the old folks' away day would not have gone down well.

"What about you, Maureen, have you heard from Tam?"

"Only a short call to say they had taken a vote and were changing the schedule, that's all. Nothing since."

Taking a vote and changing the plan for the day. What were our so-called respectable elderly residents up to? The whole day had been planned out for them. We had talked to them at length about what they wanted from their spring outing. Suggestions had come in thick and fast. I had been in the hall when they had their discussion.

"Well, how about a trip in a space rocket?" Ben the Stump suggested.

"I think that would mean a trip to America first, you daft old goat," Crabbit O'Neil replied.

"Not at all. They're going to be launching space rockets in Sutherland. I read it in the *Raggie*. That would be something – a spacewalk." Alex the Nail sat back, a smile on his face.

"Wull, if ye hiv onything tae do wi' the buildin o it, it winnae git af the gruund. It wauld be full o holes," Old Tam pointed out.

"There's nothing wrong with my building skills."

Before Alex the Nail could say more, there was a collective chant of, "That a few more nails wouldn't sort," and peals of laughter from his elderly companions.

"I think we can safely say that no space rockets will be involved," Auntie Lottie had put in.

The discussion had continued well after I had left. I'd heard sailing boats and sandcastles, a day at the dogs which was interesting in itself as I knew of nowhere around here where they ran dogs.

Someone had suggested a walk up Fyrish, but given that most of them had mobility challenges, this was more a pipedream than a serious possibility.

In the end, an agreement had been reached. We had booked the use of a community bus, and one of our volunteer bus drivers had agreed to take them out for their chosen adventure.

They were supposed to have gone for a coffee break at Dalmore Farm Shop and Restaurant, then on to Culloden Moor to the exhibition centre and the battlegrounds, lunch in Cromarty, a quick trip back on the Nigg Ferry, then afternoon coffee at the Seaboard Centre in Balintore. If there was enough time, they would have a look at the Mermaid of the North nearby.

It was a full day out. We expected that many of them would be asleep by lunchtime and happy to be home by teatime. It may not have included their hoped-for high adventure, but it had a little bit of interest for everyone.

❧

"Stroma, pay attention." Ellen brought me back from reminiscing.

"Who's driving the coach then?" I asked. We had numerous volunteers we could draw on, and most were not much younger that some of our elderly going on the day out.

"It was young Kevin. He was keen to take them. It is the first chance he has had to drive our old folks."

I was busy trying to fathom out who young Kevin was. I couldn't think of anybody who went by that name, and let's face it, he could be twenty or eighty with the word 'young' attached to him.

Ellen spotted my face. "You know, the Bandana Bairn."

"Oh him, yes of course. I never knew he was a Kevin."

He was a bit of a hippy. Long past his twenties but nowhere near his eighties. He did a school run for the teenagers to the secondary school in Inbhirasgaidh so I knew he was well practiced in delivering passengers from A to B.

"Has anyone listened to the road reports? Is anywhere closed? Maybe the Nigg Ferry isn't sailing. You know how it stops at the slightest breeze."

Ellen assured me that all the normal avenues had been checked and there was no reason why the bus hadn't arrived back.

"I've been on to the Balintore Hall." That old hall didn't exist anymore. A nice new hall with catering, office space and a fantastic outlook had replaced it. A new name had been imposed on it with the grand title of the Seaboard Centre – given to reflect that it catered for the residents of the Seaboard Villages that all ran together: Shandwick, Balintore and Hilton. However, it was built on the old site of the Balintore Hall and so those who knew such things called it the Balintore Hall or even the Hall in Balty. "Our elderly never turned up."

"Well, what about trying to call someone else's mobile?" I asked. Just as a whirlwind appeared in Ellen's kitchen.

"Ellen, Ellen, you have to help! Poor Kevin is at his wits' end. I can't get any sense out of him. I'm worried. We were supposed to be going out to a gig tonight and he is nowhere near home yet. Those bloody old age pensioners have kidnapped my poor Kevin, so they have. Right bunch of thugs they have turned out to be. The high school lot are nowhere near as bad, I'm telling you. I just can't believe what my poor Kevin has been subjected too, honestly." She was clutching her phone dramatically to her chest. "I'm keeping my line clear just in case he has to phone me back, you know, for support. He said to come and talk to you. 'Ellen will sort them out,' he said, so he did. Go to Ellen's house, she will help. Everyone knows to come to you to sort things out. People listen to you, so they do. So I'm here, like he said. I know you can help. Even those old biddies will listen to you, so they will. So how are you going to save him?"

Sleeping Beauty, so named as she was known to sleep till lunchtime, thankfully had to take a breath. Maureen jumped in as Ellen seemed in shock from the sudden appearance of this colourfully dressed character in her kitchen.

"Beauty, sit down – those shoes must be killing your feet. Can you do that in such a short skirt? But my, what a lot of colours you wear. Quite dazzles me. That's it, take a breath. Cup of tea? Ellen's cakes are lovely. Help yourself, then you can explain to us what exactly has happened to your poor Kevin. We are all anxious to know."

Beauty stared at Maureen not quite sure if she should take offence or not. However, the need to tell us all what had happened to the love of her life was too strong a lure to ignore.

"Well, he phoned when they got to Culloden Moor. That's where it all started. Them oldies met up with some Jacobites – all dressed-up, my Kevin said… the Jacobites, that is. Shields, swords, the works. When it was time to get on the bus again, them hooligans… them old people…" She wrinkled her over-powdered nose. "They are just a bunch of troublemakers. They refused to get back on the bus, at first, and then, when they did, they hijacked my Kevin."

Sleeping Beauty popped a piece of cake in her mouth and looked around at her audience. She saw she had us all captivated. We waited expectantly to hear what happened next.

24

"It's all true, I tell you. My poor Kevin, stuck he was, totally stuck, and that lot downright refused to get back on the bus unless he agreed to take them somewhere else. Not the planned route either, oh no, that wasn't good enough for them. What a state my poor Kevin was in. He was very upset, very upset indeed. Phoned me, so he did; told me all about it. Wanted my help but what could I do? Then someone took the phone off him and said they were renegotiating his contract for the day. Rene-gotiating!" Beauty emphasised each syllable slowly before continuing. "Said he would now be too busy to answer personal calls, so I would have to hang up, then she cut me off. Bloody cheek of the woman – who did she think she was? He's allowed to phone home. It's not like he's getting paid for his time. He was looking forward to catching up with a mate tonight as well. Now that has all gone out of the window."

Paul of the Sheds was looking a bit uncomfortable. Like us, I'm sure he was thinking about the woman who had answered Kevin's phone. Auntie Lottie would be the first one we had all thought of. Ellen's lips were in a tight line. If Auntie Lottie was involved in all of this, Ellen would have a few choice words to say to her.

"Please go on," Maureen urged. She, on the other hand, was loving this. No doubt it would go down among the tales of the village. She was probably now wondering how she could get Auntie Lottie to re-enact it at their next storytelling event. Her eyes sparkling, she encouraged Sleeping Beauty to continue. "And so they met up with an army, did you say, of soldiers?"

"Yes, yes, an army of Jacobean soldiers. Not real ones, of course. But a bunch of grown men all decked out and playing games." The contempt in her voice was not hard to find. "But now they're playing games with my Kevin." She sniffed and delicately dabbed at her non-existent tears, taking great care not to destroy her make-up.

Paul of the Sheds was fed up listening to her dramatics. "Beauty, can you just get to the point? I doubt very much that the Jacobean army kidnapped Bandana, I mean Kevin."

"Of course they didn't. No, no, not that bunch of overgrown kids. It wasn't them that kidnapped my Kevin; it was them old folks of yours. They wanted to follow that army. Just like all those clans that followed the prince to Culloden." She crossed herself and sniffed again.

I was getting a bit lost. "Sorry, do you mean Bonnie Prince Charlie? Are you saying the old folk wanted to follow Bonnie Prince Charlie?"

"Aye, yes, I am, in a way. They wanted to follow him, only backwards not forwards, not to Skye, well no, that would have been a lot worse if they had taken my boy Kevin all the way across to Skye."

I gave up. I had no idea what she was talking about. Maureen, to her credit, had managed to follow Sleeping Beauty's rather wandering story.

"Do you mean they were going back a few days before the battle then, Beauty? Are you saying that they have gone to some other place where a battle was fought before Culloden?" Maureen quizzed.

If she was right, goodness knows where they went. There

had been so many battles or skirmishes in the area before the awful day itself. Worse still, what if they had decided to go and visit a battlefield where something had taken place centuries before. They could have ended up at Bannockburn or Stirling Bridge or—

"Stroma, are you listening?" I nodded and fought myself back to Ellen's kitchen.

"So," Maureen said, satisfied with her logic and grasp of history, "by my reckoning, from what you have said, they could have gone up to Golspie. There was a battle held there a few days before Culloden – the Battle of Littleferry, which the Jacobites lost as well, by the way. They reckon a good few ended up drowning in Loch Fleet trying to get away. And—"

"Maureen, please stick to the point. Why would they go there?" Ellen was used to her friend reciting history. Myself, I found it fascinating and always learnt something more each time Maureen kept to the actual history and not to the local gossip.

"Well, my mother's second husband's first cousin's nephew's girlfriend, Ruth, well she works on the *Raggie, The Northern Times*. She wrote a whole article recently on how they were doing a re-enactment of events for some sort of documentary. Or it could have been a film to play at some museum thereabouts. Anyway, I think it was maybe today. So perhaps our old folks have gone up to watch. It takes place in Littleferry near Golspie and in Dunrobin Castle too. Knowing them, they have probably popped into the ice-cream factory for a cone in Brora– it's only about five minutes away anyway. Yes, I bet that is exactly what they are up too. I wouldn't worry yourselves – they will all turn up unharmed and full of strawberry ice-cream."

Someone's phone went off as Maureen finished. Sleeping Beauty dived for hers and read a message that had just come in.

"They are on their way back. Kevin says not to worry. They won't be long and he will tell me what happened when he sees me." Sleeping Beauty raised her heavily made-up eyes. They were shining with tears.

"He's okay; he's coming home. That mob of thugs have all fallen fast asleep so he can make his way straight back with them. We'll make it to that gig in Inbhirasgaidh after all. But I am telling you this – he is never going to take that bundle of old people out again. My nerves wouldn't stand for it, no they wouldn't. I'll leave you ladies to your cake." And off she rushed as quickly as she came.

A welcome silence followed the banging of Ellen's front door. Broken eventually by Paul of the Sheds as he coughed and shuffled his feet. Ellen made to say something, changed her mind, turned and refilled the kettle.

"You don't really think that—" We would never find out what Paul was about to ask as the room erupted with songs, pings and ringing as mobile phones went off. The back door flew open, and Auntie Lottie marched in full of smiles and good humour.

"Beauty said you were all here. What a day we have had. Not our planned one, right enough. But everyone, well, mostly everyone, loved it."

"We heard you changed the schedule," Ellen said. "And we know not everyone was happy. Kevin for a start."

"Ach well, he's a bit of a wet blanket, if you ask me. Our elderly have way more backbone that him. Ach, don't look at me like that, Ellen. He is as happy as can be now. Bought him his afternoon tea and then had a whip round and gave him a nice wee bundle of money to spend at that gig he is going to with Beauty. My, what a fuss she made of him when he got off the bus. You'd have thought we had kidnapped him."

"You did," Ellen said.

"Ach, away with you. We just persuaded him in our own way to follow the Jacobite boys. He was fine after we fed him in Golspie. Did you really think it was me who changed the day? Why would you think that?" Auntie Lottie looked around at us genuinely surprised. "You as well, Paul, you thought it was me?"

"Now, Lottie," Maureen intervened, "I don't know why you would be so surprised. You are renowned for going off-piste, so to speak. Remember Edinburgh?"

"Oh." She thought for a split second as a deep crimson blush took over her face. "What happened in Edinburgh, stays in Edinburgh," she declared. "Now, let me tell you what happened today."

Always adept at changing the subject, she went on to explain that they indeed went up to Littleferry and spent the day watching, some taking part in, the filming. "Alex the Nail fair impressed us with his acting abilities, I'm telling you. He seemed about twenty years younger brandishing that sword. And Catherine Cailleach got all dressed-up in shawls shouting out the Gaelic and waving her stick. We were all puggled by the end of it, so headed to The Stag in Golspie and had afternoon tea. And before you say anything cutting, Ellen, I'll say again – it wasn't me who instigated it."

We all looked at her in disbelief. If it wasn't Auntie Lottie, then who had led our elderly into battle with the driver. Any one of them was strong-willed enough, I supposed, to lead the charge. However, if I thought it through there was only one person who would set the whole thing in motion, enjoy the outcome and stay safely out of any finger-pointing as to the real troublemaker. A pair of twinkling eyes flashed before my mind. There was only one person strong enough and bold enough to carry out that plot. I looked around at my friends who all had a similar look on their faces.

"Mary," Ellen whispered, and a slow smile softened her lips. We all nodded and smiled.

Auntie Lottie humphed. "So it is okay for Mary to cause a mutiny, but not me."

"Of course it is, *mo ghràdh*. You are way, way too young – you'd never get away with it." Paul of the Sheds put his arm around his wife who was now smiling, delighted at the recognition of her youth.

25

Their heads were bent together deep in conversation. When you got right down to it you didn't need to hear Maureen's voice to work out how she was feeling. Her expressive gestures danced in the air around her.

Old Tam, on the other hand, looked a bit drawn and sheepish. As Maureen filled the space around them Old Tam somehow appeared the lesser of the two. It took a few minutes before I registered that he was alone. Where was Dìleas? He had become such a part of Old Tam that his absence was noticeable.

Maureen had finished talking; she bristled with indignation obviously displeased with what her friend had been saying. If her wheelchair could have stomped off, it would have. Unfortunately, it was heading in my direction. Malt was pulling at her lead, anxious to get to Blether who had jumped down from Maureen's lap and was making her way towards us.

"Come back here, you little monster."

"Wha are ye cawin a monster?" Old Tam called after her.

"It was not you, Tòmas 'ic Eilidh Dhùn Deagh." Oh, this was serious – Maureen was using his lineage name. "But if the cap fits feel free to put it on," Maureen yelled back without looking.

"Maureen what is going on? I can't believe you've fallen out with Old Tam," I ventured as I bent down and retrieved both dogs' leads.

"Silly old bugger. He's finally twigged that Dìleas was probably got for him, and he has handed him back to Morag to look after."

"Oh no, poor Morag – she has enough on her plate. And poor Dìleas – he won't know what he's done. I take it that's what you've fallen out about?"

"Well, yes and no." Maureen looked shifty.

"Come on, Maureen, that's no kind of answer. What's really going on? I don't recall you and Old Tam ever falling out."

"Well, he thinks I'm interfering too much in his life. I don't know where he got that impression from." Maureen appeared to be genuinely baffled by the accusation. "I mean, it's not like I give him any more attention than anybody else who has a credible story to tell."

Well, I suppose, from Maureen's point of view, that was true. No one was safe from her inquisitions. If there was gossip going around, she didn't care if you were young or old, rich or poor; she would root it out of you or your kin.

"So what makes him feel you're after him this time, Maureen? Have you heard something about him he's not happy with?"

"No. That silly man has it in his head I am keeping tabs on him. Just because I was phoning him to find out if he and the rest of the oldies were alright on their day out. I mean I could have phoned Lottie, but she was never going to give me the right answers, especially if she was involved in the first place. As to Mary, well, we all know she was never going to answer her mobile, being as she, as we now know, was the main instigator."

"Come again, Maureen – Old Tam is annoyed with you because you phoned to find out where everyone was? That's a bit strange."

"Not half as strange as him thinking I am chasing him."

"What!" This was getting stranger and stranger.

"Silly old goat thinks I am after his money and his body too. *Him*, with his washed-out look and dour nature. Humph, he should be so lucky." Maureen folded her hands on her lap, looking indignant. "Although, to be truthful, he doesn't smell nearly as badly as he used to. I'm beginning to think all that stench was coming from Old Shep. Now that he is gone so has the smell. That, or Morag has taken Old Tam in hand."

Thanks to Maureen I now had the image of her running after Old Tam in her wheelchair. The two of them had always been close but we had put that down to their shared love of gossip. *Was there more in it?* I wondered. *Surely not.* He was a good few years older than her and so gloomy in comparison. Then again, opposites are often attracted to each other.

"Stroma, are you listening to me? Honestly, you spend so much time daydreaming, what a girl. I said, what are we going to do about getting Dìleas and Old Tam back together? Neither of them are happy, and he is just being a stubborn fool, trying to prove a point."

"I think this calls for tea and cake at Mary's."

I hadn't seen her since their day out, and getting her advice on the Tam and Dìleas situation would be the perfect excuse to catch up with her. Out of us all, she knew Old Tam the best.

"Oh, good idea, and don't forget to bring along—" Maureen began.

"Don't even go there, Maureen. The only thing I will bring along is maybe Ellen or Iona if she is free."

"Well, I wouldn't hold your breath on Iona's availability. She seems to be spending an awful lot of time with a certain chef, if what I'm hearing it true. Would you care to enlighten me on that account? Or better still, definitely bring her along tonight, let's say 7.30 p.m. I'll let Mary know to expect us. Come on, Blether, up you come, my precious wee lass. Just look at your bow. I'll have to fix that now." And off she went, talking non-stop to her pup who sat snuggling on her knees.

I shouldn't have allowed Maureen space to mention Iona. Of

course she would have heard about what my sister was up too, most people had. You can't live in a small place and expect to keep things secret. I could only hope she was busy tonight – that would save her from interrogation. I went off to let Ellen know her presence was requested at Mary's.

"Morag is at her wits' end and blaming us, which to be honest, she has every right to." Ellen had joined us in Mary's kitchen after first finding out how Old Tam's granddaughter was feeling about once more being made responsible for a young dog.

"It's not that she doesn't like Dìleas. It is just the timing is wrong for her. Having a young baby to attend to and returning to work is quite enough for most people, I would think. We have to at least get Old Tam to agree to walking Dìleas, even if he's not taking him back."

"He is a stubborn old goat. He has been in a right funny mood this last wee while. I can tell you. There is no talking to him."

"Ach well, I wouldn't say that," Mary interjected. "He has a lot on his mind, what with the birth and then losing Old Shep, then the new dog, and I hear he has a woman chasing after him, is that not right, Maureen?"

"It certainly is not," Maureen replied. "I just don't understand where he has got that notion from. We've always passed the time of day together. Now he won't even be seen with me. I miss our cosy chats and cups of tea. When that man puts his mind to it, he is full of local knowledge and history." Maureen paused. "Then again, it does tend to revolve around people and things dying and horrible tales of murder and grief, but it all adds colour to our folklore."

"Lottie, perhaps you could enlighten Maureen how it is that Old Tam thinks she is the scarlet woman," Ellen suggested.

Auntie Lottie tutted and straightened an imaginary out-of-place hair on her immaculate head. "I have no idea what you are referring to."

Oh dear, what had she done. Guilt was written all over her face. She was holding herself completely still and upright. Auntie Lottie, whose normal position changed every second, was condemned immediately.

"Lottie?" Maureen asked. "Lottie, what have you done? Surely, you haven't said anything to Old Tam?"

We all looked over at her. She sighed, her normal body language returning. "It wasn't my fault." Okay that was a lie again, but then Auntie Lottie never thought anything was her fault, well not entirely.

She held up her hand as if to stop anyone else speaking. "All I said was, the way Maureen was trying to keep tabs on him on our day out was like a wife."

There was a collective intake of breath. Maureen was about to explode, but just before she did, Auntie Lottie looked contrite. "Honestly, I was trying to make a joke of it. I didn't think for one second he would take it like he has. Only, my phone had died and I couldn't get in touch with Paul and I knew he would be worried when we didn't show up when we were supposed to. And there was Maureen phoning Tam every two minutes. It wasn't fair."

"So you were jealous that I could phone Tam and you couldn't phone Paul. Are you mad?" Maureen yelled. She took a deep breath to steady herself and asked, "And just when did you let your big mouth run away with you?" Maureen asked.

"At Culloden, right after we had all finished our wee treat from Mary," Auntie Lottie said.

"What wee treat?" Ellen asked, looking over at Mary who simply took a sip of tea and refused to answer.

"It was some of those seaweed beers that the girls are developing. Really nice they were too, Stroma. Very tasty and drinkable. Some of us had a wee bit too much, I think." Auntie Lottie smiled at the recollection.

"Was that before or after you lot took over the bus?" Ellen asked.

"Well, it was after we had met those nice Jacobite people. And then we all shared a few beers… and a laugh and a wee sing-song. And maybe a bit more beer. Then… well, it was at that point some of us decided we would take over the bus."

"You got our elderly drunk and then encouraged then to take over the bus." Ellen stared at Mary in disbelief.

Mary, never one who felt the need to explain herself to anyone, merely shrugged her shoulders and changed the subject.

"If Maureen and Lottie have quite finished their wee domestic, we can move on." Mary smiled at them both. "I think I may have the answer to our wee problem with Tam and his new dog."

26

Iona was perched on a stool in front of the bar talking with Old Tam. I watched as she laughed and cajoled him. The other 'worthies' in for a wee drink were crowding around listening to the pair of them bantering. I sat patiently at our table awaiting our meal. We hadn't had much time together recently. I was curious as to how her friendship was getting on with Mateo her Spanish chef. She had been keeping him far away from the populace of Blàs.

The habit of keeping her private life away from the village had been installed in her years ago. It meant though that I would have to prod her if I wanted the lowdown on how things were developing.

"Ach away, Tam, I was always a dog lover you know that. Mary is enjoying Dìleas' company right now, but she's an elderly lady. Even older than yourself."

"Noo dinnae be so cheeky, young lass. Eh'm nae that auld."

"Oh, I don't know, Tam – they don't call you Old Tam for nothing," Archie chipped in.

"Nae tae meh face, Archie, an Eh'll thank ye fur nae usin tha term wi' meh agin," Old Tam retorted.

"To me, Tam, you will always be old. You were old when I was a wee one and you are old now, so I suppose you could say you have aged well," Iona added.

The cronies all burst out laughing.

"Well, she has the right of you worked out fine, Tam," Sandy said. "You always were the clever one, Iona. A bit wild for my liking, right enough, but clever just the same. I don't like my women to be too clever. Now that aunt of yours is a fine figure of a women, but no too bright. Well, she couldn't be – not after who she married. Oh, evening, Paul. Was just talking about your missus." Sandy had obviously seen Paul of the Sheds walking in. He winked across at his audience.

"All good, I hope. Intelligent woman, my wife. Had the good sense to marry me and keep all you reprobates at bay into the bargain. Evening, Iona, I hear when you leave, you will be taking Dìleas with you. That young dog is way too much for poor Mary to handle. Poor wee thing doesn't know if he is coming or going, being to so many homes already. Such a shame, nice wee thing too. But you are doing the right thing – better he never comes back here than gets muddled as to why he's not where he should be."

Old Tam was looking decidedly uncomfortable. "Wull, lass, ye wauldnae be goin fur a wee while yet," he said hopefully.

"Ach, you know me, Tam. I never stay in one place for long. I could be here today and gone tomorrow. Anyway, Paul's right. I will leave Dìleas with friends anytime I come back. That way he doesn't have to see he's not wanted. Although how anybody could not want him is beyond me. He's that cuddly, and you should see him when I give him chocolate, he loves it." Iona winked across at Paul of the Sheds.

"Ye cannae gie em chocolate, lass, ye wull kill em," Old Tam exploded.

"Ach, Tam, don't be such a spoil-sport. That's just an old wives' tale, I'm sure," Iona said.

"No, it's no. Aubody kens ye can kill a dug wi' chocolate. Tell er, Paul, fur goodness sake, mun, tell er."

"I'm afraid he's right, Iona. You shouldn't give a dog chocolate," Paul of the Sheds said gently.

"Ach, we'll see," Iona continued. "I mean it would only be while I was working. He's going to be stuck in the house for ten hours on his own so I have to leave him something."

"Ten hours! In th name o the wee mun, ye cannae leave a dug fur ten hours. Ee'll need oot, fur one thin." Old Tam was getting more and more agitated.

"Ach, he'll be fine. A quick run out to the garden to do his stuff, pop him back in his cage. You know one of them cold wire ones where you shut the door and leave them there." She stared into Old Tam's eyes. "Then I let him out ten hours later and take him for a wee pee and then we can have some dinner. I was thinking of giving him one of those dried feeds. I don't want to spoil him, so just that. No treats, I don't want him getting fat. Mary is feeding him chicken right now, but he will just have to get used to it all. Right, that's my tea ready. I'll see you all in the morning... or then again, maybe not. Perhaps this is my last supper here before me and my dog disappear. Oh, he is so going to like living in the city, all that noise..."

"Eez frightened o loud noises," Old Tam said.

"Hustle and bustle. It's a shame that he'll have to go back into his wire cage when I go out for the night, but there it is, a dog life, *nach eil*."

"That is nae th' kind o life at all fur a dug. Eh'm surprised at ye, Stroma, allowing yer sister to tak thon pair wee dug wi' er."

"Jeez, Tam, when could I ever stop Iona doing just what she wanted? If it comes to that, when could anybody stop her. Is that not right, everyone?"

To voices of agreement and nodding of the heads, Old Tam pushed his full pint away and marched out of the door.

"Where are you off to, Tam, you haven't finished your pint yet?"

"Wull, Eh'll nae be back th night."

"Why? What's wrong, where are you going in such a hurry?" Sandy asked as he winked at Paul of the Sheds.

"Meh, meh, wull, Eh'm off tae see a wifie aboot a dug, that's wer." And with that Old Tam slammed his way out of the pub.

Paul of the Sheds crept towards the door and peeped out.

"The coast is clear. He's marching off in Mary's direction."

A cheer broke out from the crowd in the bar.

"Well done, everyone," Pete the Froth said. "Here you go, Iona, Stroma, free drinks on me." He handed us each a large glass of wine.

"I thought you had pushed your luck a little bit there, Iona. Especially when you talked about the dried biscuit. I didn't think he would be that bothered about it," Paul of the Sheds said.

"Ah, that's because you have never had to listen to him talk about dog food. I once said he shouldn't feed Old Shep so much cake and I got a lecture on how it wasn't as bad as dried dog food and how Shep only got the best of meats and veg. I think he fed that dog better than himself before Morag took over."

The atmosphere quietened down as Iona and I turned to our food. Something was worrying me though.

"Iona, you were really impressive. I mean really good. So believable."

"Why thank you, Stroma." She clinked our glasses. "Fair praise from you."

"Only I was just wondering… You know you said you were about to leave, well is that true?" I realised I was dreading the answer. I had enjoyed having her back but knew I couldn't keep her here if she didn't want to be. She had helped to fill a part of the void left by Scott's leaving.

Iona stared at me unblinking. She leant forward kissed my cheek then whispered in my ear "I love you too, and no, I'm not about to leave. That whole thing was make-believe. I think I have finally understood why you never left."

She lifted her glass. "A toast."

We clinked our glasses together. "Sisters, *gu brath*!"

"Forever." I added, and we sat back and grinned at each other before getting stuck into our food.

27

It was rare that my fellow officers at GLADS had a chance to catch up in person. We were stationed around the country and only met up when we had to attend training or meetings at HQ in Inverness.

Unusually, I was staying overnight. Normally, I would head home after a day's training and come back the following morning. But we were having an early start on the second day, so for once, I had opted to stay in the city. Grace would be in town the following day and we had arranged to meet up for lunch. After which she would head off back to Blàs. I, on the other hand, had a meeting and presentation at HIE that afternoon. Jim would be there, thankfully, so I knew I already had one person in favour of what we were trying to do.

First, though, I had a day's training to attend and then what would be an enjoyable evening out with the rest of the GLADS development officers.

It was getting late – I knew that, on some level. Despite being insulated by the amount of alcohol we had consumed, goose pimples had risen on my skin as we hurried back to our hotel. Sleet lashed into us as we huddled along in an attempt to keep the wet and cold out. The warm April weather had lulled us into a false sense that summer had come early. It happened every year, caught out each time by the hope of a long hot summer.

"I wish I'd worn wellies instead of my shoes," wailed one of my colleagues as we tottered along together.

Why we had thought turning up at a weekday wedding reception dance was okay I couldn't quite remember. I think it had come under the guise of a distant cousin or cousin's friend, a suggestion put forward by Shona our development officer in the south. She who now lived exiled in Glasgow rather than on her native West Coast island.

"Ach, they won't mind, the more the merrier. They'll be pleased as punch that someone from the family made it. It's only the ceilidh dance anyway. It's not like we are eating a meal or anything."

It wasn't so unusual this assumption that if you knew someone having a celebration of some sort it was fine to just turn up. However, that addition to our evening had not been the first entertainment we had attended.

❧

"There's an art exhibition about animals around our sea-coast," Shona said. "Free drinks. Come on, girls, you know how much I miss the island. We can have a look at what's on offer, a quiet drink then an early night. Better than just huddling here or in our rooms. What do you say?" It wasn't as if Shona lived in the back of beyond. She could access this sort of thing anytime in Glasgow, but I guessed that going out in Inverness represented a step nearer her birthplace.

"Don't get me wrong, I love living in the city, but I do miss the homely feeling of a night out in Inverness. I mean, it's not as if we will be staying up late or anything. Just a wee cultural evening then back to bed."

The evening started out much as we had anticipated. We dutifully perused the paintings on offer as we clustered together talking quietly and sipping wine. Our reflective mood was interrupted when Shona spotted a friend she hadn't seen for ages. This led to a riotous welcome, much chatter and more wine. Shared news quickly developed into funny anecdotes which gradually took on a more competitive edge as they both vied for the funniest outcome.

Raucous laughter soon erupted from our once sedate group. You could say a lot about Shona, but one thing stood out: her laughter could wake the dead! The people in charge were heading in our direction, frowns deepening.

❧

"Now, if you really want to see some art, we should go and look at Ness Islands. They've got some statues of haggis people in all shapes and colours. Going to be selling them off to help raise funds for the hospice," Shona's friend, our new companion, informed us.

Of course, any sensible person would have said, "It's pitch dark, you idiot, and we are hardly dressed for walking around the islands."

Of course, we didn't, but that may have been because we had gone into The Tavern on the way past for a quick nip just to keep the cold out.

"I can't see a bloody thing. Jeez, I hope that's just mud I've stood in." "Shine your phone down here. Aah, will you not just look at that wee haggis man's face."

The area was covered in three-foot-tall statues of various shapes, each unique and boldly decorated. At least they looked that way when illuminated by our mobile phones.

"If this one looks like a haggis person… I think I would be

steering well clear of him or her."

After much hilarity, falling and splashing about, we exited the island and happened to find ourselves looking straight at the hotel where Shona's cousin was holding her reception. Call it fate, good planning or just luck but it was obviously meant to be, or at least, that was the consensus.

So there we had stood in our finery at the door looking in on a good old ceilidh in full swing. Only, looking back, our 'finery' was probably a bit ragged at the edges. We trailed small droplets of mud in our wake as we hastened inside.

Arms were in the air as men and boys danced round the floor yelling and birling each other around. The shyer ladies laughed and cheered them on. Shona marched happily inside and disappeared as the rest of us slunk quietly into empty chairs. Wine and glasses appeared on the table as Shona, laughing, swirled past us on the arms of a joyful male. Bagpipes droned, mixed with the fiddle and accordion, as music cascaded all around us.

People jumped up and rushed onto the floor to continue in what felt like a never-ending dance. Orkney Strip the Willow was followed by the Dashing White Sargent quickly lost in the Eightsome Reel.

Eventually the musicians took pity on the dancers and, panting for breath, took a break themselves. We all collapsed in a heap around the table grabbing what was left of our drinks.

"This is some wedding your cousin is having," I panted across at Shona.

"It certainly is. Although to say this is my cousin's wedding is maybe pushing the boundaries a bit far."

Before she could elaborate any further, we were informed that a supper was available for any who wanted it. I could see Shona's dance partner for most of the evening was now in a heated discussion with a young woman. She looked back at the bride before determinedly marching towards our table. The bride and her new husband following in her wake.

"I think that might be our cue to leave," Shona said as she grabbed her bag and hastily made for the door."

"What? Right now, when there's food on the go. Can't we stay for a wee while longer?"

"Nope, I think we may have outstayed our welcome. Besides, we still have half a day's training to get through tomorrow." And she was off out the door while we were left grabbing for our coats.

❧

Breakfast was served without much conversation. After we had consumed the equivalent of a small loch of tea, we made our way along to HQ. Our minds were obviously on the night before rather on the day ahead.

"Shona, why did we have to leave your cousin's wedding so sharp?"

"Ach well, you know it was just time to go. Anyway, it was my cousin's friend's not my cousin's."

There was no way we were going to leave it there. As our minds cleared, it was obvious something had been amiss.

"Come on, Shona, out with it – had you fallen out with her?"

"No, no, not at all. In fact, I didn't speak to her at all last night. I texted her this morning right enough to wish her well."

Steaming hot drinks sat on the board table as we awaited our boss.

"Shona," he boomed, entering. "And where were you last night? Your cousin thought you might turn up. It was a grand reception, right enough. The Drumossie knows how to put on a good wedding. A lot of singing, though I say it myself. Personally, I would have preferred some more dancing but that is what the couple wanted, I suppose, being singers themselves. What did happen to you then? Not fancy a wild night?"

Our heads had swivelled towards our work colleague at the mention of the Drumossie Hotel. It was nowhere near the centre of town. Whoever's wedding we had gone to it wasn't Shona's friends.

Bold as brass, she replied, "Ach no, we wanted to be fresh for today's session. We had a very cultured evening – went and saw some art, had a little walk, heard some Scottish music and headed back to the hotel."

❧

Grace and I had finished lunch. I patted my pocket once more. The memory stick with my presentation for HIE was firm against my hands. Despite the convenience of these devices, I often found they managed to get either wedged or lost in the depths of my bag. Having this backup was essential to my frame of mind. It wouldn't be the first time a gust of wind had blown my papers into a muddy puddle or a hastily grabbed cup of tea had spilled over my work. I tried not to take any beverages on offer but sometimes thirst overpowered my reason. At least with the stick in my pocket, if I lost my bag or misplaced my documents, I knew I had the information at my fingertips.

"So what were you so desperate to buy that you had to come up to Ness?" I asked Grace who was surrounded by shopping bags.

"Well, nothing much really." She laughed when I indicated all the bags surrounding us on the floor and slung from Cavan's buggy.

"Okay, initially, nothing much but you know me. I can't keep away from the city lights for long and I might as well make the most of things. Granny Lottie offered to come along but I fancied a day out with my son. Finding you were going to be about at lunchtime was an added bonus."

It certainly was. For one thing it meant I wouldn't have to eat on my own. The other development officers had already left for home in their various modes of transport. Train and ferry timetables had to be adhered to, which meant our morning session had had to finish promptly.

I had stayed behind to update my boss on future developments in my area. He was heading off to his own meetings which left me free to follow up on some Trust business. I was still managing to combine both jobs together for much of the time. This latest combination was a look at offering a longer language course to families. We were suggesting that Auntie Lottie spend time with half a dozen families using the immersion process. She would be with a family full-time over two days then move on to the next one. After which, all six families would meet for six sessions in each other's houses to practice and tailor the sort of language they would use.

In all, each family would receive twenty hours at their own house and a further thirty between the other houses. It would run over a short period to gain the best outcome and fluency possible. This was all tied in to the third phase of the Trust's application which focused on sustainability of language and culture within the community.

We hoped, eventually, to have a community space that would allow a full-time care facility to run in Gaelic, but once more, the shortage of children who would and could use this made it difficult to sell to funders. They tended to wrap their grant handout around numbers not quality or long-term quantity. How they expected us to find as many children to start the project as they expected in a city setting like Inverness was beyond me.

In percentage terms, if out of seven preschool children, all but two wanted to attend Gaelic preschool in a rural area, surely that was better than seven children in a population of around fifty thousand in Inverness.

Trying to get people to look past the actual numbers was frustrating.

Five children who could attend in a rural area would have a bigger impact on the amount of Gaelic spoken within their community. Their impact would be greater purely because their

Gaelic was less likely to be watered down. I knew from previous experience – if the local Gaels knew some families were learning, they would go out of their way to speak to them and their children in Gaelic. The use of Gaelic itself would increase gradually within that locality. However, most who held the purse strings had little real knowledge of how to rejuvenate a language or how to increase the number of speakers. They had no idea how to assess the viability or success of a language project that was trying to regenerate the traditional voice within a community.

I had vowed long ago that I would never give up trying, even though it required me to explain for the millionth time why those in power should look again at or reconsider how they evaluated and funded restoring Gaelic to an area.

"Right, I better get on. I'll catch up with you on Thursday night at yours around 8 p.m.," I confirmed with Grace.

Herself, Karen and I had been managing to keep up with our catch-up sessions a lot better than before. Karen's husband Jack was home from his rotation on the rigs which meant he could look after the bairns and that left Karen free to come along. When Jack was offshore, we met at Karen's so she didn't have to worry about a babysitter.

"Yes, Cavan should be fast asleep by then." Grace didn't like to call on Paul of the Sheds and Auntie Lottie to babysit too much. This meant, when we were at Grace's, our together time had to work around whether Cavan actually stayed asleep. So far, I had to admit, it was working pretty well.

We grabbed our bags and headed out to our respective destinations.

"So, there you have it, everyone, the results of our project so far. I hope you will agree with me that we have more than met your targets from the first two phases. In our third phase we hope to do even better. I have to admit our progress has even outstripped our expectations in terms of delivery."

The presentation had gone way better that I had expected. People appeared genuinely interested in what I had to say. They had asked relevant questions throughout my talk and seemed happy with my answers. Even the technology had worked. My work had appeared bright and clear from the start.

"I've also included some statements from the community. As you are aware we have residents who are not so technically minded so I have brought some of their original hard copies to back up our findings."

I smiled around the table. Jim gave me an encouraging grin. He knew I had wowed them all. Phase three money would be made available to us – I felt that in my soul.

I hoisted up my bag from the floor and opened it to be confronted by a pile of nappies. I could hear a quiet chuckle coming from someone as I placed nappies, small socks and an all-in-one small vest on the table. A small jumper was followed closely by some sort of cream and wipes.

My face instantly infused with embarrassment. Instead of stopping, I felt this weird compulsion to delve deeper into the depths of my bag. Where were my papers? My hand finally grabbed what felt like them and I hauled them out. A pen soared out of the bag and landed in the middle of the table. A collective gasp could be heard.

What was in my hand was not the documents I had hoped for but a pile of forms of some sort. Not that I was focusing on them at all. Right there, for all to see, wasn't a pen as I had thought, but a pregnancy test. Not even in a packet. One that had already been used, if the two lines on it were anything to go by. Frozen in horror, I couldn't take my eyes off the pink indicators. I was pregnant. No, no, I wasn't. What was I thinking? This wasn't my bag. I leant forward and grabbed the offending object and quickly stuffed it back into the bag.

Looking up, I saw some were offering me gentle smiles while

others looked horrified. Jim was one of them. He sought out my eyes, a puzzled look on his face.

"Right well, congratulations are in order, I feel." The chair-person stood up and held out his hand and then just as quickly withdrew it. He obviously knew how a test worked.

"But I'm not, I mean..." I looked across at Jim again and swallowed.

"The third phase." The Chair empathised, looking at my stricken face. "We had already decided, if what you had sent us before proved to be true, you would be told the outcome today. And I think everyone here would agree, Stroma, you have left us in no doubt that your Development Trust has done a more than thorough job. We wish you well in your future endeavours. Now, as you know, we have other presentations to consider. Congratulations again."

I grabbed my stuff and made a quick exit.

"Don't tell me they were that hard on you?" the woman about to make the next presentation asked as I left the room.

"What? No, no, they are lovely. Not hard at all. I'm just, well..."

"Oh, I see." She laughed and indicated the pregnancy stick I was still holding. She leant forward and whispered, "Congratulations," before she entered the room behind me.

I quickly stuffed the test into my bag or rather into Grace's bag. By now, if Cavan needed changed, she would have realised the mix-up, too. I would have to tell her I knew... Worse, I would have to tell her Jim had been in the room when I had my mishap. I could only hope he hadn't put two and two together and realised whose bag this actually was. At least Grace couldn't hold me totally responsible for what had happened. Only, I wasn't too sure she would see it like that.

28

Grace and I were in Mary's kitchen. We knew she would meddle in our affairs, so we had been avoiding each other and Mary. Of course, this hadn't stopped her. Instead, she had cornered Auntie Lottie at the hall and told her that she would expect myself and Grace for supper.

"Just the two of them, mind. No need for Karen or anyone else to come along. My legs aren't what they used to be, so I am relying on you, Lottie, to deliver this invite."

It was unusual for only Grace and myself to be summoned. Normally, when going for supper at Mary's, it would be Karen, Grace, and me or just Iona and me, so we knew it was more a command than an invitation. The fact that Auntie Lottie was chosen as the method of delivery, rather than Maureen, confirmed that, in Mary's eyes, this was a clan thing. Auntie Lottie was a part of both Grace's family and mine, therefore she was the one charged with making sure we understood the importance of the invitation.

Mary didn't need to be part of our clan. Mary, apart from being our friend, was regarded as an Elder of Blàs, which ranked above any other title, voted for or born into. Few would ignore a summons from her. Behind those glittering eyes was a strong, slightly wild and determined woman who you ignored at your peril.

I had been right in my assumption that Grace would hold me responsible for letting the cat out of the bag or, in this case, the positive pregnancy test out of the bag.

I knew, along with the funding committee in Inverness, exactly what Grace kept in her bag. My contents had not been so intimate – mostly work-related forms, notepads, mobile phone and pens… a lot of pens as it turned out. If anyone cared to check, they would be forgiven for thinking I had a pen fetish. I'm pretty sure Grace had already gone through my bag trying to find a way I could be as embarrassed as she was. Colossal amounts of pens would have been the nearest she would have got.

"Now then, Grace, what was that you were saying to Stroma?"

Grace's body language was not encouraging. We had both picked at our food like teenage girls not happy with the world. Mary's little talks always seemed to reduce us in years.

"I wasn't saying anything. I have nothing more to say." Grace spooned some trifle into her mouth, swallowed, thought for a moment then looked at me. "That is apart from: you are a total weirdo. Who has as many pens as you in their bag? I needed a clean nappy for Cavan and all I could put my hands on were pens. My poor son had to wait until I bought some more. Have you any idea how bad for the environment disposable nappies are, Stoma? I have added to that environmental disaster because you were so careless and took the wrong bag."

I squirmed in my seat. It wasn't my fault she had grabbed the wrong one. She had popped my one onto her buggy handlebars before I picked hers up.

"Stroma, your turn," Mary insisted.

"Well, firstly, Grace, you took the wrong one and placed in on

Cavan's buggy. I'm sorry you didn't have the stuff you needed to change him. But it wasn't my fault. It was an accident."

"That you compounded. I can't believe you kept hauling things out of the bag, Stroma. You saw it wasn't your stuff. And then, well, for goodness sake, now everyone knows. I had to tell Dad and Lottie after the phone call from Jim."

"He phoned you?"

"Well, how else would I know you had emptied the contents of my bag out for all to see? He phoned me, Stroma. He phoned me and now he wants to meet to discuss things. Things I didn't want to talk to him about. Things I can barely process myself. Ach, maybe it would be better if Cavan and I both left."

"No!" both Mary and I shouted together.

"Why would you even think such a thing? Depriving Cavan of a granddad and a granny and an honorary *seanmhair* like me. Why would you think running away will solve anything? Did it work the last time?" Mary's soft voice had taken on a hard edge.

"As a matter of fact, yes, Mary. I came here, and up until Stroma showed all the world I was pregnant, it was fine, so moving could well work again." Grace folded her arms defensively across her body.

"Ach, lass." Mary's tone softened. "You weren't running away that time. You were racing home – that was a different thing. You have all your support here as does Cavan. Whatever you decide, we will all be here for you."

Grace's eyes filled up. "You don't understand. There's no choice. I'm pregnant – that is not going to change. There's no question about whether I keep the baby or not. Whoever he or she is will be a sibling for Cavan. That was the one thing I wanted most in the world when I was younger – a sibling, of my own. Karen, Stroma and Iona were the closest I came to having any, but they all had their own siblings. The choice of whether I tell Jim or not, though, has been taken away. What if he doesn't want a child but feels obliged now to pay for one? What if he doesn't think the baby is his? What if he wants to become a family? How will I know it is me and Cavan he wants or just his own child?"

"Oh my. Grace, Grace, you are so like your father. All these questions and doubts, when all you have to do is talk with him." Mary leant forward and patted her hand.

"He has been plaguing both me and Karen about you, Grace. Long before he knew you were pregnant. He's been trying to find out what he did wrong and why you broke up with him. There is no question that it's you he wants, and Cavan of course."

"And whose fault is it that that he knows I'm pregnant? Tell me that, Stroma, whose fault?"

I felt wretched. She was right. I should have stopped pulling things out of the bag once I realised it wasn't mine. But I hadn't been thinking straight. I had been desperate to get the papers I needed. I was as much to blame as she was for the mix-up.

We had had a blazing row when I had arrived back. She didn't even give me time to explain but slammed her front door straight in my face. She had already known about the bag incident. I couldn't understand how she had known so quickly. It was obvious now – Jim had worked it out. He knew I didn't have a small child who needed any of the paraphernalia I had so unceremoniously dumped on the table. Jim would have worked out who the bag actually belonged to.

Grace had torn into me with angry words when she had opened her door to me. I had lashed back as she slammed the door shut and stormed home to nurse my guilt. We hadn't spoken for days before the summons from Mary had forced us to face each other, and by that time, everyone knew Grace was expecting and that we had fallen out.

"I'm sorry, Grace. You are right, it was my fault too. I just couldn't stop myself pulling everything out. One part of my brain was convinced my forms were in there somewhere. I am truly sorry. I hoped Jim wouldn't have worked out whose bag it was. I mean, it could have been Karen's with her three bairns."

"Only, Stroma, that little blue bear and those cute wee dungarees that you pulled out, they were bought for Cavan by Jim. He knew right away that was my bag."

Well, that explained a lot. I had thought the shocked look was a general look of sympathy for me, not a 'Oh my God, Grace is pregnant and what's more I'm the father' look.

"Sorry." What more could I say? If I was honest with myself, I was quite relieved that Jim now knew he was to be a father. Grace should have told him from the outset. He had as much right to know as she did. She had already run away from one disastrous relationship, Cavan being the only positive thing to come out of it. His father didn't and would never know, as far as Grace was concerned, about Cavan. But Jim wasn't like Cavan's father. He wanted Grace, even with all her hang-ups. She had to start learning to trust again.

I loved the independence, strength and determination of my friend, but sometimes these were also her greatest weaknesses. And when they were, she could turn into someone who was difficult to like. We brooded in our collective silence. Grace started to fidget.

"You know, you really are weird. Who in their right mind would have carried on pulling things out and just compounded the situation. Most folks would have stopped, not panicked than carried on. And who carries around all those pens? You are a total oddball, Stroma." She nudged my elbow and grinned.

Mary lifted our plates away and placed a golden liquid in front of us both.

"A toast to real family and friendship. It's alright, Grace – it is just apple juice. You have to be careful in your condition," Mary said, her eyes twinkling.

I gulped mine and immediately regretted it as I coughed and spluttered, tears pouring from my eyes while I tried to regain control of my body.

"As I was about to say – Stroma and I have the real thing." Mary winked and took a gentle sip of her nip.

"Weirdo." Grace smiled at me as she dabbed my eyes and handed me another hankie for my nose. No wonder she was such a great mother.

29

The yearly fishing competition had arrived. We could look forward to this annual event again after initial resistance from some of the fishermen about the seaweed factory. Now that the venture had been up and running for some time, that initial negative feeling had dissipated. Jim had helped considerably, even inviting along some fishermen from Lewis to talk to our fishermen about the impact on inshore fishing grounds. They had pointed out that the growth and development of further seaweed beds could actually help improve the quantity and diversity of fish available. Grudgingly, our fishermen had taken the wait-and-see approach.

A few years down the line, and our events were once more blessed by their participation. After all, they lived in the community and knew meeting the need for more permanent jobs was important. There simply weren't enough full-time jobs that allowed the local population to work and stay in their beloved Blàs. Young people often left for higher education and other job opportunities. After a time, many wanted to come back but only if they could find a job that paid them well enough to do so.

As part of the fishing contest, an increasing number of onshore competitions had developed over the years. Even those not involved in the fishing trade could find something to take part in or enjoy. More and more of our community were taking part in something we offered.

An afternoon of sand modelling was the new addition for this year. Unfortunately, it had come about after a rather heated argument in an Inbhirasgaidh pub one night. As a result, like most friendly rivalries between towns and villages, the competition had taken on more significance than it should have.

A mixture of men and boys had met after a hard game of shinty. Inbhirasgaidh were in a different league to the small team of Blàs which often had difficulty finding enough members to play. This had resulted in a heavy defeat. The normally friendly atmosphere had disintegrated after a few pints and Blàs' heavy loss. Insinuations that the Inbhirasgaidh team had more brawn than brains and other less than sportsmanship behaviour had festered as the night went on. Eventually, the pub had been closed and a standoff took place in the street.

Our local priest who was well used to this sort of behaviour reminded them of the fishing competition in the hope that the Blàs men would take this as an opportunity to save face. He knew they fancied themselves as the winners even before the first rod was baited. Unfortunately, his intervention didn't have the desired effect, and before we knew it, our supposedly gentle afternoon of sand sculpting had become a contest between the two communities.

I had met Father Antonio the day after the squabbling between the two shinty teams.

"Oh, I'm sorry, Stroma, but they just weren't open to seeing sense. Our young men were intent on letting our neighbours know that they hadn't a brain between them. Don't quote me on this but I think the words were 'aye, never mind castles in the sky, you lot couldn't break out of a sandcastle' or words to that effect. It was only a small leap in their addled brains from there to competing against one another in the sand modelling competition."

"But Father, it's not a competition. We've no prizes and it was supposed to be just for fun," I protested.

"Now, Stroma, you know full well, if I had not agreed to it, this situation would have gone on for months. Might I remind you how many times we have been here before with our young and, I may add, not so young men. They would have been trying to outdo each other in so many ways we would have all been suffering the consequences. They are not bad people just a little bit misguided at times. We have to nip it in the bud. After all, we don't want another situation like the gully. Now, do we?"

He was right. Poor wee Larry MacQueen would never be the same. He now limped around the village with a walking stick, and he wouldn't be going to college or university. All because he had misjudged the leap across Tinker's Gully.

No one could remember what had started the original disagreement, but it had ended with a contingency of males from both Blàs and Inbhirasgaidh setting out once more to prove who were the bravest of the brave, the most skilful and the strongest. Everything had started off well, but as each person leapt over the gully, the landing site became more slippery.

Larry, like the rest of them, was so high on adrenalin he didn't see the danger. Apparently, some of the girls who had turned up had been warning them to stop – they could see what was happening. Eventually, the lads had stopped, but it had taken Larry's accident to finally put an end to it. He had made the leap but slid on landing. The others had made a grab for him but missed, and he had banged his head on the way down. He still hadn't recovered full use of his limbs or brain. It was hoped he would recover some more, but as time went on, the belief that the person he had been before would return dwindled. His friends accepted who he was now – a new different Larry, but still their Larry.

❧

Since it had been Father Antonio's idea to take an entirely uncompetitive event and turn it into yet another contest between Blàs and Inbhirasgaidh, I had insisted that he be the judge. I knew it wasn't being fair as, like me, he worked with both communities. All this rivalry often hampered our work. Mostly it was friendly, but at times, the outcome could be harsh – to which Larry MacQueen was now testament.

Stalls and tents littered the road adjacent to the beach. Some of our elderly residents were seated together near the new bench that had replaced the old one after the storm. They watched as people milled about on the sand below.

On the beach, some were intent on building while others wandered around inspecting each creation. I entered the snack tent and saw Maureen helping Mary fill up plates with sandwiches and cakes.

"I thought you two would be out there enjoying all that artistry."

"Ach," said Mary, "I would rather be in here enjoying all the socialising than out there getting sand between my toes."

I gave her a dubious smile. It never bothered her while out guddling for fish in the pools when the tide went out, or collecting seaweed for that matter.

"I'm just helping our Mary out," Maureen added. "Anyway, getting onto the beach is such a trial, then I'd have to be moving around to catch up on news. This way, most people make their way here at some point, and I can catch any wee snippets without much effort." Maureen grinned.

I grabbed a cup of tea and squeezed my way out as others came looking for a warm drink.

It was strange seeing the beach so busy. Families worked together as far as the eye could see. Father Antonio had placed the young men from Blàs and Inbhirasgaidh at different ends of the beach. I chuckled as I saw runners for each group going backward and forward delivering news on how their competitors were doing. Father Antonio had expressly forbidden the use of mobiles. He didn't want either group filming what the others were creating.

As I passed the bench again where a few of our seniors sat, Catherine Cailleach hailed me.

"Ach, Stroma, we've been having a right laugh at the young men. Haven't we, Crabbit?" She paused and nodded towards her companion. "We were just discussing how funny they looked running backward and forward. Though to be honest, from what we can see from up here, they should be watching out for what the Smiths are doing. Is that not right, Crabbit?"

"Aye, they should. Although it is mighty difficult to see what's going on down there from up here. I was just saying to—"

Catherine Cailleach interrupted. "Oh aye, you are right, Crabbit, but look what these kind children have done. Swallow has been taking pictures of how the other competitors have been doing and young Stag has been bringing them up here to show us all."

"They have that," added Ben the Stump. "If my leg was still there, I would be right down there enjoying the fun."

"Humph," Crabbit O Neil said. "It's not your leg that's the problem, it's your age. You are not young anymore. You wouldn't be able to bend down, and just think of all that sand everywhere."

"Speak for yourself, man. I'm not as old as I... well, I'm not as old as you," Ben the Stump said, just as Stag made his way towards us.

"Here, I've got some more photos. Swallow has been along the beach to them men over there," he said, as he pointed to the Inbhirasgaidh crowd. "They're doing a big ship. They says it's a fishing boat but I don't fink that. It just looks like a boat... boat," he finished lamely. "Our lot are building a big castle. It's cool. Dad said ours is bestest."

Stag held the phone in front of Catherine Cailleach who watched as the pictures were displayed. Ben the Stump got up and peered over her shoulder.

"It would be good to get down the beach again. I'd love to see these for myself. Maybe us oldies should put a team together for next year."

"Don't be daft, man. We'd all get stuck and never be able to get off the beach again. They'd have to send for Paul of the Sheds to haul us out," Crabbit O Neil said.

"But you could win," Stag said, then thought about it for a few moments. "Well, you might come in second – Mum will be able to help us next year and everybody knows she is the greatest artist ever."

"Stag, Stag, hurry up! I need my phone back, come on."

Stag gave us a big smile and ran down towards the beach to join his big sister.

"Such a nice boy that, a nice family," Catherine Cailleach said as she watched the children run back down the beach.

I watched the modellers continue their work. Some old, some young and some in-between but nobody who was unable to keep their footing in the sand. Not many with walking sticks either. Larry was part of the Blàs team, but it was hard going even for him. That was two sets of people since getting my tea that were denied access to our bonnie beach.

They never got near enough to feel the salt spray on their faces or taste it on their lips. The beach smell was less strong even this short distance from the sand. On a day like this, you couldn't hear the waves gently breaking at the tide-line unless you were right there, down near the water's edge. Even the screech of the seagulls and the cries of other sea-birds were muted from here. Stag was right – we had to find a way to fund access for everyone to one of the favourite things that Blàs had to offer.

I had always thought how lucky our community was to have such a nice beach on our doorstep, something we could all benefit from. But I had been wrong. Not all the community could benefit, only those who were able to walk unaided. We had to open it up – they had a right to have the same opportunity as the rest of us.

I found myself wondering why Auntie Lottie hadn't been in touch about our new resident celebrity. They had offered financial help and we had a project that would allow most of our residents access to our beach and solve the problem of the storm damage into the bargain. It would be great to be able to offer something over the summer months. This was definitely something that needed following up. I turned around looking for Auntie Lottie – we needed to move on this now.

30

"I'm not sure, Stroma. I'm employed as his tutor, you know. It may be overstepping boundaries." Auntie Lottie was reluctant to introduce me to Dan Coplan our local celebrity. He was a well-known actor who, like many before him, had bought a house where he could stay hidden from the public and media.

"It's for a good cause, Auntie Lottie," I persisted. It felt strange having to appeal to her. Normally, any male within ten miles of here who was unattached and she considered 'suitable' would have her rushing me forward for an introduction.

"I understand that." She patted her hair. "Of course I do. I would love it if Maureen could get down to the beach. Could you imagine having a proper storytelling night there with the stars out and the dark sea behind us, a big bonfire and a large crowd? It would be lovely. I'm just not sure if the timing is right when I'm there to teach them."

"Please, Auntie Lottie. You said they had offered to help." Something wasn't sitting right with me. Auntie Lottie was the one who had brought up their original offer of help in the first place, so why was she so hesitant now? "I've looked up his profile. He supports a few charities, so he's obviously willing to be parted from his money. What harm could it do? He did offer. Just ask him."

"Well, for one thing, I could lose my job. No, sorry, Stroma, I just can't do it."

I couldn't get over Auntie Lottie's refusal or the stand she was taking on this. However, if she wasn't willing to help out then I would just have to take matters into my own hands.

The World Wide Web was a wonderful thing. It didn't take me long to find an email address where I could leave a message. It took even less time to get a reply from his personal assistant.

I would be meeting Mr Dan Coplan in a few days, and without Auntie Lottie's knowledge.

❧

Mist and droplets covered everything. I knew the house was here somewhere. Today, Mr Coplan wouldn't have to worry about prying eyes. No one would be able to see anything as the mist swirled around and blocked out any view or colours from the surrounding countryside. Normally, greens, purples and yellows would be assaulting my eyes right now. All round, however, was shrouded in washed-out grey.

Driving into nothingness along a road with only one track forward and back meant nerves of steel were needed. No car lights in front could be seen until the vehicle was almost upon you. Thankfully, this was not a road well-travelled. So far, I had only had to brake to avoid a Highland cow whose horns had appeared out of the gloom just before its hairy body. It had meandered back into the mist and disappeared as quickly as it had appeared.

The road was becoming more and more difficult to follow and pick out. At least Auntie Lottie wouldn't be able to see my car out on top of this moor. She still had no idea I had gone behind her back and arranged a meeting.

Just at the point when I was willing to give up, the mist lifted slightly, and I made out the structure of a gated house. I swung into the driveway and eventually pulled up outside the large stone-built dwelling.

A man immediately appeared on the doorstep and ushered me in.

"Hi, I'm Darren, Dan's assistant. Please follow me."

I was momentarily blinded when a blast of light hit my eyes. After a few moments' adjustment, I looked around a spacious tiled hall.

"In here," Darren said. "Dan was intrigued by your email. He had fully intended to become involved in your community, but he was led to believe that you all liked to keep to yourselves. Dan has no desire to intrude."

We had walked into a homely sitting room. Darren indicated a seat. As I prepared to sit down, Dan Coplan himself appeared and took my hand.

"Stroma, how lovely to meet you. I've heard so much about you and all your friends. I never expected to get the chance so early on to help and make your acquaintance."

I was rather stunned. Why did he appear to know so much about me? And why did he think I, or anyone else in the community, didn't want to meet him?

"Darren said you were inquiring about funding for a local project. I'm keen to help, so ask away. Tell me more about your project and what it is you want from me."

This was proving way too easy. I felt sure if Auntie Lottie had mentioned our project to him, he would have been just as responsive to her. He was offering not only his help but, if he was serious, a large amount of money too. I explained the challenges we had with beach access for the elderly, infirm and those with mobility issues. He listened with interest and appeared happy with what I had said.

"If you could leave me with the figures and timescales, I will see what I can do. Or more correctly, I will see what Darren here can do." He smiled across at his assistant. "I don't know what I would do without him. He arranges everything and makes life so much easier than it could be."

"Don't you be listening to him. He is quite able to do all this himself. I'm just an excuse so he can go and lock himself away and learn some of his lines." Darren smiled across at his boss.

The atmosphere was both friendly and enjoyable. It prompted me to probe a bit further.

"You know, I was led to believe you didn't want to mix with us either. Perhaps I misunderstood but you seem eager to help and become part of our community."

"Well, yes, I am. I don't know who would have led you to believe that. In fact, we"—he indicated towards Darren who nodded back—"are eager to become a part of your little community. This is going to be our home, after all. Our place to retreat to after any film work. I hope we can both become full members of Blàs when we are about, and try and lead a normal, everyday life away from all the publicity."

I wondered what they regarded as 'normal everyday'. Blàs had more than its fair share of characters and events. Our 'normal' may well be regarded as a bit quirky by some. Although, given Dan's line of work, he would probably fit in well with the rest of the community, now I came to think about it.

"Perhaps you read somewhere that we didn't want any publicity while we were here? But that's not the same as being a part of your community," Darren added.

Now was not the time to tell them that Auntie Lottie was the one who had discouraged any contact with them, so I agreed with his assessment that perhaps their need for keeping out of the public eye while in Blàs had been misinterpreted.

A look passed between them, an unspoken decision had been made. "Stroma," Dan said. "I know you are a firm favourite with Lottie. Has she said anything about our… well, how we met?"

"Only that she knew your dad years ago." Auntie Lottie had had many lovers in her past, before she become a one-man woman. I had already worked out that Dan's father was probably one of them.

People reacted differently, even these days, to the thought that women could have as many lovers as some men. It wasn't my place to enlighten Dan to how many ex-lovers Auntie Lottie had left in her wake. Nobody particularly wants to be one of many.

Dan was looking across the silence at Darren. Eventually, he spoke. "Has she said anything else? I know you are both close."

"Auntie Lottie has a mind of her own, as you will probably already know." I thought for a while before I spoke again. These people obviously knew her, but I didn't want to say too much. After all, it was up to Auntie Lottie how much she was prepared to reveal of herself. "She only tells us what she wants us to know or thinks we should know."

The community all knew, deep down, Auntie Lottie had many secrets she never shared with us. I was quite sure we only heard a little of what had actually gone on, all those times she was holidaying abroad. Never the same place twice, everywhere littered with broken hearts. If anyone knew all the interesting middle bits, it would be Mary, but she had never told us anything that hadn't first come to us from Auntie Lottie herself.

"Stroma, what are you doing here?" the woman herself strode across the carpet. She glanced anxiously from Dan to myself.

Dan held up his arms as if surrendering. "Lottie, I was telling Stroma here that we would like to help out the community in some way." He paused. "That is all."

Darren was hovering at his back as Auntie Lottie visibly relaxed her stance.

"Well, Stroma, since you are here." She reached up and patted her hair. "I have something to say."

Dan sent for tea as we settled ourselves. I hoped Auntie Lottie wasn't about to tell me one of her long, convoluted stories. I had what I had come for and was anxious to leave, only it would seem rude to leave right then. Ah well, I supposed I could always shift my afternoon's work to the evening. I might as well relax, enjoy my tea and hear what Auntie Lottie had to say.

31

A chill had descended with the mist and refused to shift. All I wanted to do was light the fire and snuggle down with Malt on my lap and think through what Auntie Lottie had told me. However, she had asked me to be present at Mary's tonight. It was the least I could do, given the revelations of that afternoon. If I hadn't gone against her wishes, she wouldn't now be compelled to tell the rest of our friends her news. Thankfully, Paul of the Sheds already knew.

"Why do you think I called off our relationship so often? I was scared he would find out, or worse, I would tell him and he would leave me forever. It was Mary who insisted the last time that I tell him."

So, I had been right all along – Mary, and probably Angus her departed husband, had known from the start.

"Paul just laughed in my face. I nearly walked out on him again until he said he was laughing with relief. He had thought it was going to be something bad or unfixable. He's already met Dan actually. They seemed to get on quite well."

She had admitted all this once we got back to Blàs and she had had time to cool off on her way home. We could only drive at about ten miles an hour due to the thick fog, so she had had plenty of time to simmer down, thankfully. After her insistence that we meet up at Mary's later, I had texted Iona and asked her to come too. As usual, since she was having to alter her plans, she wasn't happy, so she phoned to give me her reasons for not attending.

"Oh, come on, Stroma, whatever is happening tonight, it can't be the end of the world. Nothing that happens in Mary's kitchen is ever as bad as people think. I don't want to spend a night talking with you all about something that will probably not interest me and certainly wouldn't be as earth-shattering as anyone thinks. I don't want to cancel a fun night with my friend here." I heard Mateo laughing in the background.

"Look, Iona, I've told you. Auntie Lottie thinks it's important for you to be there tonight; she wants your support with something. She needs you, Iona, as much as I do. Please come." I signed off. Prolonging the discussion would only have resulted in her continuing to moan at me and end with my agreeing she didn't need to put in an appearance. I knew full well, with me ending the conversation like that, she would sigh, stamp her feet in annoyance but still turn up. Auntie Lottie wanted the rest of her friends to know her news at the same time. I picked up Malt's lead and headed out. Dampness covered my face and hair. I shivered as I walked along.

Sweet chocolate scented the kitchen. Giulietta handed me a large warm mug. I smiled my thanks and sat down. Maureen was busy fussing over Blether and feeding her some lemon cake from her hand. Mary placed a bottle of Angus' special nip on the table, while Ellen lifted out tumblers.

Old Tam, with Dìleas at his side, almost looked happy as he watched and waited for it all to start. Paul of the Sheds leaned against the work surfaces right behind Auntie Lottie, whose hair, for once, looked slightly ruffled. I knew they had both spoken to Grace before they arrived.

"Do you know what this is about?" whispered Karen as I sat down. Before I could answer, in breezed Iona. She threw her arms around Auntie Lottie and gave her a peck on the cheek. "Well, whatever it is, Auntie Lottie, it can't be as bad as anything I've got up to."

There was a peel of laughter around the room. Only, that got me wondering – if Auntie Lottie had kept something like this a secret, could Iona have done the same? She had spent lots of time away from here. Enough to do the same as Auntie Lottie.

"Oh for goodness sake, Stroma," Iona said, nudging my arm. "I've not done anything any crazier than this lot."

"Course you haven't. Thanks for coming, by the way. I know you would rather be elsewhere tonight."

"Ach, you know me, Stroma, you summon, and I appear." She hugged me, and I knew then, whatever happened in Iona's life, if it was a major event she would tell me. We may not have known everything we each got up to, but we told each other the important things. I hugged her back tightly, reassured.

Chairs moved as we all settled down awaiting a tale from our local storyteller. Only, this time there would be more than a modicum of truth behind it. This time, Auntie Lottie would be telling a story about a young girl in a foreign land, a long way from home, and the choices she made that would tangle her life for a long time to come.

America was an exciting country for a young lass from rural Scotland. Auntie Lottie had arrived without any real ties determined to live a life free from responsibility and full of excitement. Only fate, as it often did, decided to step in her way. It took the shape of a six-foot-two man called Gene from Montana.

Auntie Lottie tried not to dwell too much on his good looks, no doubt remembering her husband was standing only a few feet away. However, she still managed to leave the impression that Gene was certainly worthy of consideration. According to Auntie Lottie, he was as kind as he was rich. He had recently separated from his wife and was still hurting. Apparently, the strain of not being able to have children had been too much for the couple.

Auntie Lottie had always been a good listener, and soon they had developed a friendship which eventually led to a whirlwind romance. Gene wined and dined her, took her on visits around the country and bought her expensive gifts. They laughed and joked, generally enjoying each other's company. After six months, Gene had grown tired of nights out and rushing around. Being a good few years older than Auntie Lottie, he was ready to settle down again.

Auntie Lottie, on the other hand, although enjoying all the attention, had no wish to start a family or look after a home, never mind how many employees they could count on to help her. They parted company soon after.

Two months later, Gene was back with his wife. He appeared happy and settled. Auntie Lottie, meanwhile, had a live-in position tutoring English to the children of the family she stayed with. Unbeknown to her at the time, Gene had asked a friend to offer her the job. She had little work experience and running round the country with Gene hadn't exactly helped her with job applications.

Before long, Auntie Lottie was running to the toilet every morning suffering from terrible morning sickness. It was obvious to the family and herself that she was pregnant. Before she could seriously decide what to do, Gene turned up at the house. The family had contacted him, feeling he should know what was going on. He offered Auntie Lottie a proposal that would have an ongoing effect on her entire life.

❧

"I was young and not quite at the panicking stage. I knew I didn't want the responsibility of raising a child, but I knew, whatever happened, I was going to have this child. It was Gene who laid the choices out for me. He wasn't trying to be unkind, but he was trying to get what he wanted – namely, a child. I could have used that to pressure him to come back to me but I didn't want him any more than I wanted a baby at that time. Turns out, I couldn't afford the expense of giving birth in America, which left me the choices of coming home pregnant – and things here were not as accepting as they are now, believe me – or allowing Gene and his wife to cover my expenses and adopt the baby. After all, Gene was the father.

"It took me a long time to decide. Gene was continually coming around, talking to me and buying me things. In the end, I agreed to meet up with his wife Hayley. She was lovely. I can't tell you what a nice lady she was. You could see they were meant to be together and it was only the strain they had gone through that had temporarily torn them apart.

I agreed to stay with them at another property they owned well away from their permanent home. They looked after me well and cared for my health and that of the baby, until I eventually gave birth to a bonnie baby boy.

"All things changed for me then. I didn't want to give him up. It was the hardest thing I have ever done in my life, but I knew he would have a better life with his father. They had the means to look after him and they were a loving couple. They were so grateful to me. They understood how hard it was. They insisted on putting money in my bank account, way more than I imagined.

"As the years went on, they often invited me out to visit them under the guise of being a distant aunt. As I said, they were very kind – Hayley had known how much it had taken for me to leave my son with them. She always thanked me for giving her the best gift anyone could."

The silence was broken by Ellen asking the question that

most in the room were thinking. "So where is your son now, Lottie?"

Auntie Lottie patted her hair and shifted in her seat. "He is here."

"What? In Scotland?" Iona blurted out.

Auntie Lottie nodded.

"Well, where exactly in Scotland? Can we meet him? Does he know? What's he like?"

I squeezed Iona's arm gently. "Give her a chance. I know it's a lot to take in."

"Sorry, yes of course, but this is so exciting. Where is he exactly, Auntie Lottie?"

"Actually, not far from here, not far at all."

"In Blàs," a chorus of voices said at once. I could almost feel everyone trying to work out which males in the village were the right age as well as us knowing nothing of their parentage.

"What is his name, Lottie? He is not living in the village. I would know if he were." Maureen was right. There weren't that many males of the right age and she would know them all, and could probably recite their lineage as well.

"He's bought a house not far from here. A big house. A lodge, as a matter of fact." Auntie Lottie went to pat her hair but stopped midway, uncertainty written across her face.

"No, that can't be right. The only one who has bought something like that here lately is thon actor what's-his-name, and he's American." You could almost see Maureen's brain doing the calculations. "He's the right age. My God, Lottie, is that your boy?"

"Dan Coplan. Yes, it is. And in answer to your questions, Iona, he does know about me now. His mother died a good few years ago and his dad told him about his birth. I think it took him a wee while to adjust to the idea."

"Wow," said Iona. "My auntie has a film star as a son. When can we met him?"

"Quite soon as it turns out. Is that not right, Stroma?"

All eyes turned to me expectantly.

"You knew?" Iona gasped.

"Only very recently, almost by accident. I'll fill you in later." I felt my face infuse red with embarrassment. "He's happy that the funding he offered can be used for the beach wheelchair project, so we can start immediately, and he wants to meet up with everyone. So, he is coming with his PA to the meeting tomorrow night at the hall."

"Well, that's one meeting I will definitely be on time for," Iona said.

32

"Well, Stroma, you certainly seem to have a knack lately for rooting out secrets. I better be careful you don't take my crown." Maureen was feeding Blether on her knee and smiling across at me. I shifted uneasily in my seat. The last person I wanted to be twinned with was Maureen. Much as I liked her, being the local gossip was not my idea of fulfilment. It was hardly my fault that everyone seemed to be hiding so many secrets.

It wasn't something I could be accused of. Then I remembered how long I had kept my relationship with Scott, Ellen's nephew, secret. Or rather, I had *thought* I was being discreet but it turned out most people had been aware of our romance all along. Having to meet the sympathetic look in my friends' eyes after he left had made it all the more difficult. *He's only helping his dad while his mum recovers – he made the only choice he could,* I had reminded myself several times a day. As the weeks had turned into months and there was still no sign of him coming back, these daily reminders had become less frequent.

"Maureen, that is hardly fair," Karen jumped in to save my reputation. "Everyone knows that Stroma means well. It's just that little world she lives in means she isn't always aware of what's going on. And that's why she keeps putting her foot in it." She smiled across at me as I frowned. I wasn't always daydreaming. I did see what was going on. I opened my mouth to say something then Iona whispered to me.

"I would just smile nicely and stay quiet. This lets you off the hook, and let's face it, you do spend a lot of time somewhere other than the here and now." Iona passed me a large piece of chocolate cake. "Ellen made this – it's so tasty."

The hall was slowly filling up. People grabbed pieces of cake and drinks before they sat down. Notes had been sent out to everyone who had shown an interest in setting up wheelchair access to the beach. It had brought out a few extra people than we could usually rely on. First and foremost were our senior citizens who would normally be tucked up at home by this time, sipping hot drinks and devouring their favourite television programmes. I couldn't remember them coming out to meetings before, especially ones at night. They frequented any event we held but never volunteered to be on committees.

Mind, our projects needed residents to support them by attending our fundraisers, just as much as they needed volunteers to run things. And this the old folks did, even to the extent of sponsoring young trees when we purchased our local woods. Taking full advantage of their mutual love of gossip, Maureen had spent an afternoon with them finding out about their needs regarding access to the woods. Now we had paths that were more suitable for wheelchairs and those who found walking challenging. I often met Catherine Cailleach, Ben the Stump and Crabbit O'Neil at Cnocannach on one of their outings and they were frequently in the audience for any storytelling event there – often, it had to be said, shouting out comments and thoughts on the performance. I didn't recall ever seeing them in the woods before our improvements. It would have been almost impossible for them to gain access before that.

The beach project was one that they would benefit them the most, so I shouldn't have been surprised to see them there, sitting next to the Smith family. Jill had made it along with the new baby. If dad Ralph was coming, then so would the children. It was generally accepted that if one was there, they all would be. Adding another child to their family mix had made little difference to their attendance at events. They had become one of our most active families in the community and a great bonus for the village.

The presence of some of the elderly folk of Blàs did surprise me, though. Mostly, they were content to enjoy any benefits that our work offered without their direct intervention. It allowed them to both criticise and praise any elements they thought worthy of their interest. I suspected both Auntie Lottie and Old Tam had had a hand in their appearance. After the conversation at the hall that afternoon, I shouldn't have been surprised that they had turned up en masse tonight.

❧

"Ach, if it is a film star you are wanting to see, I wouldn't be holding your breath. Thon wee laddie at the lodge is hardly what I would regard as a superstar."

I had looked across at Auntie Lottie who was looking a bit indignant on behalf of her son. She should have known what the old folk were like though. Filling them up with hot sweet tea and cake did not lead to a tempering down of their views.

"Ach, you are right there. I mean, thon laddie is hardly out of short breeches. Never mind a heartthrob. If you will pardon me for saying so, Lottie."

"Now, John Wayne he would make my knees wobble just the thought of him." Old Betty grabbed her chest faking a swoon. She was a recent addition to the oldies table. One of the few elderly that had returned to Blàs, moving in with younger relatives who could offer a bit of care when needed.

"Ach, never mind the men folk. The ladies, now, they were so glamourous, real ladies they were. Knew how to look after a man. That Audrey Hepburn was some woman and what about the other one… you know, who wanted to be alone."

"Greta Garbo," was chorused around the table.

"But man, she was well before your time. She was in the silent movies, I'm thinking."

"Aye well, right there, that would be why I liked her. Quiet and bonnie woman, what more could a man ask?" Crabbit O Neil nodded his head sagely.

"Aye wull, ane that cauld talk tae ye. Ane that kent ye wull enough tae ken yer ane mind afore ye kent it yersel," Old Tam intervened.

"Aye well, you are right there, Tam. Your missus was such a woman, right enough. Full o words and could stand up against any of those old beauties."

Nods of agreement ran around the table. Old Tam's wife had been as lively in appearance as she was in humour. Even after all this time, she was lovingly remembered.

"You fair married above your worth there, Tam. Mark you, if she had known me first, I could have given you a run for your money," Ben the Stump added.

"Ha, she wouldn't have looked at you once, never mind twice, you old rogue," Catherine Cailleach said. "Our Tam here was the only one for her."

It hadn't surprised any of the older generation that Old Tam had married a person who was as happy as he was dour and as colourful as he was dull. It was the classic case of opposites attracting. Small wonder that their granddaughter Morag was such an outgoing person while her father was more inclined to be like his own father – never the one for looking on the brighter side of life.

"These youngsters nowadays have no idea of glamour," Old Betty added.

"Well, I don't know about that. Our Lottie here is glamourous enough for anybody. And if the rumours are true, well then, that boy of hers will be too." Crabbit O Neil smiled towards Auntie Lottie.

Auntie Lottie patted her hair and returned his smile. "I am here, you know. I can hear you all discussing me and mine. If you are interested in our latest addition to the area, he will be at the meeting tonight 7 p.m. sharp. Tea and cake will be available. No charge."

"An if ye are interested in bein able tae git on tae thon beach, I wauld mak th effort tae come. Thon boy o eers wull be saying somethin of interest tae us awh," Old Tam said.

❧

And so it was that some of the old and not necessarily the wise of the village had turned out for the meeting. Free cake, after all, was not to be sniffed at, never mind meeting a new-age film star.

As the noise level subsided in the main hall, a stirring occurred at the door. Voices could be heard before anyone appeared. Laughter heralded in Dan Coplan and Darren his PA. Paul of the Sheds walked in right behind them. It was obvious from the start that Dan was used to making an entrance. All eyes quickly took in the party that had just arrived. Auntie Lottie walked over and embraced her husband then his two companions as they helped themselves to cake. Ellen stood up and called for attention.

"As you will be aware, we have some new residents in our midst. One of which has very generously offered to fund a great deal of the project we need to get the beach wheelchair project off the ground. Stroma will fill you all in on where we stand with it right now, then I will ask Dan and Darren to say something about how they can help. So, Stroma, if you would be so kind."

I had my notes, the display and the correct bag all ready, so no mishaps could occur. I watched as Dan and Darren finished off their refreshments and took their seats.

I knew my audience were only half listening – they had come

for what they regarded as the real show. I couldn't honestly say if it was the prospect of the beach wheelchairs or the chance to meet our film star and son of Auntie Lottie that interested them more. I didn't care, as long as they were willing to help.

At the end of my presentation, all attention switched to our two Americans as they stood up. They didn't take long to summarise their offer of help nor to present themselves to the community. I could see why Dan was so successful on film. He drew your eye and commanded your attention. Darren stood at his right shoulder and passed over any information needed.

As soon as their presentation was finished, the two of them retired to mix and talk with the audience. After kissing Auntie Lottie on both cheeks, they made a beeline for the elderly and wheelchair-bound. Maureen was delighted to be included. Much laughter engulfed their walk among the folk who had turned out for the meeting. When they finally made their way to the back of the hall, they turned to say farewell and left before most were aware they were going.

It was as if a light had gone out in the hall. For a few seconds, complete silence followed them out... before the elderly resumed their debate on whether Dan and Darren could be included in the same glamorous category as the stars of the 1940s and 1950s.

33

Before the money had a chance to settle in the bank, Ellen had already been in touch with the Highland Council Access Officer, and the Community Council. This was no hardship, given the Community Council was made up of most of the Development Trust Trustees. Permission had been sought regarding the necessary works.

The part of the beach that would house the beach wheelchairs and allow access was on Common Good Land, which was looked after by our local Community Council, so it was merely a case of getting everyone together and agreeing.

I had always presumed that all our villagers and holidaymakers had access to our beach. How could I not have noticed that not everyone among us was fortunate enough to walk, ride and play on our sands? How we hadn't considered this before, I will never understand – especially given we had just improved the paths in the woods so wheelchair users could get better access.

Maureen had never complained about it, so we had been blind to the issue and just accepted that she stayed on the road above and shouted down to us if we were on the sand. We left the beach automatically when we saw her and walked beside the beach but not on it. I wasn't the only one having these thoughts, if the turnout at the meeting had been anything to go by.

"Why did you never say, Maureen? It's not like you to keep quiet about things?" Ellen placed a cup of tea in front of her once we had reconvened the following morning.

"Ach well, I never really thought about it. You learn to accept you can't do or go certain places. It's not a conscious thought process, you know. It just is, or should I say was." Maureen took a sip of her tea. "It never stopped me doing much I wanted to do. My friends have always been good about lifting my chair here, there and everywhere."

"Or rescuing you here, there and everywhere," Auntie Lottie added.

"Aye, you are right there, Lottie. If it wasn't for your Paul and yourselves here, I could well still be stuck in the mud somewhere." She took another sip. "Mind you, now that I can get into and out of the woods on my own and it looks likely I will be able to get onto the beach, I may find myself getting into all sorts of bother." She laughed as Auntie Lottie spluttered into her tea, then continued. "I'll be expecting more access to places now, I can tell you. The beach – just think, Mary, I can accompany you down to the rocks and collect seaweed. And rock pools, seeing the wee fishes swimming around. Imagine being able to get my feet into the water. How deep do you think I will be able to get the wheelchair into the water?"

"We haven't even got them, and you're already pushing the barriers. I'd better let Paul know to expect to have to rescue you from deep water." Auntie Lottie laughed nudging her friend on the arm.

"It's nae a laughin matter. Eh'll telt ye afore, ye ken whut'll happen, pair Paul wull be oot fishin folk oot o the water every day." Old Tam was nodding his head agreeing with everything he said to himself. I just caught sight of Dìleas from the corner of my eye. Had he been nodding in agreement with Old Tam? *Don't be daft*, I told myself returning my attention back to Maureen.

"I'll not have the voice of doom putting dampeners on my bid for… what is it they call swimming in the sea now? Oh aye, wild swimming. I will be 'wildchair' paddling," Maureen chuckled. "I can't wait. If only we'd had one when Angus had died. I could have come down to the beach properly to say goodbye."

Angus' ashes had been released into the sea breeze off our beach one stormy painful day. Maureen had been unable to attend but had joined her friends in the hall after a rather unfortunate incident with her wheelchair and her best underwear.

"Thank goodness you didn't," Mary mused. "Can you imagine, with your underwear flapping about in the wind. It was bad enough watching your bra swooping away into the sky. Poor Finlay has never been the same, they say."

We all smiled as we remembered Maureen's mishap at Angus' funeral. She had forgotten about her underwear drying on the back of her wheelchair. It had brought Mary back from that dark place she had disappeared to. Maureen, however, had never been allowed to forget about it.

"Wull, Eh'll be off. Eh dinnae want tae think aboot that day if ye dinnae mind." Old Tam, his face crimson, took his leave along with Dìleas close at his side.

Peals of laughter followed him out. "I don't think it's only Finlay who's struggling with that memory," Auntie Lottie added. "I think a lot of the older menfolk around here were taken aback. Anyway, Maureen, now we are getting the beach wheelchairs we can think about putting on a proper storytelling event where both of us can be on the beach. I can tell you, I felt quite exposed having to stand there all on my own at that last event on the beach."

"At least that was all you exposed, and your underwear was safely put away, Lottie." Mary laughed as Maureen looked indignant.

Our friend had long ago come to terms with the death of her husband. She manged to right it with herself by savouring the memories of the time they'd had together, knowing they were luckier than most to have had that.

Angus had left a legacy of stories and poems that Mary felt was her duty to promote as often as possible. The job of local bard was one she continued to encourage.

"She has a point though. Maureen, it would be right nice to have a storytelling event with you on the actual beach. I had a lovely time the last time, but Lottie is right – you were missed. It didn't feel right you sitting up there on the road with others who couldn't make it onto the beach. How many beach wheelchairs are we getting? We have more than Maureen to think about, you know."

"At least five," Ellen said. "We will have three that need someone to be with the person in the chair and two that can be independently worked. We may need to get a sixth at some point, but we have to consider how big the shed will be to house them."

"Aye, she is right. We've had a letter saying we will have to consider a changing table. We can't have people going home covered in sand. There is a lot more to consider regarding water supply to wash the wheelchairs down. Next year we may need to employ someone part-time if we start getting lots of requests from holidaymakers, otherwise we could get snowed under with emails and telephone calls."

We continued for a few moments longer discussing the various ins and outs of running the beach wheelchairs. We had various members of the community who could give us further advice, but in the end, what we would need was a stable subcommittee that could move the whole thing forward and keep it running.

It had surprised me how many people this project was capable of helping and how many families had at least one person among their relations who could use this service. From young children to the elderly, people who were disabled due to illness or accident, age or infirmity. The old folks' home in Inbhirasgaidh had already voiced their support and hoped to use it for some of their clients. The additional needs school had also requested to be informed when the chairs would be available.

If we took the Dornoch project as an example, we could well be catering for people from all over Scotland and beyond.

First thing first, though, we needed to get that shed up and the access area to the beach sorted out. Dan's generosity had made this all possible far quicker that we were ready for, but now that the money was there, we needed to get ourselves organised to carry it forward. His money wouldn't last long, though hopefully we would hear back from the SSE about the wind farm grant soon and that would allow us to take on someone part-time to answer emails and run the bookings.

34

"See what you think. Go on, try it." Iona had presented me with a tub of beauty cream they were developing at the seaweed factory.

"I know it isn't the best scientific experiment ever, but you are so fussy about what you use I thought you could give me your thoughts."

I wasn't used to this nervous version of Iona. It was strange to see her anxious and wanting my input about beauty products. We'd never done the whole sister make-up thing as teenagers. I had been too busy making sure I was covering all the important things like getting tea ready and having the laundry up to date to worry much about my appearance. Iona also went for a more edgy look than I would have tried. If anything, it would have been me going to Iona for make-up advice not the other way around.

"It's enriched with seaweed extracts. So full of antioxidants and minerals. It will keep you looking young, Stroma, but not younger than me obviously. So, what do you think?"

I hadn't a clue what she was talking about and couldn't care less what antioxidant or whatever the cream had in it. As long as it didn't cause a reaction, was natural and hadn't been used on animals, I was happy.

My skin was sensitive and often reacted to creams and beauty products. No immediate tell-tale nipping from my skin as I rubbed it in. It felt cool and refreshing.

"I love the smell. I was a bit concerned it would smell too seaweedy, but it just comes across as fresh. I really like it."

"That's great. You are among the first members of the public to try it. I decided to have a local sample group test it for the final check. Auntie Lottie has offered to be one of my testers. I've also included Mary since she has older skin, but really, it's more so I could give her a wee treat. The cream has already passed all the tests it needed to. We're hoping to get it in the lodges for the beginning of September, and we're close to the launch now. I'd like your thoughts on the packaging too."

You could tell they were going for quality upmarket buyers. The packaging was high-end and stylish, heavy on the natural elements of the sea. It was sure to go down well with customers. The products would be a bit out of my price range for everyday use, but as long as Iona was involved, I was pretty sure I would be able to get it at cost price for myself.

Iona had been working hard to develop these products. I was still a bit worried that once they stopped the development stage and moved on to full-blown production, there wouldn't be much left to keep her here. The grant covered her for another eighteen months but after that I wasn't sure if the factory could sustain her post. Perhaps they would have to move her to part-time but that wouldn't be enough for her. Iona liked a challenge and needed a full-time job for the wage alone. It was the reason I hadn't fought her on the brewery idea. Perhaps she could make some sort of living from that.

"Right, since I have your attention." Iona placed a glass in front of me. "This is our latest batch of beer. What do you think, better or worse than last time?"

I sniffed the glass and regarded the contents dubiously. "I'm not sure about the colour. It looks kind of yucky."

"Oh, very technical, Stroma. Here is our latest beer, tastes brilliant, notice how the lovely yucky colour enhances your experience."

"Okay, Iona, I'm only saying." I took a sip. "Actually, I quite like the taste. Only the colour does put me off. What happened to the other one we tried?"

"Well, that one is fine. Colour, taste, everything. I just feel we need to have more than one to launch. I had high hopes for this one, but I don't seem to be able to control the colour. Back to the drawing board, I suppose." Iona lifted the glasses away.

"I appreciate you working so hard, Iona. I know you're trying to make this brewery work. I'm just sorry I can't help you more at the moment, but between work and the Development Trust, I hardly have a minute to myself let alone to help you out."

I did feel guilty that Iona was left to do so much on her own, but I hadn't wanted to start this project in the first place or rather not right now. We had to make it work though as Iona had acquired the materials and equipment. I had to start being more committed to it.

"Look, Stroma, I'm pulling a wage from the factory at the moment, but I can work on the beer in my own time. It's better to do this development work now when I don't need to take a wage from our little venture. We can do this part-time to begin with. All I need you to do is give me your feedback on taste and design. Ellen is helping me out with the books. Once my 'day job' drops down to being part-time, I can devote more time to our brewery. There's already talk of prolonging my contract if I drop my hours now that we have a few products to sell. To be honest, it would suit the factory and myself right now. I just wanted to sound you out about it."

Iona's enthusiasm for something new was always energising, but like her job at the seaweed factory, as soon as it appeared the initial challenge was over, she was always keen to start something else. I was still apprehensive about how long the brewery would keep her interest. I didn't want to wake up one day to find I was having to work two full-time jobs because she had left for something new.

"Stroma, I could have gone head-first into a microbrewery but I'm taking baby steps. We can keep running as a nanobrewery with myself and Mateo. Once the factory and I agree on my part-time status, we can move into more production and become a microbrewery. Mateo is keen to learn the ropes for being a brewer, for any time I'm not around. Others have said, if it grows, they would welcome a job. Once it takes off a bit, we can re-look at it. Paul of the Sheds has been great not only helping me with the brewery methods, but the shed will easily take any expansion we want to make. Can you imagine being able to offer some of our friends a job? Maybe building in some flexible working for those with children. Auntie Lottie is already mentioning us to others. She would make a great salesperson, or at least an ambassador for the brand."

Over the kitchen table, like so many occasions over the years, we discussed and threw ideas about, only this time it was about our own brand. It cleared my mind and focused my thoughts. We could do this, my sister and I, we really could. Still not quite believing it, I laid out some thoughts to Iona,

"It would have to have a Gaelic influence. It needs to reflect our culture and language as well as our landscape. Obviously, the sea has to take centre stage to an extent, but Gaelic has to be in there."

I wasn't surprised that Iona agreed wholeheartedly. Partly, it would be to encourage me to become more involved, but also, she felt as strongly about our culture as I did.

"We don't have that much time to come up with a name. The owners of the lodge want to be able to add it to their welcome pack. Both the beauty products and our beer have to be ready by

September – that's not that long, given we have labelling, etcetera to do."

I knew she was right but other things were occupying my mind, not least of which was the email I had received from Scott. I tried to put it at the back of my mind. I had other priorities to think about – the language course for summer, for a start. And if Iona and I wanted to have a sustainable business to run here in Blàs, I needed to focus more on what she was doing, rather than daydreaming about when Scott may reappear in my life.

I gave myself a mental shake. I knew I wasn't prepared to give up my day job. I loved it, so whatever way I fitted into this new venture it would have to be on a part-time basis. I looked again at the beer Iona had handed me. I felt a bubble of excitement as I thought about owning our brand and brewery. It would be hard work, but I was used to that; it would just be a case of repositioning my workload.

Iona had one more brewing to do before we settled on our first few beers. After that, perhaps I would re-look at how we could realistically take this forward.

35

My Blàs language plan was laid out before the team. My boss wasn't totally against the idea which, under the circumstances, wasn't surprising. He tended to be open-minded about anything that could lead to more Gaelic speakers.

"It's not unlike our summer course from last year. Only the places you suggest visiting are not so exclusive so it could work better. How do you see marketing it, and where do you envisage the funding coming from?"

That was one of my main concerns about going to my boss with an idea. You were expected to come up with all the solutions as well as the initial suggestion. He felt anyone could come up with what appeared to be a great idea. The delivery of said idea was where the real skill and acumen took place. That was also the most time-consuming part. It was great that he had taken the time to listen to me.

HQ was one of the few places I could still totally converse in Gaelic, and I enjoyed getting to use the language all the time while in the building. We had a separate room used for anyone who came in who didn't speak Gaelic. HQ had decided to include this space, as even when we had several people capable of speaking in Gaelic, it only took the appearance of one person who couldn't to change the language of use.

We often had visitors who were trying to re-establish their own languages from around the world, and although they were bi- or multi-lingual themselves, the most common language between us was English. Having this room where English was spoken helped us keep the ethos of the rest of the building Gaelic.

"Stroma, *a bheil thu ag èisteachd rium*?" My boss' voice pulled me back. It didn't matter what language was spoken, my daydreaming was fluent in both.

"Sorry, yes, of course I was listening. We have a promise, in principle, of help from the local Development Trust, a tutor who is happy to deliver the course."

"Well, I don't have to guess who that is – Lottie, I take it?"

I nodded. "Our HIE Project Officer for the area is also willing to fund some of it. I haven't had time to talk to SSE about wind farm money, but I am hoping they could be another source. As I said, it's early days yet and I just wanted to mull over the idea with you first. The Development Trust could set it all up and run it, but I thought it would be better for us to do it. We don't want to be building up competition for ourselves or, worse still, making ourselves redundant."

He sat back for a few moments, deep in thought. We openly encouraged communities to stand up on their own and take projects forward. At the same time, the more we did that, the less our funders saw any reason for us to exist. They found it difficult to recognise that, if it wasn't for us laying the initial groundwork, most communities would never get their projects started, never mind completed.

Politics, unfortunately, did come into it. We knew that we had to make ourselves more visible and shout about what we actually did. We needed our communities to say we were there helping them and often coming up with the ideas to begin with.

"Okay, right, we will put this forward as one of our pilot

projects for the autumn. I can give you some hours to work on this as part of your remit. But remember, you still have to cover the workload you have. I can't take on anyone else – we don't have the resources – but I can allow you to work as many hours on this as you can. Remember, it will all have to be accounted for in your annual report."

I sighed my relief. In reality it would make my job easier. With the go ahead from HQ, it meant that many of these extra hours I would be working would be included in my day job.

Hopefully, given the projects we had set up from the previous year, I could use some of the initial administration and set-up costs and merely tweak them, instead of coming up with a whole new set of everything. Working in my own community for a while would suit me fine, given how many projects locally were coming together at the one time. Now all I had to do was timetable it all in.

I left HQ and took out my mobile phone. No new notifications. I swallowed my disappointment – Scott had not been in touch. Before my mood could sink lower, I pressed Iona's number.

"Right, Iona, get a meeting organised and make sure Auntie Lottie and Ellen are there, and whoever else you think should be involved." I listened as she whooped down the phone. "Yes, okay, tonight would be fine. See you in a wee while. Yep, I love you too."

It's amazing how three little words can lift your spirits. I smiled. Talking with Iona, even for those few minutes, had made me feel so much better. Knowing you are loved and having someone tell you that… well, how can you not smile?

The hot, sweet smell of Ellen's baking filled my nostrils. Thankfully, Iona had arranged for the meeting to take place in Ellen's kitchen rather than ours. It would have been a tight squeeze fitting everyone in, plus bought biscuits just didn't soften anyone up in the way Ellen's homebaking did. Her kitchen was perfect for informal meet-ups, and never mind how short the notice, she always seemed to have the time to rustle up some cake.

Iona would be a few minutes late. Some habits were just too difficult to break. Old Tam was already there. I wasn't quite sure where he fitted into all of this, but Iona felt it was important to invite him. Dìleas came over to sniff and greet Malt who was just as happy to see him. Blether simply extended her neck so I could tickle behind her ears better. She had long ago sussed out that humans could pet her a lot better if she stayed up on Maureen's knees. What she hadn't grasped was sometimes her wee extras that her owner insisted on her wearing made it difficult. Tonight, she had on some sort of sparkly tiara... Maureen saw me looking at it.

"Isn't it lovely, Stroma? She looks just like the princess that she is," she purred, misunderstanding my look. "I can give you the web address I bought it from if you want." Before I could answer in the negative, Maureen went on. "We have our eye on a lovely pink shiny cape for our next purchase, don't we, my wee precious."

Honestly, Maureen was sounding more like Gollum from Lord of the Rings every time she talked about her dog. Blether took it all in her stride, gratefully accepting all the attention she could get.

"Right, if we're all here, let's get started." Just as we all settled down, laughter erupted from the hall, and Iona appeared, along with Mateo.

"Sorry, a bit of a hold-up, don't wait on us."

"We weren't, dear," Mary said. "Ellen?"

"Well, actually, I think we should ask Stroma and Iona to lay out their plans, then we can see how the Trust can help them."

Once more, I presented my thoughts. This time, I knew the

audience would definitely back us. However, they wouldn't be shy about asking questions either.

"So basically," I finished, "we are looking at having a permanent part-time language school here, run by the Trust but supported by GLADS. There would be enough places here that learners could visit to develop their language skills."

Iona broke in. "For example, we could develop the use of existing native speakers such as Old Tam here. Stroma told me that day the bairns had on the croft was really successful. It could become an established part of the course." Iona smiled across at Old Tam, and there was a flicker of movement beside him. I stared at Dìleas then shook my head. No, I couldn't possibly have seen him nodding his head as if in agreement. I continued where Iona left off.

"Learners would also visit the brewery and take in the language from there. The woods and the dig will also feature as a permanent part of the course. Of course, there is also the seaweed factory and other areas slightly outwith but near Blàs that we could use."

"So where exactly are you expecting this course to run when it isn't out and about?" Maureen asked.

"Our brewery is only taking up a small area in our shed at the moment. Eventually, we would like to expand, but until then, we can use the other side as the classroom. It wouldn't take much to divide the space up. We could include a small area for having coffee, but it is near enough to the hall that students could nip over at lunchtime, and we can even hold a class in there on the language around soup making for example. There are enough B & Bs around for travelling students, and the hostel at Inbhirasgaidh could take any who are on a more limited budget. There's still enough of us who speak Gaelic here so that students can hear it within the village. The pub, the shop and most at the hall speak Gaelic, so the students can have an immersed time. Blàs could become a Gaelic learning centre, in its own right. If it proves popular, who knows, we could add a classroom-cum-cafe onto the brewery in the future," Iona said.

"My," said Mary, her eyes sparkling in delight. "Well, wouldn't that be something. Reviving a real Gaelic community. We could give Sabhal Mòr Ostaig a run for their money."

"Well, I don't think that will happen. We're not looking to offer certificate courses or degrees, purely language courses. But you're right – hopefully, it we will lead to the growth off a real Gaelic community again. It will certainly encourage lapsed speakers to start talking in Gaelic again."

"Well, definitely, the Gaelic words regarding alcohol will be well used," added Auntie Lottie. We all looked at her. "Well, what with the pub and the brewery involved – I might never have to leave Blàs again."

36

"Digger Dodds is fair getting on with her work," Auntie Lottie shouted above the din.

Digger Dodds had offered to scoop out the area we needed to allow access to the beach for the wheelchair users. Her great yellow machine was like a magnet. Young and not so young hovered close by, watching her excavate and flatten the area. Personally, I found the sound too overwhelming and turned to go.

"Tea," Auntie Lottie shouted at me and moved her hand up to indicate drinking. Thankfully, teaching in the immersion way allowed her to communicate her meaning non-verbally without too much trouble. We made our way over to the hall, neither of us speaking. Our voices would have been lost in the noise that encompassed everything.

The door lazily closed behind us stifling the sound.

"That's better. I feel I can breathe now." I shrugged, shooing away the last remnants of the digger.

"Ach, you're just not used to that noise level. In the city, you know it was never quiet. It took me a long while to adjust to the lack of sound back here," Auntie Lottie said as she straightened her hair and found a table for us.

On hearing, Ben the Stump said, "Well, lass, there is always sound around. It is just different. You can hear the bees buzzing and—"

"The blackbirds singing and the—" Catherine Cailleach interrupted.

"Children laughing," Mary added, joining us.

"The sheep baaing," Old Betty said.

"And the midges feeding," Crabbit O Neil said.

"You can't hear midges feeding. What are you on about?" Alex Nail said.

"Of course you can. You hear them all the time, eating away at people here on holiday – nawt, nawt." Crabbit O Neil wasn't going to give up his point.

"I've never heard anything so daft – midges eating. What a lot of nonsense," Alex Nail said.

"You hear the people shouting and screaming the minute they attack – that's the same thing," Crabbit O Neil said.

"No, it's no. That's the people. You can't hear the midges," Alex Nail stated.

"I'm telling you..." And so the debate would go on and range around as many subjects as they cared to discuss.

I tuned out of the old folks' conversation. It could go on like this for hours. I wondered if Doctor Seuss got some of his ideas from listening to the older generation's conversations. They seemed so nonsensical at times and just weird. In the end, who cared if midges slurped as they stole our blood. What we did care about was not having too many of them here on the East Coast. If we had been on the West Coast, nobody would have been out watching Digger Dodds and her machine working – the midges would have run them all off.

"Stroma."

I jumped as Auntie Lottie snapped my name.

"You're not even listening to me. Where had you gone? Don't be listening to the oldies; they will addle your brain."

"Says the one who enjoyed their company so much she kidnapped them all," I retorted.

"Oh ha-ha. You know fine and well that is not what happened. I still can't believe I've been banned from any future trips for two years. It wasn't as if it was just me, you know. There are some around here who never have to face up to what they have done. All they have to do is smile sweetly and immediately all is forgiven."

Mary set down her teacup. "Ach now, Lottie, you wouldn't be wanting to have me banned now at my age, would you?" Mary smiled and her eyes sparkled with mischief.

"Fat chance of that. Ach, get down now, Whisky. I'll give you a treat in a minute."

Two pairs of brown eyes pleaded doggie starvation at her – Malt was not prepared to miss out on any free treats that might be on offer. Ignoring them, Auntie Lottie continued. "I thought we could use this as a business meeting."

That sounded fine with me. I couldn't think of a better place to hold one. Nice cakes, good tea and my dog was with me. It made for an enjoyable working environment.

"I thought I would give you an update. The courses with the local families are going well. I've been considering the beach element. Is there a way we can use that too?"

Auntie Lottie did take her tutoring seriously; she had obviously put a great deal of thought into how to get the best out of her student families. Exploring the language that children and families use together on the beach was a great idea. Play and fun helped the learning process. A beach language day open for everyone would work. We could include lots of elements, have a story session and beach-themed phrases. I was sure the school and others in the community would come up with something of their own. As long as we included the expected ceilidh, we were on to a winning event. If we had taken delivery of the beach wheelchairs by then, we could have a real celebration of Gaelic and the beach. Mary and Auntie Lottie were of the same opinion. We smiled, raised our teacups and clicked them together.

"Here's to our Gaelic Language Beach Wheelchair Grand Open Day."

"That's a wee bit of a mouthful, is it no?" Crabbit O'Neil butted in.

"Ach, away with you, man. It is not that bad, I remember now that day when..."

And off the old folk went again, down memory lane, complete with grumblings, competition and debates on who was right.

Whatever the name of our day would be, I felt sure it would be a great celebration.

37

"It wull nae be th same agin." Old Tam was shaking his head as he downed his pint in the local bar.

"What are you on about now, you daft old man?" Archie, one of the Twa Pinters, asked.

"Oor beach, that is," Old Tam said, "or waz. It's nae like oor beach at awh, ye ken."

"For the love of God, man. What are you complaining about? You're hardly that clever on your legs and you're getting older by the second. You'll be pleased to be able to get down that slipway now to the beach," Sandy, the other of the Twa Pinters, added.

"Ach, that's no slipway. A slipway is for boats, you old goat. That there is an"—Archie put on what he thought was a posh voice—"access road."

"Ach, help ma boab. Eh dinnae ken whut ye wauld caw it, but it's juist nae right tae be shiftin the sand and movin the beach aroond," Old Tam said. "That there is whair the *ùraisg* used tae be, Eh telt ye that."

Ben the Froth shook his head and refreshed the men's drinks. "And what is the difference between how the wind howls in the winter and changes the beach and how it looks now?"

"Ah wull, that is different. That is nature, this isnae the same thin."

Old Tam didn't like change, unless of course it was either forced on him or had happened through a naturally occurring event like a winter storm. As far as he was concerned, you shouldn't muck about with nature. He was a firm believer in many of the old superstitions that still surfaced periodically around the area.

The last time he had caused such a fuss it had resulted in some of the revered in the community becoming involved in switching an old skull for a modern duplicate. Hopefully, Old Tam hadn't remembered some old tale that was going to compromise our beach wheelchair project. Prevention in advance of his stories getting out of hand was needed. Before anything could be done, however, Old Tam continued.

"Ye ken that area thon wee folk foound. Wull, Eh've been hivin a wee think aboot that."

Oh God, no, please don't come out with some fable we will have to circumnavigate again.

"Wull, whut if that hole waznae storm damage. Whut if it waz caused by someit else." All around him were now awaiting his latest proclamation. "Whut if'n someit came oot o that hole an is noo on the loose? Eh've hid some bad vibes, ye ken. And Eh'm nivir wrang!" Old Tam lifted his head and looked his fellow drinkers in the eyes. I wanted to intervene before it got any worse but as I was listening my limbs seemed to be set in slow motion and were unable to move fast enough to put a stop to Old Tam's predictions.

"Thon area, Eh'm sure it wauld hiv been cursed."

And there it was – the start of yet another tale of fate and bad luck and goodness knows what else that would fall on Blàs or its inhabitants. It didn't take much for the old stories to leave a mark on the people who had lived here for generations.

Technology and the modern world were well and truly used and loved in Blàs. However, tales, fairies, curses and other worldly things were ingrained in the highlander's psyche. It didn't take much to revert back to long-ago beliefs. Second sight was commonly referred to, and Coinneach Odhar, the Brahan Seer, was often quoted as the gospel-truth. Ancient beliefs had never truly left the area.

"Ach, next you will be telling us it was guarded by the fairies you are always on about," scoffed Sandy.

"Wull, since ye mention it. Eh happen to ken that, wull, ye all ken that broonies or *gruagach* wer wull kent tae be foound aroond here."

"Aye, well that is true. Our Jean, bless her sweet soul, swore we had a *gruagach* in our home. She would leave out a bowl of cream every night for it, aye she did that," said Sandy, looking thoughtful.

The men around the bar were all nodding now in agreement. I knew, even if I could get up and intervene, no one would be prepared to listen to me. Old Tam had them just where he wanted them.

"You were right enough, you know, Tam. Once our Jean died, I forgot to leave out that bowl of cream. And it never forgave me that *gruagach*, you know. Never came back, never mind how much I left out. My house was never as tidy. Always stuff lying about, and dishes – you know they were never washed-up and put away. Never had to do anything before Jean died, as that *gruagach* did everything, everything, I tell you." All the men were deep in thought.

"You don't think it was because he never lifted a hand to help poor Jean, ever," Iona whispered in my ear.

"Well, I happen to know that Mary started to feed an old stray cat every night, once Jean died," I informed Iona. "But I don't think that lot are about to believe me if I say Jean was feeding an old stray, and by the way, Sandy, you are renowned for being a lazy old bugger. Oh, and by the way, it wasn't some house fairy that had a love of milk that cleaned your house but your hard-working wife."

"Aye, we may be better keeping quiet," Iona said.

"I'll still have to let Mary know. If Old Tam is stirring things up with tales of *gruagach* and disgruntled fairies, goodness knows where it will all end up. We need to get this stopped before it starts to impact on our beach project."

A few days later, I wished I had taken action sooner. Old Tam had once more been whispering into the ears of the twins. They had been telling the bairns in the playground of the strange *gruagach* that could be found on the beach where you least expected it. Unfortunately, his tales dovetailed nicely with a new TV series based on the book, *Five Children and It* by E. Nesbit where a sand fairy grants five children wishes.

"The bairns are full of it at the moment," Karen informed me. "Most of the younger ones are watching the series on TV. And with Old Tam filling their imaginations with even more stories, we are finding that many of the bairns are heading off down the beach on their way home. It's only a matter of time before the parents start complaining that their children are always covered in sand when they get home. I'm going to have to come up with a way of taking the wind out of his sails without the children losing their enthusiasm for our folklore. I'm considering asking Auntie Lottie or Maureen to come along and do a story session around our traditional folk tales, but I don't want to make matters worse."

"I'll have a word with Mary I'm hoping she can have some influence on Old Tam," I said. "We don't want to get into the same situation as we had with the skull."

"Ach, I wouldn't worry too much about that," Karen informed me. "I mean, thankfully, there wasn't anything found in that area, so it's not as bad as that yet. I mean, no bones were inside that hole, as far as I know."

"No, but Old Tam was trying to convince the other old

worthies at the pub the other night that something climbed out of that hole. He kept talking about it being near that ancient Pictish site. So, of course it's connected with an old evil spirit or something. We haven't quite got to the 'something bad is going to happen', but he's working up to it."

"Oh, for goodness sake. Did they learn nothing from before?" Karen asked. "We'll have to get this stopped before my entire class of infants are found unsupervised on the beach or, worse, start ducking school to find this bleeding *gruagach*."

"Oh Karen." I wagged my finger at her and smiled. "Don't tempt the *gruagach* – you never know what will happen."

"Oh ha-ha, drink your tea and tell me your news. You've been very quiet about what it's like to share with Iona again."

We finished our tea and caught up on what was happening in our daily lives. Grace hadn't been able to come along that night as Cavan was running a temperature. Although we had more or less made up, there was still a slight edge to our friendship. She still hadn't completely forgiven me for Jim knowing about her pregnancy. If I was honest with myself, I wasn't comfortable with the thought that she had never intended to ever tell him he was going to be a dad. I understood it was her choice, but I still felt somehow it would have been wrong not to have let him know eventually. That was no longer a consideration however, and things had moved on. It would all settle down in the end. Right now, though, I could enjoy having Karen all to myself without any hurt feelings to tinge the evening.

38

"Did you hear? I expect you didn't. About Old Tam."

I had bumped into Maureen on my way back from the shop. Blether and Malt were ecstatically jumping around each other as though they hadn't been together for months. Maureen must have been waiting to ambush me, I could tell. Her eyes were gleaming, and anticipation was coming off her in waves. The dogs felt it too which was probably why they were so over-excited. I had only been away up north for a couple of days, so it had probably been three days at the most since they were last in each other's company. I had looked for Iona the night before when I returned but there had been no sign of her. I assumed she was with Mateo.

"I've not seen anyone for a few days, Maureen, so no, I haven't heard anything. What's Old Tam up to then?" I wasn't feeling full of patience. I had a report to do and lots of other loose ends to tidy up after my trip to Caithness.

"Well, you will never guess what happened—" Maureen's delivery was interrupted by the sight of Malt tugging at the huge blue bow around poor Blether's neck. "Malt, you stop that right now, you jealous wee thing. If you want a bow for yourself, I can give Stroma one for you. Blether, come here, precious. That's right, come to Mummy." Maureen helped the little dog as it jumped up onto her knees.

"Sorry, Maureen, but I've got work to do, so unless this is really important, I have to go and start my report right now."

"Well, if ending up in hospital as a result of the work being done isn't important, I don't know what is."

That stopped me heading home. I turned back to her to find Old Tam hobbling towards us, Dìleas at his side. I inwardly groaned. But at least I could see Old Tam appeared fine.

"Eh telt ye, Eh did. Ye heird meh at the pub. Eh telt ye someit bad waz goin tae happen." Old Tam shook his head and stroked Dìleas. I did a double-take as Dìleas looked up at him and appeared to move his own head slowly back and forth. I rubbed my eyes. That late drive home last night had obviously affected my vision.

"That *gruagach* fae Sandy and Jean's hoose, it wasnae ane, after awh. It was an *ùraisg*. Can be quite a handfoo an *ùraisg*, ye ken, if thay are in the mood fer it, aye, quite a handfoo."

Despite my better judgement, I asked, "What are you talking about, Tam? An *ùraisg*?" Even as the words left my mouth, I felt something tickling my brain, a distant memory of a tale told about them. Probably courtesy of Angus or Mary. In fact, I had been hearing that word a lot lately.

"Ah wull," he continued, shaking his head. And there it was again – Dìleas was watching and slowly copying him. "Ye young anes. Ye didnae believe meh. Juist look at meh. Limpin Eh am noo, limpin. Hurt meh ankle, ye ken. Eh should oh listened tae mehsel, so Eh should hiv."

"What happened, Tam? I can see you are hirpling."

"Eh've nae time right noo, lass. Eh've got tae git hame. This ane needs ees dinner, so ee does. Eh'm off tae Mary's th night, so Eh'll tell ye awh aboot it then. Awh Eh'm saying noo, is that it twaz awh that Parnell an Spuit, that *ùraisg*'s fault, so it waz."

I watched Old Tam hobble his way past, Dìleas matching his slow progress home. What had happened to him and who on earth was Parnell an Spuit or the *ùraisg*? Then I remembered – hadn't Mary mentioned something before about Angus talking to someone called Parnell an Spuit?

Maureen broke into my thoughts. "Looks like I'll be seeing you later at Mary's then. About 7.30? I'll get her to pop the kettle on." And with that she was off up the road, catching up with Old Tam and Dìleas, no doubt talking over the events that had led to Old Tam's injury.

❧

As I was walking towards Mary's croft, little pieces of information about the *ùraisg* kept coming to mind. Until all this talk about them recently, I had forgotten the old tales Angus had told us about them. They were around long before we had heard of the word Bigfoot. Angus had told us all about our own version of these beings. They were reputed to live near water. Apparently, they could be shy and kept to themselves. I smiled as I recalled how Angus had described them.

"Not unlike our very own Tam, in that they are melancholy in nature. They can make you feel a bit sad, even just being in your own company. Big though they are, they can sit for hours on a rock or mountain without moving."

As I reached Mary's, the rest of the story became lost in my memory, but I knew Mary would not disappoint me. Surprisingly, Karen, Old Tam, Maureen, Ralph and Auntie Lottie were already there, drinking tea and eating cake.

If Old Tam had been spreading his thoughts about the *ùraisg*, then Ralph would be anxious that his twins didn't become embroiled in yet another legend thrown up from our rich past. Honestly, sometimes I despaired of the old tales that many still believed in.

"Take a seat, Stroma. I'm hearing you want to know about our local *ùraisg*." Mary smiled.

"Yes, but really, I would like to know what happened to Old

Tam here. I can see he's been hurt. Maureen left me with the impression that something awful had happened."

All eyes swivelled to Maureen who merely shrugged and continued to feed Blether cake.

"Tsk," Mary started. "As you can see, he's fine."

I fidgeted. This didn't tell or reassure me very much. If something had happened at the site on the beach, all works could stop, and that would lead to a delay in the beach wheelchair project.

I knew we already had a few bookings from the old folks' home and even some from holidaymakers who were coming to Blàs later in the summer. These tourists had opted for Blàs because they knew they could get access to the beach for their disabled child. We couldn't afford any hold-ups in the scheme.

"Anyway, it is all mixed up together in a way. Tam, here, thought he saw an *ùraisg* on that big rock beside the access path. Silly old fool got such a fright when it moved that he fell over and twisted his ankle."

"Juist wha are ye cawin an auld fool, Maureen? Ye are ane tae speak. Eh'm nae that auld," Old Tam said. "An Eh ken whit Eh saw wi' meh ane eyes. Eh saw em, Eh did, Eh seen that *ùraisg*."

"That's as may be, Tam, but what he's not telling you, Stroma, is that he had to phone Paul of the Sheds for help. He picked him up and took him to the doctors. Ended up in Inverness as he needed an X-ray. He was lucky."

"An jusit hoo waz Eh lucky, Maureen? Eh hurt meh ankle."

"Ach well, Tam," Maureen continued, "it's not every day you see our own Bigfoot as they would call them in America. Not everyone gets to see an *ùraisg*. Is that not right, Mary?"

"Should I be warning the parents about this?" Karen asked.

"Ach away and don't be daft," Mary said "I've invited you here, Karen, as I thought you could maybe do a lesson on it, seeing as the younger generations don't seem to know much about them. Really, my Angus should have done a better job on this and told more stories about them instead of his own exploits."

Mary chuckled, knowing full well what her husband had got up to. "I can tell you what I know, but it is up to you all to spread the word so no one has the fright that Tam here got, if they come across it again. Or if it comes to that, they don't chase the poor thing away. It has been here a long time, and I don't want it having to move away because of a few silly folk."

39

Mary began. "Our *ùraisg,* are a mythological folk, equivalent to Bigfoot, as Maureen said. They bide in and around lonely and remote places. Like here in Blàs, some would say. According to our folklore they were often seen up in the mountainous areas during the summer months, eager to stay away from any summer visitors. They would come down in the worst of winters where it was said they would huddle next to the campfires of the farmers and drovers. There were others of their ilk that lived permanently beside water and rivers."

Mary went on to claim that our local *ùraisg,* Parnell an Spuit, had lived in this area for centuries. He was shy and a kind soul at heart, helping many out when they were in trouble. According to her, he would sit for hours on end in full sight but unseen, often mistaken for an outcrop of rock. If she was to be believed, he frequented the area where the burn met the sea. Very close to where the storm damage had occurred.

"Thon big rock that was dislodged and caused that hole during the storm – mind, it was never found. Well, that's because that boulder was him, I believe. Everyone took that boulder for just being that, a big rock. You wouldn't have known it was him. He sat so quiet and still. Unless you were fortunate to see him move, you wouldn't have known he was there.

"There's not that many of the *ùraisg* left. There used to be a few around. He'd tell my Angus where his other kin were and talked about the places they could be found. My Angus would come back home and check out the old maps. You can see the old Gaelic names where they could be found, right enough – my Angus showed them to me. One on Skye and others spread around the Highlands and down in Perthshire too. You can see where they lived even today by the place names. You will have heard of some of them yourselves such as Allt Corrie na h-Ùruisg and Clach na h-Ùruisg; there were others as well. Parnell an Spuit even told us there used to be a meeting place where they would all gather occasionally. Lottie here can tell you there is one near Bealach nam Bò where she spent many a summer – Coire na Ùruisgean, they call it.

"Parnell an Spuit was quite a lonely soul. I think it had been a while since he had met any of his kind. We haven't seen him around for years so thought he had gone off to their gathering place. I hoped perhaps he had met a nice female, you know, and maybe gone with her. But it would seem not, if what Tam says is true. As back he has come." Mary paused into the silence that filled the room. We sat mesmerised in her telling of Parnell an Spuit, the *ùraisg*.

We had heard of these creatures as we grew up, but as people often do, we had dismissed the likelihood of their existence. No one had seen or talked about them for so long that, like many an old tale, they had fallen out of fashion. No photographs had ever been taken of an *ùraisg*, and apart from Angus, I couldn't remember anyone who actually admitted to seeing one. That was until now. Suddenly, it seemed I knew at least two. Old Tam from a few nights ago, and Mary who had apparently known this Parnell an Spuit for years.

"Eh wanted tae see hoo Digger Dodds hid gotten on. Came fae th other side as Eh hid been walking Dìleas eftir th pub, ye ken. Juist takin a quiet wee while, lookin at the sea an hivin a wee rest against th boulder. And then it slowly dawned on meh – th boulder hid gone in thon storm. And then ee moved – th boulder moved. Eh thought it waz topplin or'er but ee stood up. Eh'm tellin ye, Eh got such a fleg. Eh fell backwards an bumped meh heid. Eh wasnae sure what happened next but Eh foound mehsel on th road. Thon Parnell an Spuit, ee must hiv picked meh up an carried me or'er. Eh should o thought it cauld o been an *ùraisg* when ee stood up, but it's been sae lang since we hid ane here, Eh didnae think o it. Eh tried tae walk but meh ankle was tae sair. So Eh hid to caw Paul. Eh cauldnae caw Morag she wauld hiv telt meh off fur walkin there eftir th pub."

"That's my Paul, always ready to help. I followed him out, you know. But we didn't see any sign of anyone around, no footprints, no boulder, nothing. I thought it was just the bang on the head that was causing Tam to say what he did. But Paul seemed to believe him. He said there was lots of things that couldn't be explained, and I should keep an open mind."

We talked some more in hushed voices about Parnell an Spuit and others of his kind. It never ceased to surprise me how much folklore we had in these parts.

Karen was more concerned that we were losing these old stories that told of the beings that once frequented the area. Whether these beings actually existed would be a debate that would continue. However, it couldn't be argued that enough folk had believed in them. Ancient places names bore witness that our forbearers had believed in their existence too.

Malt and I left the meeting, leaving Maureen and Auntie Lottie arranging to meet up in the hall to talk to some of our elders about the old stories and, in particular, any about Parnell an Spuit, no doubt over a few cakes and cups of tea. Myself, I kept a close eye on the shadows and boulders I passed on my way home.

❧

The following day, after meeting up with the pensioners at the hall, Auntie Lottie and I got together to discuss our event for the opening of the beach wheelchairs. It had been agreed that, if possible, all six chairs would be rented out for the day. Snacks would be provided in a tent up on the now widened parking area, and once more, Heritage Rangers would be engaged to take groups of people around the beach and explain about some of the wildlife.

One ranger would be assigned exclusively for the wheelchair users and their families or carers. As the light drew down, a huge bonfire would be lit, and Maureen (using one of the chairs) and Auntie Lottie would perform a storytelling session. It was looking like the *ùraisg* would be the main character in the tale.

It was a great idea, given we had a way of linking it into our theme. Hopefully, it would also counteract any rumours of gloom and doom that Old Tam was spreading about. Mary had been very stern with Old Tam the night before.

"*Ùraisg* do not bring bad luck or anything else anyone should be worried about. I'll not have you miscalling them or causing them trouble, Tam. If you start your nonsense and the *ùraisg* gets caught up in it, I'll never forgive you. You keep your thinking to yourself."

Rather than displease Mary, and to everyone's surprise, Old Tam agreed. "Eh'll noo be causin ony trouble. Thon Parnell an Spuit did meh a good turn, helpin meh back tae th road. Ye'll noo find meh cabin eem bad."

We all knew that wouldn't stop Old Tam and his doom-and-gloom stories, but at least he wouldn't be pointing the finger at the *ùrsaig*, not if it meant he would have to face Mary's wrath. She was a woman who was slow to rile, but once her temper was up, everyone ran for cover. I suspected even the *ùraisg* would take to its heels.

Auntie Lottie brought me back to the present. "Well, what do you think, Stroma? I had forgotten all about the *ùraisg* before Tam had his wee accident. All that information Mary gave us has helped me build a good picture of the *ùraisg*. I'm sure I can unearth and develop a story around Parnell an Spuit. I have to say, though, I am a wee bit upset that I have never laid eyes on one myself. Paul, bless him, swears he has seen him. Up in the mountains during the summer, he says. Far away from any path folks would take and—"

"Right, Auntie Lottie, that's enough. I can see you're getting into story mode but we have work still to do here. If you are determined to do a story on Parnell an Spuit, then I suggest you go and find Maureen and get your story sorted out together."

"Well, seeing as you are too busy to listen, I'll do just that. And don't tell me you don't believe in some of our stories, Stroma – we all know you do." And off huffed Auntie Lottie.

I did feel a bit bad, but really? A Scottish Bigfoot, whose existence was even older than any other Bigfoot in the world. And not just one, but a whole tribe of them. But then again, if you looked at all those old Gaelic names, there could well be some truth in their existence. Our ancestors obviously believed in them, and who was I to argue with our folklore.

40

We were refurbishing the shed for the beach wheelchairs. Things had moved on at such a pace that we couldn't wait any longer. The wheelchairs were already ordered so we needed to get on with the shed that would house them. Shed seemed such a small word for what was a substantial building. Paul of the Sheds had long since moved his many bits and pieces of machinery out.

"You've helped me clean out a lot of things that haven't been used for years," he told us. "I always thought I would clear up some of this stuff and reuse it but even I can't use it all."

"He never throws anything out," said Auntie Lottie, smiling, "unlike myself now. I don't like to horde stuff, as you well know."

I looked at her in disbelief. Had she forgotten the amount of stuff she had acquired over the years. It had almost broken me when I went down to help her move back up to Blàs. What had been a simple two-bedroom house had exploded out into a garage, garden shed, conservatory and floored attic. Three times we had to go down with a so-called removal van, man and his shadow before we had fully emptied her house. Scott had even been roped in to help to finally finish the move.

Auntie Lottie chose to ignore my indignant look and carried on. "Paul, bless him, thinks he can fix everything. On saying that, he normally does – so good with his hands."

"Ach, Lottie, is that you boasting about your love life again," chuckled Maureen.

Auntie Lottie smoothed her hair. "I wouldn't stoop so low, but since you're asking—"

"No, she wasn't," I broke in, before the conversation deteriorated any further. "What time did we ask people to come again?"

A call to arms had gone out in the village and surrounding area. We needed this last push so we could meet our deadline. There was little point, we felt, in missing out on the summer months when people could get access to the beach if we had everything ready. The shed had been overlooked as we had known it was there. Paul informed us that the electrics was still in fairly good order.

Dan Coplan, true to his word, had covered the cost of insulating the shed and fixing up some cupboards. A grant had bought a hoist which was now attached to the outside of the building to allow people to go straight from a car into a chair. All joinery and fixing works had been finished. Now the whole thing needed painted, cleaned down and sorted out.

Ellen and Giulietta had agreed to supply some soup and snacks to everyone who volunteered to help. People had been asked to come with a paint brush and be prepared to help in any way they could. As was usual in these circumstances, some musicians had turned up to help move things along. Maureen and Auntie Lottie were attending, so we could expect that a poem of some sort would also be one of the end products.

Our elderly shuffled down to see how we were getting on and sat around on convenient big rocks and portable seats, others sat in cars parked around the area. Children ran in and out the dunes and across the machair, running down to the beach with dogs chasing after them and their families. Malt and Whisky had joined Stag and Fawn as they raced around diving between working adults and spectators. Old Tam was talking with Ben the Stump.

"Eh'd be careful if Eh wer ye," Old Tam warned his friend "Fur awh ye ken, thon rock thar cauld be Parnell an Spuit eezsel, ye ken."

"Ach, don't be so daft, Tam. I think I would know if this was an *ùraisg*." Ben the Stump moved slightly shifting his weight away from the rock. When he thought no one was looking he gave it a shove. A small stone fell off the top and he stumbled back.

"Eh telt ye tae be careful," Old Tam said and shook his head. I watched to see if Dìleas copied him, but he was too interested in all the running and excitement coming for the bairns and dogs all around.

"Okay *a bhalach,* af ye gan if ye want tae join in." Dìleas lowered his head and looked up at Old Tam."Af ye gan noo, awa wi' ye." His dog took one more look then rushed off to join in the fun.

As the afternoon wore on, we began to see all the work and tidying up gradually making a difference to the shed. The second coat of paint was on and the whole area was looking clean and sparkling.

Inside, the changing table was ready and the kettle in place. All that was now needed was the arrival of the wheelchairs themselves. The sun, which had shone all day, was losing some of its warmth as was normal this early in May. Children returned to their parents looking tired but with a healthy glow to their cheeks.

Iona and Mateo arrived with some of our beers for the adults. The musicians, spotting them, drew their session to a close and took a well-earned rest.

We sat and listened to the waves hit the beach and the *bi glic, bi glic* (be wise, be wise) call of the oystercatchers on the shore.

"Ah the *gille-Brìde,*" Maureen said, watching the black-and-white bird flying low. "Such an important place that wader has in our folklore."

Auntie Lottie took up the tale. Many of us had heard this story before, but its importance never diminished in its telling.

"Back in Celtic times, before even Christianity, although there are some who would argue that point, lived a young woman named Brìde. If she were alive today, we would recognise her as an eco-warrior. She was brave, strong and kind-hearted, at least to animals and beast of all kinds. She worshipped the many spirits of the forests and the Earth mother. Not all agreed with her. Eventually, this led her into mortal danger.

"After escaping numerous attempts on her life, the tales of which I leave to another time, she eventually found herself on a beach with nowhere to hide. Her end was coming; she felt it in the call of the wind and the taste of the salt on her lips. Exhausted, she fell to the ground and prayed to the spirits of the Earth to take her soul and join it with Mother Earth. The spirits, loath to lose this warrior woman, sent her the oystercatcher. As Brìde lay awaiting her death, the oystercatcher returned again and again, covering her in seaweed. Those who looked to kill her moved on, unaware that, under the sea's harvest, lay Brìde.

"Realising the oystercatcher had saved her life, Brìde placed a blessing on the birds. As she graced the bird, its plumage changed to black upon its back and white across its breast."

As if in acknowledgement to this tale, we heard again the oystercatcher, or *gille-Brìde*, call as it flew past.

Maureen finished the tale. "Brìde was such a strong figure in our Celtic past that the Christian Church rewrote much of her story and then named her a saint to quell any mutterings." Silence descended, even the waves seemed to hush before the gentle voice of Mary took up the notes of a Gaelic song.

One by one, people joined in, and the melody ebbed and flowed with the waves of the sea. Children cuddled closer to their parents, and tired dogs settled at the feet of their loved ones. We listened again to the *gille-Brìde* as its call ended our song. Slowly, families rose and headed for their homes, tired and satisfied.

Our shed was complete. Now we only awaited the chairs themselves to complete the interior. This may have been the shortest project we had worked on from conception to finish, but it was one that would bring a lasting benefit for all the community.

Finally, hopefully, all our inhabitants would be able to access one of our best assets – our wide and spectacular seashore.

41

Our *'Fàilte,* Beach Wheelchair' event dawned bright and fair. Bubbling white foam crested the waves as sea-birds swooped in the sky above. Laughter floated across from the group beside the rock pool. Auntie Lottie, true to her word, had developed a session focusing on Gaelic phrases that could be used on the seashore. Buckets and spades were held tightly by children as the group peered into the pools. I had no doubt crabs, shells and other creatures would find their way briefly into their containers. Wellies were the common footwear, but I knew as the heat of day increased these would be tossed aside. Then bare feet would take over as the bairns raced along the sand.

I wandered along to our beach wheelchair shed, soon to be given its official new title, the Wheelchair Bothy. People were still arriving. Karen was organising the schoolchildren into two groups. Fiddles, a bodhrán and accordions were being readied by some of the children. The others stood waiting to sing a variety of songs.

Peter the Pipes along with three of his pupils were positioned at the start of the new access road. I felt my stress levels ebbing away – Peter the Pipes and his rather fluid timekeeping was the most difficult element to plan into any event. Like many musicians, his impeccable timekeeping when playing music was not matched by his timekeeping regarding his presence.

"I was just apologising to Peter the Pipes before you arrived, Stroma." Mary smiled as her eyes twinkled "Apparently, I got the time wrong when I asked him to come along."

I returned her grin. "Oh really, Mary, that isn't like you at all. So, what time did you tell him he was needed then?"

"Ach, about an hour ago, I think. It is my mind, you know – at my age, I can often get the hours mixed up." Her smile broadened. "Still, just as well really, as he only arrived twenty minutes ago."

I burst out laughing. There was nothing wrong with Mary's mind. She was sharper than most of us. No one else would have managed to get away with such a blatant lie to Peter the Pipes. He would never question Mary. If anyone else had made that 'mistake', they would have been left in no doubt about how annoyed he was. The truth of it was Peter the Pipes was such an amazing piper and so generous when asked to play for community events that we were all prepared to put up with his flexible understanding of timekeeping.

Dan Coplan was going to officially open the Wheelchair Bothy. Jill had decorated some old rope recovered from our beach clean. Along its length were cut-outs of tiny, shiny fish made from old tin cans – reused from their 'scarecrow mermaid' entry in the village competition earlier in the year. Shells and other flotsam were woven into the rope's length. She had thinned out a piece so Dan could break the 'chain' and open the Bothy.

It was all thanks to his generosity that we were able to offer this facility so soon. Dan and his PA, Darren, would be paraded down our new access road. After a short welcome speech, I hoped he would be afforded the privacy to enjoy the rest of the day like everyone else.

❧

The day had gone better than we had hoped. All the wheelchairs had been rented out. Inbhirasgaidh Old Folks Home had used three of the chairs for two different sets of their residents. The look on the faces of their elderly clients as they enjoyed being on the beach once more filled the soul. An additional needs child had spent the day laughing and enjoying the seashore along with the rest of her siblings and family. Locals had also booked out chairs. Catherine Cailleach and Old Betty had spent a happy few hours talking and joining in the fun on the sand. They had arrived back at the Wheelchair Bothy with pink cheeks and sparkling eyes. Their next visit was already booked.

A mutual feeling of wellbeing and high spirits engulfed the community. It even appeared to have infected Grace, who finally seemed to be making an effort with Jim. I'd heard Cavan's laughter throughout the afternoon as Jim and Grace searched the rock pools with him. As the day drew to a close, Grace appeared relaxed as she strolled alongside them, sandals in one hand, her other in Jim's grasp.

To my delight, Dan and Darren had been allowed to enjoy relative privacy. They had tried the varieties of seafood on offer and spent time with Auntie Lottie and Mary in the tea tent. Now, with many others, they sat around relaxing beside a large fire, awaiting the storytelling event.

Sparks and bright orange flames leapt skywards, keeping the slight chill in the air at bay. Lit braziers flanked either side of the storytelling tent casting shadows on the sand.

Maureen was in the circle of people that surrounded the fire. It was she who had pulled my heartstrings the most. After an afternoon parading along the water's edge, she had made her own way to the gathering in one of our beach wheelchairs. Finally, she could enjoy the freedom of our beach as much as the rest of us.

A mellow feeling descended with the darkness as people slowly made their way off the beach. The storytelling finished. Maureen, flanked by Auntie Lottie and Paul, was making her way back to the Wheelchair Bothy to return her chair. On event nights like these, it had been decided that users of the wheelchairs could book out the chairs to attend our gatherings. It meant a late finish for our volunteers, but it was deemed worth it for such occasions.

I watched as families carried half-asleep children back to waiting cars and homes. Grace and Jim walked past, a sleeping Cavan resting on Jim's shoulder. They appeared to have resolved their differences, at least for now.

Other couples strolled off into the gloom, hand in hand, no doubt seeking some private moments on the shore. I felt a moment of wistfulness and contemplated the heavens above. I had no desire to watch as others enjoyed a romantic walk along the beach together.

I sighed. No amount of wishful thinking would change the situation between myself and Scott. I just had to be patient. But I was finding that harder to do. I felt a paw on my shin – Malt no doubt sensing my mood change.

We turned for home, reminding myself that the event had been a success, and our benefactor appeared to have enjoyed his day as much as the community had. I had my dog at my side and a hot chocolate beckoned at home. Life was not bad, not bad at all.

42

Gillie Dubh thumped into my legs. The screeching of the seagulls overhead couldn't hide the excited voices of the twins as they raced across the sand to retrieve their dog.

"We're going treasure-hunting," Stag bellowed over before he had reached me.

"On the beach. We are looking for pirate treasure," Fawn added.

"Yes, and when we find some, we're going to let everyone know we are the greatest treasure-finders ever, in the whole wide world." Stag threw his arms wide and birled round and round in sheer exuberance.

"With all these treasures you two keep finding, we are going to need a bigger museum." I smiled.

Stag stopped twirling, shook his head to clear his dizziness and leant into his sister for support.

"Do you really fink so?" he asked. "Maybe we can find another skull, Fawn, or that *ùraisg* rock giant, person, fairy fing, fing, Old Tam is always taking about." He turned to his sister full of hope. "Come on. Fawn, let's go and hunt."

"Can we take Malt with us?" Fawn asked. Never mind how

much she loved her own dog, Fawn was always looking out for taking on another one.

"I don't think so, Fawn. Malt is looking forward to meeting up with Blether and Whisky later. If you find any more treasures, let me know. You two be careful now and don't let Gillie Dubh lead you astray."

I smiled and watched the bairns heading off to seek their fortune. I was to remember my warning to them much later.

❧

"So, that is it then. We need to really dig in and get this museum up and running. Any last-minute thoughts?" Ellen was just winding up our meeting when Auntie Lottie's phone went off.

"Ach, I'd better answer it. Sorry, it's just Paul, no doubt he will be wanting me to take him a few bits of cake."

Auntie Lottie left the room, just as a text message arrived on my own phone. I heard other phones going off as well. Mary's and my eyes met. We could sense something was up. As if in answer to our unspoken question, Auntie Lottie burst back into the room.

"It's the twins. They haven't arrived home. That's why Ralph didn't appear tonight; he's been waiting for them to show up. He's already been out looking for them. Paul wants us to start a search party. If there is no sign of them soon, we will have to call out the police."

"Agin," said Old Tam. "Wull, Eh hope they arnae on ane o their adventures." However, he was up and on his way out the door, anxious to be of some help.

Ellen was already organising a team to help with hot drinks and snacks, should they be needed. I ran home to grab my head torch and more suitable shoes. Thankfully, May evenings are long and bright, so hopefully, I wouldn't need my torch unless we were going to be out into the early hours.

I dropped a voicemail to Iona in the hope she could help.

By the time I arrived at the meeting place, Paul of the Sheds and many members of the community were already there.

It appeared I had been one of the last people to see the twins. They were now about two hours later than expected. Ralph who had been through this before was no less stressed for that.

"The bairns are a lot more sensible and savvy about the place now, Ralph. I'm sure they will be okay."

Auntie Lottie was right in one respect. They had been running free about the area for a long time now and knew a lot more about the hidden dangers than when they had first arrived. There had been no more eco-warrior campaigns that required them to disappear overnight. But like most children, adventures of one kind or another were never very far away.

Swallow and Lark, their elder brother and sister, had grown to understand the many dangers that could lurk in such bonnie surroundings if you weren't careful. They had managed so far to keep their younger siblings out of any more trouble.

We were split up into two large groups. One heading along the beach in the direction I had seen them going. The other group, including myself, starting along the rough grass towards the moor.

"With the new baby, we've been letting the twins out a lot more. They've been so good. I thought I could trust them. Jill is beside herself and feeling so guilty she can't join in," Ralph said.

"Now, of course the bairns have been out more with the weather and the lighter nights, it's only natural. Neither of you have any reason to be feeling guilty," I heard Auntie Lottie say, trying to calm Ralph down as we set off.

There was no way either Swallow or Lark was going to wait behind. I had offered to take them with me.

"Why hasn't Gillie Dubh come back for his tea? He normally takes off home and they follow," Swallow informed me.

I relayed this to Paul of the Sheds. If Gillie Dubh's tummy wasn't bringing him back, maybe he couldn't or wouldn't leave the bairns because something was wrong. He was only a young dog, but he loved his family. I couldn't decide if the thought was making me feel worse or better.

Twenty minutes into the search, and the midges and heat were awful. I knew we only had a few minutes left before we would have to call in more official help. Shouting out front dulled the sound of my phone ringing. It was Iona. I signalled the children to stop.

"We've got them. Up on the moor. That crazy puppy of theirs has got itself stuck down a hole. Oh, I can see some of you now. Are you with the ones on the moor?"

"Iona, thank goodness. Yes, it's us, we're just coming." I hung up. "Look there, Swallow, Lark, in front. Your brother and sister are there beside Iona. Look you—" Before I could say anything else, the pair of them ran off in front towards their siblings. I phoned the other search party to let them know we had found the twins.

It was a sorry sight I was met with. Fawn was inconsolable, and as usual, Stag was covered in dirt.

"He's stuck, he's stuck, my puppy, he's stuck." Fawn sobbed into Iona. Iona looked at me helplessly, tears in her eyes.

"I don't know what to do," she mouthed at me, hugging and patting Fawn on the back.

"You're doing fine," I said. "Just reassure her."

The other part of the search party arrived quickly afterwards.

Stag barely noticed any of us as he continued clawing away the earth which Mateo, who lay flat on his front, kept pushing back.

"Have you got any meat anyone?" Paul of the Sheds asked, after he had assessed the situation and spoken with Ralph on the phone.

"We do," said Iona. "In the car, some nice beef." And off she ran at speed towards her car.

I wiped Fawn's tears. "Can you tell me what happened, Fawn?"

"We was searching for treasure. Stag fought we should try the moor."

"If I was a highwayman, I would bury my treasure in the moor," added Stag, without stopping his earth removal.

Fawn ran her arm across her nose and sniffed. "It were all your fault, Stag. If we hadn't been playing highway-robbers and stayed being pirates, Gillie-Gillie Dubh wouldn't have gone down that hole."

"It was not. You was playing too."

"Twas, twas your fault. I wanted to stay and play pirates on the beach, looking for treasure. It… is… your… fault," she yelled at her brother.

Is this the same wee girl who refused to speak last year? I wondered. Back then, we would have welcomed any sort of sound she would have made.

"I don't think you can blame yourselves. Gillie Dubh comes from a line of hunters. He probably followed a smell right down into that hole. Hopefully, that piece of meat that Iona is putting there will bring him out when he gets hungry," Paul of the Sheds explained.

People started to drift off back home when they realised the bairns were okay. Paul of the Sheds assured them, if we needed help to dig the dog out, we would get back in touch. Ralph arrived and hugged his sorrowful offspring.

"We couldn't leave, Daddy; Gillie Dubh is stuck. We couldn't leave him." Fawn threw her arms around her dad. "You said we have to stay together if anything happened. You said you'd find us, and you did, you did, Daddy – you found us."

"Hush now, Fawn, we need to keep quiet and see if your dog comes out. Be still now."

Silence descended mixed with the smell of newly dug earth. A lone lapwing called overhead. The twins stood huddled together; Mateo's arm was slung around Iona. All attention was fixed on the dark hole. Midges continued to feast on our skin while we waited and prayed to any who could hear that the bairn's wee dog would somehow be able to get itself free.

As hope appeared to be fading, we glimpsed a sprinkle of earth exiting the hole just as the entrance began to collapse. Paul of the Sheds and Mateo quickly sprang forward and pulled clumps of fallen turf out of the way. After an age, we spotted small, dirt-covered hindquarters slowly reversing their way out of the hole.

Gillie Dubh's long back shuddered and half jumped its way slowly out of the ground. Eventually his long body was free, his head emerging covered in earth. A rain of peaty earth flew in all directions as he shook himself clean. He sneezed twice and shook his head again. Before we could stop him, he dropped down, leaned one side of his body on the ground, then propelled himself with his back legs along the heather, head and ears scraping the vegetation before repeating the process on his other side. One shake later, and he was staring at us all, tail wagging in glee.

Fawn wrapped herself around her dog. "You came back, you came back. I love you, Gillie Dubh. You came back."

Stag picked up the piece of meat and fed it to the Dandie.

"Will you look at all that muck trapped inside his collar?" Auntie Lottie bent down and started to remove bits of moss, debris and lumps of mud that had got tangled between Gillie Dubh's collar and his neck.

"Oh, what have we here?" she asked as she began pulling what appeared to be a piece of dirty string away from a clump of mud she had just removed.

Gillie Dubh, happy to no longer be the focus of Auntie Lottie's attention, immediately went for a long drink of water that Paul of the Sheds had supplied.

Auntie Lottie was still busy scrubbing and rubbing at the object she had removed from the mud. What had appeared to be a small clump of mud had something hidden inside. Auntie Lottie turned it over again and again, before exclaiming, "Well, would you look at that. It's my old St Christopher necklace. Look, you can see my name engraved on the back: Lottie. I lost this years ago when I was walking on the moor. What a clever puppy you are." Auntie Lottie bent down and rubbed Gillie Dubh's grubby head.

"Well, it seems the bairns aren't the only ones capable of finding treasure then," Paul of the Sheds said. "Perhaps the twins' talent for finding treasure has affected their dog."

"I can tell you something else that will connect them tonight," Ralph said, as he ruffled his son's grubby hair, "and that's a bath."

"Ah, Dad," the twins groaned together. But there were huge smiles on their faces as Stag said, "Gillie Dubh, you get to come in the bath with us."

"I don't think that's what their dad had in mind." Auntie Lottie laughed at Ralph's discomfort as we all headed happily for home.

We all chuckled as much in relief as anything else.

43

Blàs was awash with gossip, which in itself wasn't unusual. Only this time, it did not concern our native population; this time it was about our new 'locals'. The news however was not allowed to travel outwith the village. An unspoken agreement had been reached in the community. People could discuss it as much as they wanted but only with inhabitants of the village.

Silence or a quick change of subject resulted if visitors or strangers got within hearing range. Our tourists must have thought we were either the most unfriendly folk they had encountered or the maddest. Not everyone was as quick at following an abrupt change in conversation though, which led to half-finished exchanges and some confusion among the slower on the uptake in the area. Others were going about talking in hushed tones as if listening devices had been placed all around. The exception to this, of course, was the village hall where coffee steamed as hot as the gossip.

"Well, I never saw that coming," Crabbit O'Neil said.

"What? What is coming?" Old Betty asked.

"Did you say someone was coming?" Catherine Cailleach ventured.

"Oh, visitors – I like that. Who is it?" Ben the Stumped enquired

"I never knew we had visitors coming. Nobody told me," Crabbit O'Neil, added unaware that it was his opening conversation that had gone slightly awry.

"Told you what?" Catherine Cailleach asked.

"That we had visitors coming. Keep up, you old fool." Crabbit was living up to his name.

"Visitors. Are you sure? I never knew," Catherine Cailleach said. "And anyway, who are you calling old?"

It often puzzled me how our old folk, who were so hard of hearing, could somehow always hear an insult, never mind how softly said.

Old Tam shook his head and wandered up to our table, Dìleas hugging his side. "Aye wull, juist shoot meh wen Eh git tae that age, wull ye. Honestly, ye cannae hiv a decent blether wi' eem; they end up talkin nonsense."

"I heard that, Tam. We know fine what we are talking about, don't we, Betty?" Ben the Stump shouted over.

"Well, mostly, aye, I suppose so." Old Betty sounded a bit dubious. She could be heard quietly asking, "Who exactly are these new visitors that are coming?"

"I hope you are not proposing to shoot me, Tam?" Mary said in an over sweet voice.

"Ach noo, Mary. We awh ken yer nae ane of thon auld folk. Ye are juist, wull"—Old Tam scratched his head—"wull, ye."

Mary smiled and took a sip from her cup as Auntie Lottie entered the hall. Whisky, unleashed, ran to our table. The slamming of the door froze all conversation. Auntie Lottie stopped for a second, patted her hair and sashayed her way towards us, the clicking of her heels echoing around the hall.

"If only I was a couple of years younger," Alex Nail said.

"A couple of decades, more like," Catherine Cailleach said as the rest of the elderly women joined in with her cackling.

Auntie Lottie reached us, a slice of cake in one hand and her tea in the other. She placed them on the table and slowly sat down. At the last minute, she turned and winked across at the elderly males across the way.

"You are totally incorrigible," Maureen muttered. "You will have their blood pressures going through the roof."

"Ach, away with you, Maureen. It will do them no harm. I've probably made their day." Auntie Lottie smiled at us all. "Now then, I'll expect you have all heard from Maureen here. My boy." She grinned wickedly, obviously enjoy herself immensely. "My son, that is, is getting married."

"Yes, my dear, we heard," Mary said. "Not such a chip off the old block then."

Auntie Lottie scowled. "And just what do you mean by that?"

"Well, my dear, he knew the right person for him straightaway, which is more that can be said for you."

"Well, yes, of course," Auntie Lottie huffed.

"Remind us again, dear – how long did it take before Paul managed to get you down the aisle or, more correctly, down the wooded path?" Mary smiled.

"Well, once we had made up our minds, not that long," Auntie Lottie said with a straight face.

There was a moment of shocked silence before we all burst out laughing.

"Years," shrieked Maureen and dabbed her eyes.

Auntie Lottie tried to regain her dignity as she pushed back a strand of hair. "Well, perhaps it may be that we took a bit longer than the average couple."

"Oh my, Lottie, you were a legend in your lifetime. Even my Meg used to talk about it. Bless her soul," Crabbit O'Neil said.

"Lottie and young Paul, we gave up thinking we would ever dance at your wedding," Old Betty added.

"Aye well, some of us didn't. By the time you got married, it was more like hobbling." Our laughter had infected the elders' table and they carried on as we settled down again.

"Just what did she mean by young Paul?" Auntie Lottie said in high dudgeon. "I'm younger than him, cheek of her."

"Come on, lass, tell us all about your good news. Where exactly is your lad getting married? We know the date and we all know that it has to be kept quiet. Are we all going to their lodge?" Mary asked.

As ever, Auntie Lottie jumped from annoyed to good mood in less time than it took for a butterfly's wing to flap. The table lit up with her smile as she told us of their plans.

"They want as many of the community to come to the service as they can. They truly love it here and want to share their day with us. So yes, you will all be transported up to their lodge. But as for the service itself, they have other ideas. Well, as long as the weather is good, that is."

She had pipped our interest. We had all assumed everything would be held at the lodge where it could be kept private.

"They are hoping to get married where Darren proposed," Auntie Lottie informed us.

We all looked blankly at her, most of us having no idea where Darren had proposed to her son.

"And where exactly did that take place? Is it somewhere exotic? Oh, this is exciting," Maureen said.

"Well, it can be, I suppose, to some," said Auntie Lottie. "It does hold a special place in their hearts of course."

"Oh, fur the love o God," Old Tam said. "Juist tell ous."

"Okay, okay." Auntie Lottie smiled. "Well, boys and girls, get your swimming trunks on, as we are having a beach wedding."

"Oh my goodness," Maureen shrieked. "Where? Where are we going? I wonder where I put my passport?" Then her face fell as she patted her canine companion. "Oh, oh then, perhaps I may not go. What would I do with Blether? I can't just leave her with anyone, you know. She is of a delicate nature. She would pine without me."

Auntie Lottie frowned at her friend, looked at Blether, was about to say something and then thought better of it. She regarded Maureen with a puzzled look on her face before asking, "What do you mean, where are we going? Here, of course. Darren proposed after the opening of the Wheelchair Bothy. Actually, Maureen, it was right after our storytelling event. They went for a nice romantic walk along the sand, and that's when he asked Dan. So, they are holding the wedding on our beach."

"Do we really have to wear swimming stuff then?" Maureen asked rather desolately. Forgetting that just seconds before she had been voicing her concern about leaving her dog behind.

"Of course not," Mary said. "We will all be wearing our very best for such a grand occasion. Lottie, I think that is the most romantic thing I've heard in a long time – our beach as a wedding venue."

"Wull," muttered Old Tam, "Eh juist hope th *ùraisg* doesnae decide tae come along as wull."

44

"Wull, Eh telt ye." Old Tam had resumed his position as harbinger of all woes and bad ailments. "Eh telt ye awh that lookin fur thon *ùraisg* wauld bring naethin but trouble, Eh telt ye, so Eh did."

"Now, Tam, I have warned you about badmouthing the *ùraisg*. I'll not have it, do you hear? It had nothing to do with poor Lottie's accident," Mary said.

"Eh ne'er seid it waz thon *ùraisg* that caused it, noo. Eh ken it wasnae – it waz because we went lookin fur eem. They dinnae like tae be foond, nor looked fur, no they dinnae. Eh ken, Eh've heird the auld tales tae, ye ken, Mary."

We were all back at the hall only a few days later discussing news of a different kind. Auntie Lottie, the mother of one of the grooms, had fallen on the very beach that her son was getting married on. The last most people had heard was that Paul of the Sheds had been seen driving her to hospital in Inverness. Rumours concerning her health had been whipping around Blàs like sand in a storm, ever since. As with most things built on hearsay and no facts, Auntie Lottie's condition ranged from nothing more than hysterics due to her hair now being out of place to her dying on an operating table. Maureen, thankfully, for once wasn't involved in spreading any rumours about her friend.

"Have you heard how she is, Stroma?" Maureen asked, petting Blether on the head. "She gave us all a right fright. What was she doing on the beach at that time of night, for goodness sake?"

I wondered if I could save Auntie Lottie's blushes but decided Maureen would sniff out the truth eventually, so I might as well tell her now.

"She was walking Whisky."

"What? At that time? Why wasn't Paul there, and why was she walking her so late?"

Mary smiled. She knew why, I felt certain about that.

"Well, it would appear she was trying out a new pair of shoes for the wedding."

"Nothing wrong with that," Maureen said.

"There is if they have sixteen-centimetre heels," laughed Iona.

"And in real sizes, what would that be?" Maureen asked.

"Just over six inches." Iona took a slug of tea. "She went for a walk on a sandy beach in the middle of the night to try out walking in a very high-heeled pair of shoes so she could walk… What was it she said, Stroma?"

"So she could walk elegantly down the aisle on the day of the wedding."

"I believe Paul put it another way," Ellen added. "He said, so she could swish her way down. He looked quite proud of the fact, until he remembered what she had done."

"Well, I can't see her walking anywhere in the short term. She has a support on from the knee down to her toes and she won't be getting it off before the wedding. She's quite upset about the whole thing. She had her outfit picked and her matching bag and shoes. Well, you all know what she's like. And now, she doesn't know what to do."

"Oh, that's easy," Iona said as she helped herself to another cake. "All we have to do is book her one of the beach wheelchairs and she will be all set. Not a problem."

We all looked at her. Of course, how could we have not thought of that ourselves? We were so focused on how she was feeling and her injury that we had completely forgotten about our wheelchairs. I looked across at Iona who simply shrugged her shoulders and said, "What? Why are you all looking at me like that?"

Mary looked across and lifted her hand. "You are such a blessing, Iona, and we all love you so much."

Iona went bright red, adjusted her tammy and grinned back at us all.

45

Dan and Darren's guests had started to arrive in the village and surrounding area. There was suppressed excitement fizzing throughout the community. All of our beach wheelchairs had been booked out for the event. Auntie Lottie had asked Jill if she could dress hers up a little for the day.

"You know, as befits the mother of the groom. I want to look my best and that includes the wheelchair."

Old Betty and Catherine Cailleach had also booked a chair each, ready for the big day.

"It is such a lovely thing to do, and Betty agrees with me, don't you, Betty?" Catherine Cailleach then continued – as usual, not waiting for her friend to answer. "Asking the community to come along and see them getting married and on our beach too. So nice of them. We're both so looking forward to taking part, aren't we, Betty?"

Catherine Cailleach and Old Betty had been regular users of the beach wheelchairs. Most days, regardless of the weather, they could be seen down on the shore.

It had become such a regular occurrence it was difficult to remember that they had only recently been able to access our beautiful sandy seafront again. They were making up for lost time. Hopefully, as word got around about the chairs, they would still manage to book them as much as they did now.

Iona was kept busy brewing away. Her hours at the seaweed factory had been reduced as she had expected, allowing her to focus more on our venture. Our beer was looking good in its own Ùraisg label. A whole marketing campaign was being developed around the name. Mateo, when not working, could be found at her side. It was early days, but I hoped Iona had found someone who shared her passions and valued her need to feel free. I was often the recipient of his cooking so was extra happy to have him around.

The seaweed factory was continuing to expand. It would be a while yet before we reaped all the benefits, but it was providing year-round employment for some, including Iona. Markets were beginning to open up, and the demand for natural sustainable products was continuing to grow.

It was nice to think the community might be able to take a step back and just enjoy living here. But Mary had been right. It was all these things combined, all the voluntary work, all the developing involved, that helped make the community what it was. Despite finding the idea of less work appealing, I knew that, if the Development Trust and Ellen, in particular, weren't here, the community would have faded by now. We would have lost many more of our young people.

Both my old school friends were expecting again. Two more children in a few years' time would help secure the future of our local school. Jim and Grace were at least speaking now. I hoped his patience would be rewarded by Grace accepting she could trust his feelings for her.

Not everything was moving in the way I hoped, though. I still watched in despair as more and more of our smaller houses disappeared into holiday lets. These smaller houses were often the way people of my age and younger got their feet onto the property ladder. Local families were still being priced out of the market. What could have been future homes from them were being bought and rented out as holiday lets. Disillusioned and without much choice, young families had to move away to find accommodation and get on with their lives. Unfortunately, that meant away from their beloved Blàs. This impacted on our amenities, such as banks, doctors, schools and other vital services needed to keep a community thriving.

Thankfully, because of an earlier project the Development Trust had completed, we had our own stock of accommodation to rent out, but there wasn't nearly enough for the demand. I knew we would still have to build more. That, however, was a challenge for another day.

I was on my way to Mary's house. She was putting on a meal for some of her closest friends. Ellen and Giulietta would be there, as well as Maureen and Old Tam. Auntie Lottie was expected, but Paul had been called out to yet another rescue. Iona would grace us with an appearance but who knew if she would be there for the first course. And then there was me.

Although Mary had insisted she needed nothing brought along, we would all arrive with something that would enhance our meal, and she knew that too. I had picked up some cheeses from a local crofter as my contribution. Iona would bring some beer. I had no idea what the others would bring, but I knew it would be something tasty. It had been a while since we had all had a meal together and this was extra special as Iona was now a constant member of our little group.

"Stroma, thank you, lass. Sit down right there. Now, Malt, no playing with Blether, there's a good girl. We don't want the table to be knocked over." Mary ruffled the dog's head while I took my seat.

Maureen's hand went down and both dogs stopped playing and eagerly awaited the treat they knew would come next.

"Tch, Maureen, these dogs will become like fat sausages if

you keep feeding them like that," Auntie Lottie chastised as Maureen threw a treat towards Whisky.

"I see you've had your hair done then, Lottie. I'm right impressed you would go to so much bother for our meal." Mary twinkled towards her, knowing fine well the new style was not on her account.

Auntie Lottie's hand drifted up to her head. "I'm well pleased with it myself. I thought I would try out a new style. I'm not sure if I will wear it like this to the wedding, but I'm happy with it."

"Oh, it's the wedding you have had it done for then, not the present company. Second fiddle, that's us," Maureen huffed and lifted Blether onto her lap.

Ellen intervened before the conversation disintegrated further.

"Now." She raised her glass. "I would like to propose a toast to ourselves, who have worked so hard over the last few years and managed to pull off so much. I know before you say anything that we have had more help than from just those in this room, but it has been mostly you all here who have been constant and helped each other and our community pull together and achieve so much. I am proud to be a part of all this and thankful to have you as friends into the bargain. So, if you will raise your glasses, *mo charaidean, slàinte.*"

We all took a sip and returned with, "*Slàinte mhath.*"

"What have I missed out on?" The dogs erupted as Iona burst into the room.

"Nothing, *m'eudail,*" Mary said as she welcomed her late guest. Nothing much had changed with Iona, regarding time-keeping and the community. Work was one thing, but the rest of us knew, where we were concerned, Iona would always be late.

"What in the name of the wee man have you done to your specs?" Maureen barked.

Iona's specs had fallen off her face. "Ach, these. They only stay on when my hat is on. The legs have become a little loose."

I bent down and picked them up. One leg immediately flopped. I looked again. "Iona, there is only one lens in here."

"Ach aye. It fell out ages ago, but I only need them really for reading and driving so I can get by for now."

"Weren't you driving yesterday?" asked Ellen.

"Yes, and I managed." Iona was becoming evasive. I was secretly praying that they would stop. If they tried to mother her too much, she would react. She was used to her own ways and didn't like to act in a way others might expect. She knew she could manage well on her own without input and advice from anyone, never mind how well intended.

"Stop," Auntie Lottie said, "before you say one more word, Iona 'ic Annag 'ic Ruairidh." The room went silent. It wasn't often that anyone used the formal family Gaelic version of her name.

"I will not have you coming to my son's wedding wearing a woolie tammy that quite frankly has seen better days, just to keep your one lens specs from falling off your face. Opticians tomorrow in Inverness for a swift pair."

All eyes focused on Iona to see how she would react. She simply, shrugged, took a large gulp of beer, burped loudly, landed a kiss on Auntie Lottie's cheek and said, "Okay, Auntie Lottie, seeing it's you. I'll go."

I was glad I was sitting down, or I may have collapsed in shock.

As Iona returned to her seat, she whispered to me, "I had every intention of going tomorrow. I'm sick of them falling off my face, but I'll let her think she made me. It will score lots of brownie points with her and she'll give me some slack for a while too now."

I shook my head. I was glad Iona wasn't prepared to change to fit in with us. She was a free spirit and I wanted her to stay that way, as long as she did too.

"When did you break your specs anyway?" I asked.

"When I stuck my head down that hole trying to rescue that

daft dog of the Smith's. I just didn't get around to making an appointment for a new pair. You can come with me, if you want, and we could make a day of it."

I was tempted but work beckoned. Hopefully, my sister would arrive back looking or, more correctly, seeing a lot better.

46

The big day arrived. Thankfully, no spring tides were expected. We could look forward to a beautiful sunny June day. Our little beach was teeming with colour as locals gathered together. Used to our changeable climate, shawls or thin matching jackets adorned most of the women. We all knew how quickly a cold wind could whip up and destroy a fine day. However, hardly a breeze stirred the floaty dresses or shifted the soft sand.

Paul of the Sheds and Jim had set up an area for the nuptials away from the regular beach goers who wanted to indulge in sandcastle-making, boarding, surfing, swimming and the many other things people enjoyed on the beach.

It was easy for anyone to see that something special was about to take place. Those taking part in the many activities respected our space and carried on with their own enjoyment and entertainments. If they had known who was involved in this wedding, I doubt they would have been so happy to ignore what was going on. Dan had a huge fan base. If any of them had known what was happening today, he and his groom would be mobbed.

Our beach wheelchairs, largely funded by the couple, were once more being put to good use. It seemed fitting, somehow, that so many of them would be used at their wedding. Maureen was beside herself with joy. She was our local celebrant, and now that we had the beach wheelchairs, she could take the service on the beach. She sat happily in the chair waiting patiently for Darren to arrive. Blether was attached for once to a lead, although all you could see of her was a large blue bow bobbing as she changed position.

Catherine Cailleach and Old Betty, true to their word, had booked out their favourite chairs. We still had a couple left for anyone else attending the wedding who might need them.

Thankfully, despite Auntie Lottie's injury, she could attend her son's wedding in style. The beach wheelchair project had been worth every penny and all the hard work to get it ready. Given Auntie Lottie's condition, it added a whole new relevance to the scheme. Auntie Lottie, of course, was not to be outdone as mother of the groom. She had asked Jill to help her decorate her chair with ribbons and flowers. We would have a job cleaning it all down afterwards, but it would be worth it. She radiated happiness with Paul of the Sheds standing next to her.

I had thought I knew Auntie Lottie pretty well before, between visiting her as a beloved aunt when we were younger and then as an adult when we had become friends in a different way. Ours was a friendship I would always value, but regardless of how close we were, she had not confided in me or anyone else, apart from Mary, about what had happened to her in America.

It never ceased to amaze me, even when you thought you knew someone, how they still had that power to surprise you. Who else here had an untold story that had majorly impacted their lives but was buried far beyond Blàs and their daily lives?

Music filtered into my thoughts. One of the local musicians stationed near Maureen was playing the Clarsach. Its haunting sound floated on the breeze as we awaited the happy couple. It would be the robust sound of the bagpipes that would herald the start of the ceremony. All the musicians here would join others who were waiting up at the lodge for a ceilidh afterwards.

Dan was beginning to look nervous. He turned around and winked but I could see him shivering with nerves. Darren's close family and friends stood opposite. Their numbers were small. It had been so important to keep the whole thing quiet and the fewer people who knew outside of Blàs the better. Neither wanted their special day to turn into a media circus. Instead, the happy couple were content to include the local community and a few close friends and family to help them celebrate.

Iona fidgeted at my side. Mateo would meet us later. Right now, he was busy preparing a feast for us all to enjoy.

"You know, I still feel guilty. I should be helping Mateo and making sure our beer is ready rather than being here."

"No, you shouldn't. Dan is almost family – we are almost cousins. Auntie Lottie would have been hurt if you weren't here to witness the big event. Look at her."

Auntie Lottie, even sitting, still managed to ooze her big personality. Her hair was wound and bound into an elaborate design. There was no way, even with a slight breeze, that any hair would dare fall out of place. As if feeling our eyes on her, she raised her hand and patted her crown. Paul of the Sheds looked down at her and smiled, no doubt happy that his wife had made it to the wedding, after all.

A whirl of pipes could suddenly be heard drowning out the seagulls' cries, announcing the arrival of the other groom.

All eyes on the beach turned towards him as he marched down the aisle towards his partner. Music hung in the air for a split second after the pipes finished, before the call of the oyster-catcher could be heard once more.

Some tourists had come to stand on the machair to watch the proceedings. Other beach lovers had slowly made their way up towards us as the ceremony began.

Maureen's voice filled the air as she proceeded through the

wedding vows. The grooms made their commitment to each other in clear voices. Strangely enough, Dan, who was used to using his voice as an actor, sounded the more nervous of the two. Darren's words came over loud and clear, and we all smiled as they sealed their commitment to each other with a kiss.

Auntie Lottie dabbed her eyes. As with most of these magical events, the whole thing was over far quicker that we had anticipated.

Dan and Darren strolled back up the beach behind the piper, stopping briefly to kiss Auntie Lottie's cheek, shake hands and hug some of their friends and relations.

I found myself beside Ellen, Giulietta and Mary as we made our way back up the beach to catch the bus that had been laid on to transport the villagers to the newlyweds' home.

"Well, that was a nice wee ceremony. I can see now why couples are happy to be wed on a beach," Ellen said.

"Eh wull, it wauldnae hiv worked if'n we hid a stiff breeze n some rain," Old Tam interjected. "But at least thon *ùraisg* didnae show up."

"That we know of, Tam. Just because we didn't see Parnell an Spuit, doesn't mean he isn't here," Mary said.

Old Tam looked around nervously.

"Well, I thought the service was beautiful, but like Tam, I don't think you'd find me trusting our weather so much. I don't think a beach wedding would be for me."

"Is there something you're not telling me?" joked Iona.

"I was just wondering that myself," Auntie Lottie broke in as she caught up with us.

"Of course not," I said. Honestly, they never stopped, and now Iona was in on it too. In desperation, I tried deflecting it back on to my sister. "If you're looking to marry someone else off, there are lots of others here about. Iona and Mateo, for a start."

Iona burst out laughing "Aye, that will be right, Stroma. I am not the marrying kind, as you well know. And we were talking about you, anyway."

"Well, neither was Auntie Lottie the marrying kind, and then there's always Grace and Jim." I was sounding like Maureen; I needed to stop this but weddings always seemed to lead to people speculating on who was next. I had no desire for all their expectation to fall on me.

"Hmm, my Grace is not much better than Lottie here, and look at how long it took me to get her to agree to a wedding." Paul of the Sheds was obviously deeply disappointed by his observation. He had hoped that with Jim back in Blàs, and Grace finally starting to speak to him again, that she would have presented Jim as a future son-in-law by now. There appeared to be some thawing on Grace's part towards Jim, but it was too early yet to say what would happen. Like Paul of the Sheds, though, I was hoping Grace would give Jim a chance.

"Oh my, Stroma." Mary interrupted my thoughts. "But don't I recognise that figure there walking towards us?"

I looked up and immediately recognised the person making his way across the machair. Even with the sun behind him, I knew the minute my heart skipped a beat.

"Now, what was that you were saying about getting married?" Mary said, her eyes twinkling as she walked past. "Come on, you lot, we have to get ourselves loaded, or that bus will be away and we will be marooned here."

My legs refused to move. The others walked off in front while I stayed rooted to the spot. Iona turned around after she passed the man and gave me the thumbs-up behind his back.

He stopped in front of me.

"Stroma," he said and smiled.

"Scott, you made it then."

"It would appear I did. Can I give you a lift to the lodge? The bus is already leaving."

I watched as Iona and the rest of the bus waved at me. A couple of volunteers were pushing the beach wheelchairs back to the Bothy as Auntie Lottie and Maureen settled themselves in Paul of the Sheds' car. I caught a glimpse of their huge smiles towards me before I turned back to Scott.

"Aye, that would be nice," I said, as he took my hand, and we left our footprints behind in the sand.

FOLKLORE

You can't write about the Scottish Highlands without at least a nod to the local folklore, traditions and, of course, the Gaelic language.

ST. BRÌDE

Tales and stories develop and change in the telling. I'm sure there are plenty of people who would disagree with my interpretation of St. Brìde. She was reputed to be around from about C.E. 450. Some believe she was a saint; others, more controversially, believe this was made up in the hope of converting more pagans to Christianity.

I like to think she lived and fought to protect the wildlife and beauty of nature. If around today, she may well have been one of our eco-warriors. At least, that is how I like to envisage her. After all, many of our ancestors appeared to be more in tune with the seasons and nature than we are today.

ÙRAISG

According to our legends, these people did exist. The original Bigfoot. The Gaelic names referred to in the story are real places. They are all linked to areas beside streams, burns and water. I checked out my rather battered copy of *Dwelley*, the foremost Gaelic–English dictionary (after reading something online in scotlandsnature.blog) where, to my surprise, a whole column is devoted to the *ùraisg* or *ùruisg*.

I had taken a bit of a liberty, or so I thought, in changing him from a small house Brownie/*brùnaid*/*gruagach*/Brounie into a large *ùraisg*. (Given how many words we have for a Brownie, you can see we take our fairy folk pretty seriously.) My *ùraisg* liked milk and was generally good-natured, much like a Brownie. Surprisingly, it would appear my imaginings were not that far away from the truth if what I read in Dwelly's is true, which is both worrying and sort of magical at the same time.

MACHAIR

The machair features both within the pages of this book and on the cover. It is an important and stunning part of the environment in Scotland. In the Highlands, we are blessed with some spectacular beaches. The machair borders our beaches usually, but not exclusively, in the north-west and on the islands. How it grows and develops is affected by the weather, the sand dunes and grazing animals. All these elements allow for an amazing show of flowers in early summer. If you have never witnessed this I urge you to do so, it is wondrous. I have taken a bit of a liberty in that I included this amazing habitat on the east coast. Who knows, perhaps with the same management we could have some of that machair right here too.

SEAWEED

The best time for harvesting seaweed is from January to May. My grandmother and my mum both did this. I remember eating seaweed as a young girl. I don't know when it stopped making a regular appearance on our plates.

Once the food of the poor, it is now regarded more as a luxury food with many heath benefits for those who eat it. I wonder what our poor ancestors would make of that.

Seaweed factories are indeed being looked at by various rural areas around Scotland. The factory on Lewis does exist, and I'm sure others will soon join it.

BEACH WHEELCHAIRS

Thankfully, beach wheelchairs do exist.

When I first thought of including this as a theme, very few places in Scotland offered this service. Today, North Berwick, Portobello and Haven at Seton Sands can offer this facility, as well as Dornoch in Sutherland.

Luckily, one of these places, Dornoch, is not that far from home. As I said in my first Blàs of the Highlands book, Sutherland has some of the best beaches in Scotland. Many are long, golden and sandy with fantastic open views of the sea. Certainly, Dornoch can be included in that description.

There can't be many families who couldn't make use of a beach wheelchair facility for a relative or friend. My best friend Lindsay would have loved to have had access to something like this, if the facility had been available in her lifetime.

There are many others today who I know will benefit from the existence of beach wheelchairs and the help and dedication of the volunteers who organise and run these projects.

SCOTLAND'S LANGUAGES

SCOTS

Old Tam speaks Scots, English and Gaelic. Much of his Scots words are Dundonian, although, like many Scots speakers, he has a mixed accent. Many speakers have moved away from their roots and with that their language use changes.

Fife and Dundonian are often intertwined, depending on which part of Fife you are from. North-East tends to include many Dundonian words. The East Neuk, on the other hand, is full of words the fisher-folk would have used. Then there are the old mining areas which had their own words. Occasionally, you will even hear Doric (Scots usually heard in the north-east around Aberdeen and Moray) words within Fife.

In general, though, Dundonians have quite a different accent from Scots speakers of the West Coast or the Scots speakers of the old mining towns of Fife. We are lucky to still have such rich languages, given how both Scots and Gaelic were under siege for so long.

GAELIC

Thankfully, despite huge attempts to eradicate it through policy and persecution, the Gaelic language still survives today. Through those years of persecution, communities kept their language alive. In more recent times, it has been rescued (although there is still work to be done) from the brink by speakers, learners and activists, who have been working to revive the language since the middle of last century.

Today, many Scots have learnt to value again the rich commodity that Scots, Gaelic, their culture, music and language bring to Scotland and its peoples. They enrich our lives and our heritage.

If you would like to see the exact translations of the few Gaelic phrases in the book, please check out my website. I'm hoping to build up a list of phrases there I use in all my books. In *Blàs Across the Machair,* the phrases are mostly endearments.

'An Coineachan' is a traditional Gaelic lullaby. A sad one of course which I haven't translated as it is such a beautiful song in its original form.

There are many useful websites you can find online about the world of Scottish Gaelic. Here are few I've used in this book.

For the odd work check out Am Faclair Beag at faclair.com

For help and information (including audio) for parents and learners of all ages, check out gaelic4parents.com or their Facebook page gaelic4parents

For information on and about Gaelic Medium Education try Comunn na Gàidhlig (cnag) at cnag.org

For Gaelic books and help for Gaelic writers and publishers go to Comhairle nan Leabhraichean/The Gaelic Books Council at gaelicbooks.org

For The Royal National Mod, a week long Gaelic festival of competitions that runs in October, check out An Comunn Gàidhealach at ancomunn.co.uk/nationalmod

There are lots of other organisations and information out there on Gaelic history, music, culture and language. I hope you find the above ones a useful start.

ACKNOWLEDGMENTS

It takes a team to produce a book. First, though, I would like to thank my readers for buying my books and for their feedback and kind words. Special thanks to all those who have left reviews. These are so important to a writer.

The inspirational Dornoch Beach Wheelchairs also deserve a particular mention. Not only for their initial project but for their continued commitment. My special thanks to June MacLean and Isla Fullerton-Smith who spent a frosty morning drinking tea and generously allowing me to pick their brains regarding how to go about setting up something like this. Seeing their beach wheelchair 'shed' was so helpful. I decided to give my fictional volunteers an easier time by providing them with more space and a mains water supply.

Thanks also to my editor Fran Lebowitz who didn't quite pull out all her hair during her edit of my manuscript. This story is much improved after her suggestions and comments.

To Kat Harvey of Athena Copy, who I know loves the Blàs area, for her edits, professionalism and help during the copy-edit and further proofread.

Also, thanks to Annemieke Leverenz for yet again producing a cover I love.

To fellow writers and authors who understand what it is like to follow this way of life – I feel your support each time we talk, and it is so nice to be able to meet up again. Thanks go to Jane Mackenzie, Barbara Henderson and Pauline MacKay, in particular.

Thanks to the Gaelic Books Council and Liza Storey who sent me off on this path.

To my family and friends for their support and patience when I'm trying to work out deadlines and storylines.

Special thanks, as always, to Malcolm (especially now I have the whole desk to myself) for the cups of tea, space and time to work on my writing.

ABOUT THE AUTHOR

C C Hutton lives and works in the Highlands of Scotland. She spent many years travelling the Highlands as a Gaelic Development Officer. She loves sprinkling her English writing with Gaelic, Scots and old traditional tales. She is also an award winning writer of Gaelic children's picture books.

Ceitidh is registered what the Scottish Book Trust Live Literacy Programme and is the Rùnaire/secretary of the Society of Authors in Scotland.

When not involved in the world of being a writer she delivers Gaelic Bookbugs, walks the dog and helps to promote Gaelic. She can be contacted on her website or through her social media.

Website: cchuttonwriter.com

Facebook Facebook.com/cchuttonwriter

Instagram @cchuttonwriter.com

Gaelic writing: facebook.com/ceitidhhuttonauthor

Printed in Great Britain
by Amazon

27728556R00158